the vengeance code

(a remi laurent fbi suspense thriller—book 4)

ava strong

Ava Strong

Debut author Ava Strong is author of the REMI LAURENT mystery series, comprising six books (and counting); of the ILSE BECK mystery series, comprising seven books (and counting); of the STELLA FALL psychological suspense thriller series, comprising six books (and counting); and of the DAKOTA STEELE FBI suspense thriller series, comprising three books (and counting).

An avid reader and lifelong fan of the mystery and thriller genres, Ava loves to hear from you, so please feel free to visit www.avastrongauthor.com to learn more and stay in touch.

Copyright © 2022 by Ava Strong. All rights reserved. Except as permitted under the U.S. Copyright Act of 1976, no part of this publication may be reproduced, distributed or transmitted in any form or by any means, or stored in a database or retrieval system, without the prior permission of the author. This ebook is licensed for your personal enjoyment only. This ebook may not be re-sold or given away to other people. If you would like to share this book with another person, please purchase an additional copy for each recipient. If you're reading this book and did not purchase it, or it was not purchased for your use only, then please return it and purchase your own copy. Thank you for respecting the hard work of this author. This is a work of fiction. Names, characters, businesses, organizations, places, events, and incidents either are the product of the author's imagination or are used fictionally. Any resemblance to actual persons, living or dead, is entirely coincidental. Jacket image Copyright Authentic travel, used under license from Shutterstock.com.
ISBN: 978-1-0943-9432-9

BOOKS BY AVA STRONG

REMI LAURENT FBI SUSPENSE THRILLER
THE DEATH CODE (Book #1)
THE MURDER CODE (Book #2)
THE MALICE CODE (Book #3)
THE VENGEANCE CODE (Book #4)
THE DECEPTION CODE (Book #5)
THE SEDUCTION CODE (Book #6)

ILSE BECK FBI SUSPENSE THRILLER
NOT LIKE US (Book #1)
NOT LIKE HE SEEMED (Book #2)
NOT LIKE YESTERDAY (Book #3)
NOT LIKE THIS (Book #4)
NOT LIKE SHE THOUGHT (Book #5)
NOT LIKE BEFORE (Book #6)
NOT LIKE NORMAL (Book #7)

STELLA FALL PSYCHOLOGICAL SUSPENSE THRILLER
HIS OTHER WIFE (Book #1)
HIS OTHER LIE (Book #2)
HIS OTHER SECRET (Book #3)
HIS OTHER MISTRESS (Book #4)
HIS OTHER LIFE (Book #5)
HIS OTHER TRUTH (Book #6)

DAKOTA STEELE FBI SUSPENSE THRILLER
WITHOUT MERCY (Book #1)
WITHOUT REMORSE (Book #2)
WITHOUT A PAST (Book #3)

PROLOGUE

Richmond, Virginia
10:15 P.M.

The house stood at the end of a little cul-de-sac in a fashionable area of Richmond. Not the rich old part of town, with antebellum mansions sporting columned facades, that was home to the old money, but a more modern area of established professionals. The kind of neighborhood for lawyers and bankers, real estate agents and physicians. If the Lion of Judah had been a common burglar, he would find rich pickings here.

But the Lion of Judah was not here to steal jewelry and computers. Material wealth did not interest him. Things were of this Earth and therefore unimportant, and money was simply a useful tool to achieve one's ends.

No, he wasn't after computers or cash. He was here for something far more valuable.

Information.

And among all the neighborhood's resident M.D.s and C.A.s and A.A.L.s, the lone Ph.D. at the end of the road stood out.

Professor Edward Hale of the University of Virginia, a tenured professor of Old Testament history and theology, knew more about early Judaism than anyone else in the United States, so he was a good place to start. He had spent his career sharing that knowledge with students through his years of lectures, and with readers through his countless academic books and articles.

Or at least some of his knowledge. The Lion of Judah knew he was holding back on the most important knowledge of all.

Tonight, Professor Edward Hale was going to share that knowledge, one way or the other.

The Lion of Judah parked his car across the street, checking the area to make sure no late-night pedestrians were around. He saw no one. Good. Neighborhoods like this tended to be quiet, and he knew, from scouting the area for several nights in a row, that the dog walkers and joggers tended to go to a well-lit park just a quarter mile away.

Checking himself in the rear-view mirror, he could see he would not make a threatening impression. Nice summer suit, carefully combed hair going a bit bald in late middle age, and an intellectual air. He grabbed a book from the passenger's seat. Not a history book or theological treatise, just a novel about Navy Seals fighting terrorists. It didn't matter. All the professor would see was a book, and that would make him think of the Lion of Judah as a kindred spirit.

He wouldn't have time to see any more.

After a final glance to make sure the coast was clear, the Lion of Judah locked his car and strolled across the street to the professor's front door and rang the doorbell. The lights were on, and the Lion of Judah knew Professor Hale would be alone. His wife had died a couple of years before and his children had all grown and moved away. This late on a school night, he would not have any company.

The sound of approaching footsteps from the other side of the door. An aging, intellectual face briefly appeared at the window flanking the door. The Lion of Judah gave the man a smile and clutched the book close to his chest so the professor would be sure to see it.

As he suspected, the door opened. How many murderers brought a book to the scene of the crime?

Professor Edward Hale looked every bit the favorite professor—swept back white hair above an open, wide, and smiling face, and rugged health and good looks despite his seventy-one years. Even though it was a warm evening, he wore a tweed sportscoat and slacks. The Lion of Judah caught a whiff of bourbon as the professor greeted him.

"Hello. How may I help you?" Professor Hale asked.

The Lion of Judah, poised to spring, tried to put him at his ease with an uncertain smile and a question. "Hello, is this the MacGregors residence?"

"Heh." A short, one-syllable chuckle. It sounded at once both contemptuous and ironic. "The MacGregors live two doors down, but I think you know that." The professor opened the door. "Come on in. I don't want you breaking a window."

The Lion of Judah, taken aback, passed over the threshold.

"I presume you're here about the Ark?" Professor Hale said, closing the door behind them.

"Um, I did have a few questions."

"Don't they all, don't they all," the professor muttered. "Come to my office."

"Other people have questioned you about it?" the Lion of Judah asked, suspicion rising as the professor led him through an oak-paneled front hall and through a comfortably furnished living room. A bottle of bourbon and a glass sat on the coffee table, next to a stack of books. The Lion of Judah wondered if Professor Hale was drunk. His manner seemed to hint at it, but his movements did not.

He'd have to watch Hale's every move.

"Oh, a few over the years." The professor stopped, gestured at the bottle. "May I offer you a drink?"

"No, thank you."

"Straight down to business, eh?" the professor inclined his head, making a show of reading the novel the Lion of Judah still clutched close to his chest. "*Seal Team Special Killers: Terror in Tunisia*."

The Lion of Judah gave him a sheepish grin. "I can't read ancient Hebrew all the time."

"Ha!" the professor clapped him on the shoulder. "We all have our guilty pleasures. Mine are bourbon and the Indy 500. You're a veteran, aren't you? I can tell by the erect bearing and overall physique."

"I served." *But not in the way you think I did.*

"I was in the Army for a few years. Stationed in Germany and Korea but never saw combat. But I suppose you know that. Come into my office. It's the best place to talk shop."

The Lion of Judah followed, utterly bewildered. This was not how he pictured the meeting at all. He thought he'd have the old academic in a headlock by now.

The next surprise came in the back hall, a narrow space leading to the open door of a cluttered office at the end.

The walls of the hallway were lined with framed photos of *Gilligan's Island*. They looked like original film stills, some signed by the actors.

Professor Hale chuckled. "Surprised to see something like this in the home of one of the world's leading theological historians? My uncle was Alan Hale, Jr. He played the Skipper."

The Lion of Judah looked from Professor Hale to one of the photos showing the Skipper and back again.

"I see a family resemblance."

"Sometimes I show an episode in class. Most of my students are too young to remember the show, but they get a kick out of it. Some humor is timeless. Come."

They continued toward the office. The Lion of Judah tensed again. This familiarity, the photos, was all this just to distract him? Professor Hale was smarter than he thought. He'd have to be careful. Only one man would die tonight, and it would not be him.

At the end of the hall, the professor gestured at a black and white photo of a bunch of men in medieval garb standing in the woods.

"That's my great uncle, Alan Hale, Sr. He was an actor too. He played Little John in the silent version of Robin Hood."

"I didn't know that. Are you an actor too?"

Professor Hale cast a smile over his shoulder. "I'm acting casual around you, aren't I?"

The Lion of Judah shook his head in wonder. This was not going as he expected. Not at all.

They entered an office. Oak bookshelves lined the walls, stuffed to overflowing with books. An overly large desk was too big for the room, making it cramped. Professor Hale edged around the side and sat down, gesturing for the Lion of Judah to sit. The only available seat was a small stool he suspected the professor stood on in order to reach the highest shelves. The Lion of Judah remained standing.

"So …," the professor leaned back and crossed his legs. "You want to know where the Ark of the Covenant is."

"Yes," the Lion of Judah replied, his throat going dry.

"I suppose Axum in Ethiopia is not the answer you're looking for?"

"It doesn't take much research to know that's a red herring."

"Pier Paolo Manetti thought it was there," the professor said with a smile.

"He was a fool."

It took all of his self-control not to spit at the mention of that man's name.

Manetti was the Italian host of a cult TV show *Misterio 2000*, that investigated mysteries. The man, famous for his long moustache sticking out from the sides of his head and his habit of breaking into opera, had been arrested by Ethiopian authorities for trying to break into the St. Mary of Zion Cathedral in Axum. Great television. Poor history.

And he ended up getting murdered several months ago. Interesting that Professor Hale would bring that up.

"A fool, yes, but a richer man than you or I will ever be. Mind if I smoke?"

The Lion of Judah shrugged. "It's your house."

He watched the professor's every move.

Professor Hale pulled out a pack of cigarettes from the pocket of his tweed jacket. He offered him one, got a shake of the head as a response, and put one to his lips.

Next, he pulled out a lighter and brought it to the cigarette. He flicked it and got only sparks. The Lion of Judah moved his feet a bit further apart and turned slightly so he wasn't facing the professor full on. Professor Hale, his eyes hooded, did not seem to notice as he flicked the lighter several more times and didn't get a flame.

"Damn," he muttered and opened a drawer in his desk.

The Lion of Judah whipped out a compact 9mm automatic from inside his jacket just as the professor started to pull out a .45.

"Drop it," the Lion of Judah commanded. "I won't say it twice."

Professor Hale grimaced, dropped the pistol back in the desk with a heavy *clunk*, and shut the drawer.

"Your lighter works," the Lion of Judah told him. "I saw you flicking the wheel but not hitting the lever."

Slowly, the professor reached down, picked up the lighter, and lit the cigarette that was still between his lips.

"I admire your cool-headedness," the Lion of Judah said.

The professor cast a look at a framed photo on his desk, showing a younger version of himself with a smiling blonde woman.

"After Jenny died, I haven't cared much what happens to me." He turned his gaze back to the intruder. "Which means you won't get what you want."

"Life is precious," the Lion of Judah said, aiming right for the heart. "You look healthy. Another ten years of research and teaching. Twenty, maybe. Vintage bourbon, fine meals, good books. All you need to do is tell me where it is."

Professor Hale kept his eyes fixed on the man holding a gun to him. He did not waver as he said, "You know I won't tell you."

The Lion of Judah slumped a little. "You're one of them, are you?"

A slow nod. "Yes, I'm one of them, and a quick draw and some clever research won't make you safe from my compatriots."

"Last chance. Tell me where the Ark of the Covenant is."

"Go to hell."

Fine. I'll torture it out of you.

Before the Lion of Judah could put that thought into action, Hale reached for the drawer where he kept his gun.

The Lion of Judah fired.

The shot sounded deafening in the enclosed space. Professor Hale jerked in his seat, hit his head against the bookshelf behind, then slumped face first over the desk. His last cigarette tumbled over the desk to land on the carpet, where it started to smolder.

The Lion of Judah ground it out with his foot.

"Wouldn't want to set fire to all these important books," he said. He put his gun back in his shoulder holster and saluted. "Sorry to have to do this, old soldier."

From one of his other pockets, he pulled out a clasp knife and moved over to the professor.

He began to cut.

CHAPTER ONE

Washington, D.C.
The next morning

Remi Laurent, former professor of medieval history at the Sorbonne and guest lecturer at Georgetown, was turning out to be a natural.

The gunnery range at the FBI branch office in downtown D.C. was located in a cellar, well soundproofed so as not to worry the businesses and office buildings surrounding it. Remi stood at the range, firing the last from a clip of her FBI-issued Glock at a man-sized paper target 20 meters away. Her instructor, a former U.S. Marine three times her size, watched in admiration as she created a tidy cluster in the chest.

"Go for the main body mass," he always said. "That has the best chance of hitting and has good stopping power. Don't shoot at the legs. Don't tiptoe around and be gentle about an armed confrontation. If you must take a man down, he deserves a bullet through the torso. And don't aim for the head. Not even Army snipers do that. A 9mm round through the body will stop anyone but a meth freak. If you're facing one of them, unload your whole clip on the nutcase."

Remi finished emptying her clip and hit the button to bring the target back to the shooting position. Her instructor whistled.

"Nice one. Except for this." He poked a finger through the hole made by one clear miss, a good two inches outside the silhouette of the body. "What happened here?"

"I didn't cool off before the next shot," she recited.

"That's right. You got to make each shot an individual action. Don't rush it. Aim. Focus. Breathe. Fire."

"Sorry." Remi could feel herself redden. While she knew she was doing far better than most recruits at this stage of training, thanks to juvenile target practice with her father, a member of the Paris gendarmerie, she didn't like making mistakes. She'd seen enough fieldwork already to know how a single mistake could lead to serious consequences, even fatal ones.

She had always been a perfectionist. Now that she was a couple of weeks into a special accelerated training program for the FBI, that perfectionism was all the more important.

Her instructor glanced at the wall clock.

"Time's up. Clean, reassemble, and stow your piece."

"Yes, sir," she said, turning away.

"Laurent," he said. She turned back to him. "Perfect is the enemy of good."

Remi blinked. Did this man mountain just quote Voltaire at her?

"What do you mean?" she asked.

"This isn't some academic book where you get everything just so, where all your facts are lined up and no one can say you're wrong. This is law enforcement. It's never going to be perfect. You're never going to hit the bullseye every single time. And you're never going to get every criminal you go after. Instead of beating yourself up about not batting a thousand, just be happy you're in the major leagues."

Remi had no idea what batting a thousand meant, and he had an overly optimistic opinion of the mental rigor that went into academic publishing, but she got the general idea.

"Thank you, sir."

Her instructor nodded to the door to the arsenal. "Go on, then, Agent Laurent."

Agent Laurent. The words filled her with pride as she strolled past the other shooters to the arsenal. It still didn't seem real, and in fact was only partially real. Just a couple of weeks before, she had been a university professor visiting Georgetown for two semesters. Three times she had been called by the FBI to work as a civilian advisor, helping out its new Antiquities Division with cases involving medieval and Renaissance art. She had nearly been killed at least twice, been run ragged across half a dozen states and two continents and had loved every moment of it.

She sat in the armory, putting her Glock on the counter in front of her, and went through the steps of stripping and cleaning it. A simple step by step procedure suited to someone with her meticulous nature and attention to detail. This was easier than target practice, and much easier than the physical training program they had put her on.

While Remi had always maintained good health through long walks and a healthy, non-American diet, she hadn't been athletically active since high school. Now she felt constantly sore, constantly run down, but she could see herself toning up every time she looked in the mirror after a shower. And she had cut her time for running a mile from twelve minutes to just under eleven. She had been ordered to get it down below ten.

Remi's boss at the Antiquities Division, Assistant Director Keiko Ochiai, needed her on call and ready for duty, which put the agency in a bit of a bind. If they sent her to the academy down in Quantico, she'd be unavailable for months. So instead, they used a little-known workaround, an intense, individual training program used for recruits that were needed at a moment's notice. Thus, Remi's days were filled with target practice, hand-to-hand combat training, and one-on-one courses on investigative techniques. Her nights were filled with the study of procedure and law.

Everything else had to be put aside. She hadn't even had time to do any more research into the cryptex, her lifelong obsession that had gotten her into the strange circumstances she now found herself in.

Her social life had become all but nonexistent. She saw little of the other students, who had their own schedules and were occasionally called for fieldwork. She saw little of anyone else either. Dr. Cyril Mullen, her lover and the head of the history department at Georgetown, was not happy about that. Not at all.

After a whirlwind fling at a conference a couple of years before, and an agonizing long-distance relationship, he had arranged for her to do a year-long guest lectureship at Georgetown so they could be together.

At first it had been wonderful. The funding was good, and while the university had very American attitudes about relationships between colleagues, they had managed to keep it secret and see each other for a large portion of every day.

The only dark spot was the increasing pressure Cyril had put on her to get married. While she loved him, she didn't like the feeling of having to make a decision on a timetable. She understood how he felt. Having come out of a rough divorce with a woman who did not deserve such a kind, intellectual man, he was past fifty and eager to put down roots again. When her work visa expired at the end of the academic term, she would have to return to the Sorbonne in Paris, leaving him in the United States. It was get married or have no future in the relationship.

She understood, and she loved him but …

It all felt wrong somehow. Cyril was so obsessed with bringing them together in a permanent bond, he didn't see how it would be the end of her academic career. Full-time teaching jobs for medievalists were rare, and there were none in D.C., or even in the region. What was she supposed to do, sit home and make curtains?

Then there was his staunch opposition to her freelancing for the FBI, and the difference between what he said and what he felt. Cyril said it was dangerous work for which she was unqualified (true enough) and that it took her away from her academic duties (also true). Secretly, Remi suspected, he really objected because it took her away from him for long and unpredictable stretches and also gave her independence outside his academic world. He thought she was slipping away from him.

Well, she wouldn't be slipping away if he hadn't been trying to hold onto her so tightly. Yes, her life had taken a dramatic new turn, but couldn't he celebrate that, be happy for her? Couldn't he see that now that the FBI had given her an indefinite work visa, they could enjoy a longer engagement, freeing themselves of the pressure to marry immediately?

No, instead he tried to get her to give up this important and fulfilling new work and remain an academic.

An academic with no secure future if she married him.

With a sigh she finished cleaning the Glock and stowed it in its individual locked container. Then she gathered her things and left, handing the key to the armorer on her way out. She had lunch with Cyril in half an hour. That gave her time to go over some of million regulations an FBI agent had to know by rote. After lunch she had some more physical training followed by hand-to-hand combat. She still needed to work on that. While she had always been healthy and fit, at age 38, punches and flips didn't come so easily.

But first, those regulations. Time to hit the books, as her students said.

Ex-students, she reminded herself. *You're not a professor anymore.*

She trembled a bit. Every now and then, the magnitude of her life-changing decision hit her, and hit her hard.

All that was forgotten a moment later as she was climbing the stairs to the ground floor and saw who stood at the top.

Daniel Walker, her partner.

She hadn't seen him for the past two weeks since she had started training.

Daniel Walker a tall man about her age with broad shoulders, handsome except for a habitual frown and a belly that was beginning to take on middle-aged proportions. He wore the black suit and tie that was all but a uniform among FBI agents, the regulation sunglasses tucked in his breast pocket. He kept his brown hair cut short. Brown eyes, so hard most of the time, and especially when grilling suspects, softened as she looked up.

"Hey!" she said, running up the last of the steps. "It's good to see you!"

Surprisingly good. As busy as she had been in her weeks of training, she hadn't realized just how much she had missed this uncouth, multilayered, fascinating man.

"Good to see you too," he said with a grin.

Remi stopped, a tad too close, almost going in for the kiss to both cheeks customary in France. A handshake seemed inappropriate too (does one shake hands with someone when they've shared life and death experiences?), so she settled for a nod and a smile.

"Got time for a coffee?" he asked.

"Sure. I have … an appointment for lunch."

A brief sense of betrayal. Why not just say she had lunch with Cyril? The two knew each other, after all. Well, they'd met two or three times. Handshake. Polite small talk. Little to no mention of the other in later conversation.

They headed off to a nearby Starbucks favored by the FBI crowd, where the baristas joked it was the safest coffeeshop in the world. Clusters of men, along with a few women, all in dark suits, sat drinking coffee, eating bagels, and talking shop in quiet tones.

Remi ordered a black coffee, having to repeat her order since no one ordered black coffee at Starbucks. Daniel, like most people, ordered some giant confection with cherry syrup and whipped cream, plus a garlic bagel with cream cheese.

They sat at a small table, crowded in by the other agents, knees brushing against each other before Remi shifted position.

"I see your dietary habits haven't improved since I last met you," Remi joked. "Is that going to be your lunch?"

"Huh? Oh no, I've already had lunch."

"I see. McDonald's, Burger King, or Pizza Hut?"

"Sloppy Yo."

"I beg your pardon?" Remi thought she had misheard.

"Sloppy Yo, the hip-hop Sloppy Joe place on third."

"I understood every word but not the sentence they created."

"A Sloppy Joe is a bit like a hamburger but with ground beef that's still all loose instead of being cooked into a patty. It's got onions, Worcestershire sauce, ketchup, and a bunch of other stuff. Sloppy Yo is run by Ice Berg, that Jewish rapper that made it big about twenty years ago. His music career fizzled so he opened a restaurant. Best Sloppy Joes in town."

"I'll take your word for it. So how is work?"

Daniel shrugged. "Routine. Chased down a guy who was selling stolen stamps."

"Stolen stamps?"

"Stamps can be big business. This guy was teamed up with a burglar who targeted stamp collectors. He'd nab stamp collections worth tens, even hundreds of thousands of dollars, break up the collections, and sell them bit by bit on the private market. Almost untraceable. Stamps don't have serial numbers, after all. I only nailed him by matching up some of his sales with missing stamps. Tough job, though, because he'd sell the rarest stuff overseas, often after sitting on it for years."

Remi could hear the boredom in his voice. Daniel was more of a man of action. Tracing stolen philatelic treasures was not his idea of a good time.

Or hers.

"Did the burglar give you any trouble?"

"None. Knocked on his door and he had his hands up almost before I flashed my badge."

Daniel sounded disappointed. He could be a bit rough with suspects who resisted arrest. She had heard a rumor that he had even stuck a drug dealer's head down a toilet and flushed. Opinion was divided on whether or not he used it first.

"I've heard your training is going well," Daniel said. "Class act on the shooting range. Getting good on the track too. Still getting your ass kicked by Agent Herrero."

Agent Herrero was the hand-hand-hand combat instructor. He had black belts in Muay Thai, Judo, and Shotokan Karate.

Remi smiled at him over the rim of her coffee cup. "I'd like to see you take him on."

"Been there. Done that. Got my ass thrown ten feet."

"You probably lasted longer than I do. This sort of thing doesn't come naturally to me." Remi couldn't keep the dissatisfaction out of her voice.

"It sure comes naturally when some knife-wielding psycho is trying to kill you."

Remi laughed, and instantly felt that strange sense of disassociation she had been feeling ever since joining the FBI. The old Remi Laurent would never have laughed at the fact that more than one man had tried to kill her, and nearly succeeded. That would have traumatized the quiet academic she had once been. The speed at which she had changed made her feel at times like a stranger in her own body.

The laughter died down. Perhaps Daniel sensed something about her mood by her expression changing, or perhaps he had gotten to know his partner better after three dangerous cases, because his next question was right on target.

"So how are you adjusting?"

Those brown eyes were fixed on her, as incisive as when they interrogated a suspect, although far more sympathetic.

Remi shrugged and gave an uncertain smile. "It's … strange. When I was just a civilian advisor, it was all one big adventure. Terrifying but exhilarating at the same time. Now that I'm actually a trainee agent it feels so different … "

Her words trailed off as she became unsure, or unwilling, to continue.

Her partner/interrogator was not about to let her off the hook. "Different how?"

Remi searched for the right words. "It seems more real now. More in earnest. Beforehand, while I was eager to solve the cases, it was really your case. The FBI's case." Daniel laughed. "I know, I know. It probably didn't seem like it, but that's how it felt. I've been reading about the history of the FBI and speaking with my instructors and hearing their stories. Now I feel like I'm part of a long tradition. It makes me nervous."

"Imposter syndrome?"

"Exactly!"

"We all get that. 'Who am I to find a serial killer or bust some international smuggling ring?' It's such a big job, and such an important one, and I think a bit of imposter syndrome is good for an agent. It keeps them on their toes and focused on doing their best."

Remi nodded, smiling. While Daniel could be closed off and prickly, often about the strangest things, it was nice to know he understood.

She had a feeling that would be important whenever they got another case.

The agency had promised to keep Daniel and Remi as partners, and she felt surprised at how important that partnership had become for her.

And how much she wanted to impress him once they did get a new case.

Daniel checked his watch. "Aw, crap."

"What is it?"

"I need to go. I have an appointment with the boss."

Remi perked up. "Assistant Director Ochiai?"

"Yup."

Daniel stood.

"A new case?"

"Maybe. Just focus on learning the regs and kicking Agent Herrero's ass."

"Has she said anything about a new case?"

"No. And stop looking like a kid in a candy store with a hundred-dollar gift certificate."

Remi settled back into her coffee, giving Daniel a wry smile. "Is it so wrong to want another case?"

"Is it wrong to want to case thieves and killers across the United States? No, not really. A bit weird, though. But being weird is why I like you."

Daniel closed one eye, made a pistol with his finger and said, "Click, pow! See you later, Trainee Agent Laurent."

Remi giggled, then caught herself and put a hand over her mouth. When was the last time she had giggled?

With a wave and a smile, Daniel was gone, leaving her alone to drum her fingers on the table and wonder if whatever work the assistant director was calling him in for, if she'd be called upon to help.

CHAPTER TWO

Daniel Walker smiled to himself as he walked into Keiko Ochiai's office. It was good to see Remi again. He'd been keeping tabs on her ever since she had started training. All her instructors said she was coming along nicely. Even Agent Herrero, although the martial artist had told him in no uncertain terms that in any physical conflict, Daniel should take the lead.

Easier said than done. She went off on her own so much that Daniel sometimes felt like he was taking care of one of his friends' kids.

As he passed into his boss's office, he switched his focus to the here and now. Assistant Director Ochiai didn't call people in for routine stuff like tracking down stolen stamp collections.

The office interior was modern, with ergonomic chairs and one wall entirely of glass, overlooking the D.C. skyline. The other walls were decorated with excellent black and white photos of Japanese-American cowboys and farmers, taken by the assistant director herself, mostly on her father's ranch and those in the surrounding community of west Texas. She had won several agency photo competitions.

"Good afternoon, Agent Walker, please sit," Assistant Director Ochiai said in her Texas drawl.

"Good to see you again, assistant director."

Good to see you because this probably means I'm getting a real assignment.

"We have a case I'd like you to look into."

Bingo.

She slipped over a file from a stack on her desk. One of the thin ones. That meant a new case with a lot of legwork. Ah well, legwork was part of the job. Most of the job, as a matter of fact.

"Professor Edward Hale was murdered last night at his house in Richmond. He taught history and theology at the University of Virginia. Unknown assailant, unknown motive."

"I see," Daniel said, taking the file and opening it. "Why involve the Antiquities Division?"

"Because three years ago Professor Hale was found innocent of antiquities smuggling."

"Oh." *Now it's getting interesting.*

"Information on the trial is all in there. To summarize, he was accused of trafficking Biblical-era objects stolen from archaeological sites in Israel, Syria, and Jordan."

"How did he get off?"

"A good lawyer and lack of evidence. You see, no money changed hands."

Daniel looked up. "I beg your pardon?"

"He traded. At least on this end. He might have bought the items from dealers in the Middle East with cash, but as far as the prosecutors could make out, he traded the artifacts for different artifacts."

"Such as?"

"Rare books, mostly, including some quite early manuscripts. While some are in a safety deposit box, others were apparently at the home."

"Gone now."

"Yes."

"But that's not the motive?"

"The thief picked an evening of a school night when Hale was likely to be home. Indeed, most of the lights were on."

"Forced entry?"

"No."

So Hale knew his assailant, or at least didn't suspect he came with murder on his mind.

"Can I call in Agent Laurent on this?" he asked. It would be good to have her in on this.

"Of course. The accelerated training program allows for fieldwork. Indeed, fieldwork is the best training."

"I agree. I'll grab her and head down to Richmond immediately."

He rose, already excited for the chase. Assistant Director Ochiai raised a hand.

"Agent Walker."

"Yes?"

"Agent Laurent is still in training. And according to the reports from her instructors and your own comments she is impulsive. It is your duty to keep her in line and keep her safe."

Daniel paused, then nodded.

"I will, ma'am."
Easier said than done.

* * *

"What's the matter?" Remi asked her lover quietly, a sense of dread growing in her chest.

Lunch had not gone well. Cyril had been strangely quiet and physically distant. They had sat in one of their favorite Italian restaurants, eating quietly. Cyril had ordered a carafe of wine and drank it almost by himself. Dessert had come and gone, and over their coffee Cyril had squared his shoulders and looked her in the eye. It was the first time he had done so for the entire meal.

He put his coffee cup down with a loud clink.

"I can't do this anymore." The words came out hard, accusatory.

Remi blinked. "What do you mean?"

Cyril gestured at her impatiently. "You. Running off to join the FBI. Giving up your career. Giving up on Georgetown."

Remi leaned forward and put a hand on his. "That doesn't mean I'm giving up on us."

He pulled his hand away. It took a moment longer than it should have if his anger was entirely genuine.

"Yes, you have. You've put off our wedding date ever since I proposed. You keep disappearing on cases at a moment's notice, and you come back bruised and exhausted. When you sleep over, a rare thing these days, you toss and turn and mutter in your sleep. When you're awake you look like you're a million miles away. And you never talk about our future anymore. Hell, I found a house for us, and you let it slip through our fingers because you were on a case in Europe!"

That wasn't fair. He had already admitted that she couldn't buy a house sight unseen. He couldn't use that as ammunition now.

"I'm still serious about us, Cyril, I—"

"This is the first time we've had lunch in more than a week. Remember how we used to have lunch nearly every day?"

She remembered. It seemed like a long, long time ago.

"I'm very busy with training. I told you how intense it is."

"Yes, and then you'll be busy with cases, and what if they want to transfer you?"

"The Antiquities Division is based here in D.C."

"Sure, it is now. But what about six months from now? What if they decide to base it in New York since that's where so much of the art smuggling is based? Or what if they want you on a long-term assignment in another country? What happens to us then?"

Remi leaned forward, feeling a growing sense of panic and trying to get him to look her in the eye again. "We can work through all that. We had a long-distance relationship before and—"

Even before Cyril interrupted her, she knew she had said the wrong thing.

"Oh great, we go back to having a long-distance relationship. Don't you remember how agonizing that was? We hated it. Both of us. That's why I arranged for you to come to Georgetown. I thought we were going to make this permanent."

Remi bit her lip. Of course she knew all this, and knew the hurt he was feeling even if it hadn't been apparent in every word he spoke; and yet she couldn't say what he wanted to hear.

He wanted to hear that she'd cast aside this silly new career before it was too late, go back to academia, and marry him.

But she couldn't cast aside this career. It made her feel more alive than she had felt in years. And she couldn't go back to academia. Her status at the Sorbonne had been canceled the instant that stuffy Parisian institution had heard of her career change, and she knew that the old men who ran the university had only ever accepted her on sufferance and would never take her back.

And marrying Cyril?

She could. She might. She had assumed that one day she would.

And now it was him who was calling it off.

"Look, Cyril, just give me a few weeks. I know I haven't been spending enough time with you and I'm sorry. But once things settle down, we can work it out."

Cyril shook his head sadly. "No. It's not going to work. You made your decision when you left Georgetown. I can see you wanted another way to stay in the United States without having to marry me. Maybe it's my fault. Maybe I rushed you too much. But I did it because I loved you. I still love you. But I can't go on like this. I'm sorry. Goodbye."

He got up, squeezed her shoulder, and walked off.

And Remi realized this conversation had never had the chance to end any other way. Much of what he said had sounded rehearsed. He had made his decision before they had even sat down to eat.

She was so stunned by what had just occurred that by the time she turned around to call after him, he had already stepped out of the restaurant …

… and out of her life.

Just then, her phone rang.

Daniel.

"Oh God, not now," she muttered.

It kept ringing. Wiping her eyes, she cleared her throat and answered it.

CHAPTER THREE

Remi didn't know how she managed to hide her emotions from her partner on the two-hour drive down to Richmond. Daniel was driving, and so she read from the file, the folder up to shield her face.

While she had never met Professor Edward Hale, she had of course heard of him. He was one of the leading Old Testament scholars of his generation. She had even heard rumors of his trial for illegal antiquities smuggling, but that had been a few years ago, when she had been focused on building up a very different career than the one that she now found herself in, and she hadn't paid much attention. She had heard he'd been found innocent and the case had dropped from her mind.

"Interesting that he was trading and not selling," Daniel said.

His sudden words made her jump. He hadn't talked for some time.

"Yes," she said, collecting herself. Remi felt like the turmoil of emotion she felt must be plainly obvious to him. "He sounds like he was trying to complete a collection of something."

"Yeah," Daniel replied. "Reminds me of child molesters. I know a guy who works in our cybercrime office tracking those people. How he does that job I have no idea. Busted a bunch of them, though. He says that the vast majority of child porn distributed on the Internet is done by trade. Money hardly ever changes hands."

"I would think they'd be afraid to be tracked that way."

"Oh, there's ways around that. Bitcoin or other cryptocurrencies. In-person cash drops. That's not how they roll. They're more interested in expanding their own collections, not getting money," Daniel grimaced. "Most of that stuff is produced by the offenders themselves and traded around the Internet for years."

"How horrible."

"Bastards should be shot," Daniel grumbled, gripping the wheel and looking ahead.

A cold silence filled the car. Remi, suddenly feeling awkward, said, "Are we almost there?"

"Yeah. Next turnoff."

Daniel turned off onto a leafy residential street. Large homes with tidy lawns. Porch swings and new cars in the driveways. She suspected that if it wasn't a school day, kids would be playing baseball in the street. Remi was surprised she didn't spot any picket fences.

At the end of the street, a squad car and police tape across a front porch ruined the All-American effect. Although, Remi mused, this was All-American too. Crime was so high in this country. It was getting worse in France too, especially in the sprawling *banlieues* in the outskirts around Paris. They hadn't existed when she was young and her father was a police officer. Now those neighborhoods had sprung up and become no-go areas.

She had heard the same about other cities in other countries. Antwerp. Berlin. And especially London. It seemed like the entire civilized world was sinking.

While she couldn't save the ship, perhaps she could at least plug one of its holes.

Daniel parked and they got out. As they approached the police tape, a stocky policewoman in her forties came out the front door and down the steps to meet them. Daniel pulled out his badge. A moment later, Remi remembered to do the same.

"Agents Walker and Laurent. FBI," Daniel said.

Remi felt a childish sense of disappointment. She wanted to say that!

"Officer Teller," the policewoman said. "I've been expecting you."

She nodded her head toward the house. Remi and Daniel ducked under the tape and headed inside.

"CSI has come and gone," Officer Teller told them. "Lots of prints and hair samples, but from what we've heard, the victim liked to entertain. He was shot at point blank range but didn't die of his wound immediately."

"We'll need the ballistics," Daniel said. "Our initial report didn't include them."

Officer Teller grimaced. "That's because there aren't any. Here."

A large manila folder lay on the side table in the front hall. The policewoman picked it up and handed it to them. Remi took it and opened it up.

And immediately suck in a sharp breath through gritted teeth.

The first photo showed a close-up of the bullet wound, a ragged hole inside a ring of puckered, torn flesh in the center of a pale chest fluffed with white hair. She had seen bullet wounds before, both in real life and in her FBI textbooks. She had still not grown accustomed to them and did not want to.

But she had been learning about them, and this bullet hole looked strange.

Daniel looked over her shoulder. "Did the perp dig out the bullet?"

"That's what the coroner said," Officer Teller replied. "A short-bladed knife with a curve up at the tip, like many brands of hunting and clasp knives. It's all in the report, which I've attached for you."

"So the body has been moved?" Remi asked.

"Yeah. The responding officers and CSI cleaned all that up this morning."

"Why didn't they wait for us?" Daniel said. He did not sound happy.

The officer gave a little shrug. "We didn't realize the FBI would get involved. We thought it was a simple case of a burglary gone wrong. There's an open case full of rare books with a lot of empty spaces. We figured that's why he was robbed."

"Maybe," Remi said. That would be the simple explanation. With the cases she'd been on so far, simple explanations hadn't gotten them very far.

Especially when a leading Old Testament scholar was trading in Biblical antiquities.

Much as Remi liked to believe that people were "innocent until proven guilty," as the law states, when someone is accused of a crime and then gets murdered, you have to wonder.

She flipped through the other photos. The coroner had taken shots of the rest of the body. No other visible wounds. Another photo, before the body had been washed, showed the hands covered in dried blood, no doubt from Professor Hale's feeble attempts to staunch the bleeding.

"He survived the shot and survived the killer digging the bullet out of the wound," she said.

"But the killer didn't notice, otherwise there would have been more signs of a struggle," Daniel said. "He played possum."

"Played possum?" Remi asked.

"American expression," the policewoman said, picking up on Remi's accent. "It means to pretend to be dead."

"How could he do that when someone was digging a bullet out of his chest?" Remi asked.

Daniel and the officer could only shake their heads in wonder.

"Maybe the gunshot knocked him out and the cutting of the wound woke him up, but how he stopped himself from screaming and thrashing around? I have no idea," Daniel said.

"A pity he didn't live long enough for someone to respond to his 911 call," Remi said.

"He didn't call," the officer said.

"What?" Remi and Daniel exclaimed together.

"A neighbor heard the shot," Officer Teller replied. "He wasn't sure if it was really a shot. You know how most civilians are. But then he saw someone he didn't recognize hurrying from the house with a pile of books under his arm and getting into a car."

"Please tell me the guy got the make, model, and license plate number," Daniel said.

"Sort of. Late model Nissan four door. Black or some other dark color. Hard to tell colors in dim light. But the license plate number was a fake. The perp must have painted the numbers to change them."

"Our man is careful to get rid of any clues, and yet he walks right into the house of the victim," Daniel mused aloud. "The initial report said no sign of forced entry."

"That hasn't changed," the officer said.

"Let's see the room where it happened," Remi suggested, impatient to get on with it. They could read the full report later.

They moved through a living room and down a hallway. Daniel stopped to look at some film photos on the walls.

"*Gilligan's Island*?" he said. "What theologian is interested in *Gilligan's Island*?"

"What's that?" Remi asked.

"Old comedy show. I guess you never got it in France. Funny stuff. Not exactly university professor humor, though. This case keeps getting more and more mysterious."

They walked into a cramped office. Dried blood stained the desk and floor behind. A trail went out of the room and around the corner to another room.

"CSI says he was shot while sitting in his office from someone standing just about where I am now," the officer said. She stood on the other side of the desk, almost close enough to reach out and touch someone sitting on the leather chair behind it.

Remi looked around. There was nothing obviously missing, although given the clutter it was difficult to tell.

"A M1911 .45 automatic was in the desk drawer," the policewoman said.

A popular handgun. For many years the U.S. Army service pistol. Remi had been forced to memorize all the common types of firearms and their calibers.

"Looks like the killer surprised him and he couldn't reach it in time," Remi said. Daniel nodded.

"Strange that a Biblical Studies professor has a gun," Daniel said. "But this is Virginia."

"Don't all Americans have guns?" Remi asked.

"Forty-four percent of all households. That will be on the test."

Remi rolled her eyes. They passed into a small extra room. A neatly made bed didn't look like it had been used in a while, so perhaps this was a little-used guest room or had once been the bedroom of a now grown child. The trail of blood ended in a large dark stain on the carpet and an outline of white tape. Professor Edward Hale had breathed his last with one leg flexed and the other straight. One arm had been bunched underneath him, the other extended in the direction of a bookshelf. A splotch of blood had dried on the lowest shelf.

Frowning, Remi edged around the stain on the carpet and squatted in front of the bookshelf. It housed a collection of texts on Hale's specialty, the Old Testament, its archaeology and history. The spot of blood was right in front of several works on the Book of Exodus.

Had he been trying to reach these books? Or perhaps using his last moments to point them out to investigators?

"May I touch these?" Remi asked.

"They've been dusted," Officer Teller said.

"It would have been nice if you hadn't moved the body," Daniel grumbled.

"Look, I just got here. I don't make any decisions; I was just told to watch the crime scene and show you around."

Daniel grunted. Remi supposed that was a stand-in for an apology.

Remi pulled out one of the books.

"There's a bookcase in the living room with a bunch of old books," the police officer said. "It's one of those cases with glass sides and a little door. All the books in there look antique and valuable. Several books are missing, and we didn't find any other antique books lying around the house."

"You wouldn't," Remi murmured. "It's best to keep old books in a case. I do that with mine."

That got a look of surprise from the officer, but Remi wasn't paying any attention. The book she was looking at was a modern volume, a detailed analysis of the Book of Exodus, detailing the Israelites' forty years of wandering in the desert. She flipped through it and didn't find anything underlined. Remi never liked people who marked up or dogeared pages. She would have forgiven Professor Hale in this case. It would have been helpful.

She pulled out another volume and saw a bookmark. Opening it, she found it was a 50 shekel note from Israel. It marked the beginning of a chapter on the Ark of the Covenant. There were no other bookmarks or notations in the book.

Putting the bookmark back, she used her phone to photograph the cover page of the book in case she needed to look it up later, put it back, and took out the other three books on Exodus.

Only one had a bookmark, this time a 20 shekel note. This one was for a chapter on Moses's forty days atop Mount Sinai, talking with God.

She took a photo of this book cover too and put it away.

Standing up, she turned to the police officer.

"Let's see that bookcase."

Officer Teller led them out to the living room. As they went, Daniel looked at Remi. "Find anything of significance?"

"I'm not sure yet."

The living room had a lived in, bachelor feel. Rather messy, although clean. A nearly empty glass of bourbon sat next to an old bottle on the coffee table, Professor Hale's last drink. A couple of oak bookshelves lined the walls, and in the corner, a narrow oak bookcase with glass sides so one could see the titles inside.

Remi walked up to it. Four shelves. One full, the other three with significant gaps. While Biblical studies was not Remi's field, just a glance at the spines showed her the books all dated to the 18th or 19th centuries and would probably fetch a good price with the right dealer or collector.

"We dusted this for prints," the police office said, indicating an ornate brass key in the door. "We got a partial print that wasn't the victim's."

"Surprising he'd be so careful and then mess that up," Daniel said. "He could have used gloves or just a Kleenex."

"Can I open it?" Remi asked.

The officer blinked. "Of course. I just said the CSI people dusted it."

Remi realized she was asking permission like a civilian, instead of taking charge like an FBI agent. Flushing, she turned the key and opened the little door.

While the books all covered Old Testament subjects, there was no obvious order among them, perhaps because the narrow bookcase could only fit a couple of dozen volumes. She pulled a few books off the shelf and leafed through them, taking photos of the oldest and rarest looking.

Replacing them and closing the door, she got on her phone.

She went to the website of the largest rare-book dealer in the United States, one she had used herself on a number of occasions, and looked up some of the titles.

She stopped looking after the first three.

"These books are averaging several thousand dollars apiece," she said.

Officer Teller took in a sharp intake of breath. Most non-academics didn't realize just how much a rare book could go for.

"Makes you wonder how much the missing ones are worth," Daniel said.

Remi nodded. "Yes, it does."

"I think we've done all we can do here," Daniel said. "Let's go to the University of Virginia. I've already arranged for the history and theology faculty to meet us. Maybe some of his colleagues can shed some light on this."

CHAPTER FOUR

"Did Professor Hale have any enemies?" Daniel asked the elderly, smartly dressed woman sitting before them in the staff conference room at the University of Virginia. He was getting frustrated. This was the fifth faculty member he and Remi had asked, and she gave an almost identical reply to the previous four.

"Not at all. Even those he debated in the journals respected him. I have been his colleague for more than three decades now, and I have never heard of a threat against him or even any serious anger."

"What did you think of his trial?" Daniel asked.

The professor made a face. "At the very worst it showed a lack of judgement. Ed was a very driven man, and he felt frustrated that so many institutional barriers got in the way of research."

"Institutional barriers such as the law?" Daniel said, trying to goad her into saying something that didn't sound scripted.

The professor, old enough to be his mother, would not be drawn out.

"Bureaucracy, poor funding, slow publication cycles," she said in an offhand way. "He was a vocal critic of the Israeli government when they dragged their feet over translating the Dead Sea Scrolls."

"Weren't they discovered in the Forties? Isn't that a bit before your time?" Daniel asked.

"Yes, but a full publication didn't come until the Nineties. The Israelis insisted on only their scholars working on them. He, and I, and many others, said that an international team would get the translations done far more quickly."

"What about his book collection?"

She seemed confused by the question. "What about it?"

"It appears several of his books are missing. Rare ones, by the looks of it."

"They would be quite valuable on the international market."

"I'm aware of that." Why did these academics always lecture people? "Do you know of any specific titles the thief might have been after?"

"No, I'm sorry. I'm a scholar of Aramaic, not Old Testament studies."

Daniel sighed. This was getting nowhere. None of Professor Hale's colleagues had any idea why someone would murder him. Neither did the department head or the dean.

"Thank you, Professor Kirkland. You can go now. Please send in the next person."

Not that they'll have any more to say than you did.

The elderly scholar left, to be replaced by a portly man with a neatly trimmed beard and messy brown hair that looked like it needed a wash. Ditto for his tweed sportscoat. He sat down opposite Daniel and Remi, gave them a nervous smile that vanished almost as soon as he made it, and asked, "How can I help you?"

"First off, what's your name and focus of study?" Daniel asked.

Professor Kirkland wasn't the first of Hale's colleagues to claim ignorance because they were in a slightly different subfield. The Balkanization of academia had always annoyed Daniel. People called themselves geniuses because they knew everything there was to know about 13th century France, but if you asked them about 14th century Spain they were as ignorant as the average employee of the Sanitation Department.

"My name is Professor Thomas Utterback, and my field is Old Testament studies."

Finally, someone who studies what the victim studied. But I really don't think "professor" is your first name, buddy.

"Did you work closely with Professor Hale?"

Professor Utterback gave a sad nod. "I did, and it was an honor to. I'm one of the youngest here at the department, and Hale was a leading figure even when I was in grad school."

"Did you know anyone who wished him dead?" Daniel asked, already knowing the answer.

"Of course not! And before you ask about the trial, I think he was one hundred percent innocent."

That's not what the others thought. Kirkland was typical: "I'm not saying he did it, but if he did it's not really his fault."

A bit like Mom and Uncle Roy.

"Bastard," Daniel muttered.

"Excuse me?" Professor Utterback looked shocked. Out of the corner of his eye, Daniel could see Remi staring at him.

"Sorry. Nothing. Thinking of an old case. So if Hale was innocent, why was he murdered?"

"Robbery, I suppose. Isn't that what the police said?"

The police weren't supposed to have said anything. Before Daniel could ask his next question, Remi cut in.

"What was Professor Hale working on?"

"He studied a wide variety of subjects. Are you French? I didn't know the FBI hired non-Americans."

Ignoring the question, Remi said, "I've looked through his publication list. He published articles or books every year for more than thirty years. Except for the past two years, when he didn't publish anything."

"I noticed that too," the academic replied. "At first I thought it might be grief at the loss of his wife, who died a little more than two years ago, until I realized he had been working harder than ever. Too much. I wasn't the only one to think that. I suppose he used work to cope. He grew more serious after her death, but also a lot more driven. So I asked him if he was working on his magnum opus, perhaps a synthesis of a lifetime of work. He said he had a new research project."

"And what was that?" Daniel asked.

"He was pretty tight-lipped about it, which was strange since he was usually so eager to talk about his projects. I do know that it involved a couple of research trips to Israel, however." A look of doubt passed across Professor Utterback's face. "At least I think so."

"What do you mean by that?" Daniel asked, remembering the shekels Remi had found being used as bookmarks in Professor Hale's home.

"Well, he said he went to Israel. That made sense. He's done a lot of collaboration projects with Professor Cohen at Hebrew University in Jerusalem. I have some contact with Cohen too. Now here is where it gets strange. About a month after his first trip to Israel, this being in February of last year, I had a Zoom call with Cohen and he was happily talking about a guest lecture Hale did for him. His second trip was just two months ago. I happened to exchange emails with Cohen again shortly after Hale came back and asked if Hale's second guest lecture was as big a hit as the first. Cohen gave me a confused reply saying that he hadn't been aware Hale had been in Israel."

"Could he have gone and not visited Hebrew University?"

"I suppose, but he always paid it a visit. He was in the habit of going once or twice a year. They give him a guest office to work in, and he's always consulting their library. Plus he and Cohen were good friends. To go to Israel and not tell him would be very strange."

"Did you ask him about it?"

"No. I figured it wasn't any of my business. Ever since his wife's death he had been acting strange. More secretive. He would often miss faculty functions on the weekends and not mention why. And he called in sick an unusual number of times, even though he's always been the picture of health. Once again, I didn't ask, writing it off as grief. Now that he's been killed, I have to wonder."

Remi leaned forward. "Did he ever mention researching the Ark of the Covenant?"

Professor Utterback looked surprised. "Why, yes. Although he didn't actually mention it. I noticed that when I visited his office, he'd often have books and papers on the subject. He never brought up the topic with me, though."

"Thank you, professor," Daniel said. "Here's my card. Please email me the contact information for that Israeli researcher."

"I will. Shall I send in the next person?"

"Not yet."

The professor left, closing the door behind him. Daniel turned to Remi.

"We'll check Hale's flight records. It will be easy enough to find out where he went. Also, I'll get a court order to check his bank and credit card information to see what other purchases he made. Maybe we'll get a lead. What's this about the Ark of the Covenant?"

"A hunch. Hale dragged himself all the way into another room and reached his hand out for a section of books on his bookshelf. All the books in that section were on Exodus. The Book of Exodus, as you probably know, deals with the Israelites wandering in the wilderness after getting out of Egypt. A big part of that story is the Ark of the Covenant, which God ordered them to build after Moses was given the Ten Commandments."

"Yeah, and they put the tablets inside. I've seen *Indiana Jones*."

Remi smiled for the first time since he had picked her up for the case. Something had been bothering her. Daniel hadn't asked, because he hated it when people were nosy. Hopefully whatever it was, she was getting over it.

"Careful," she said. "Some people take it very seriously."

"Oh, I'm not knocking anybody's religion, but that's just an old story. And what does it have to do with the case?"

"One of the books had Israeli money marking the start of a chapter on the Ark."

"Yeah, I saw that. The other book that had a bookmark was marking something else."

"Yes, a chapter about the time Moses spent on Mount Sinai. That's when God gave him the Ten Commandments, and also instructed him to make the Ark to house them. So it could be related."

"Interesting. A bit of a stretch, though. Maybe he wasn't going for that section of books at all. Maybe he was going for a section further up but couldn't reach it. The shekels, though … that's interesting."

He paused, thinking.

"Wait, you're not saying he was looking for it, are you?" he asked.

Remi shrugged. "Perhaps. He did have a taste for Old Testament antiquities. And considering some of the other cases we've had, is it all that unbelievable?"

"I know enough about history to know there's no solid evidence for the story of a forty-year trek around the wilderness, or that the Egyptians ever enslaved the Israelites. They used Egyptian peasants to build the pyramids and temples, not the Israelites."

"True, but that doesn't mean people can't believe. I've even had questions from my students at the Sorbonne about it, because there's a legend that the Knights Templar hid the Ark in the cathedral at Chartres. The story has been proven untrue. Some monks created a fake Ark to attract pilgrims, a common enough practice in that era, but the legend has continued as folklore even into modern times."

"Huh."

Daniel pulled out his laptop and Googled "Professor Edward Hale" and "Ark."

He got an immediate hit.

A blog titled, "The True Ten Commandments" had an entry from just six months before titled, "Professor Hale, University of Virginia: Keeper or Cover-up Artist?"

"Take a look at this," Daniel said.

Remi leaned in close to look at the screen. Daniel noted that she was wearing some subtle perfume, probably an expensive one from France. His previous partner, Carmella Nomellini, a loudmouth Italian-

American from New York, never wore perfume, unless the smell of onions from her last hoagie counted as perfume. Daniel and Remi read the blog together.

Or at least tried to. It was a mishmash of angry diatribe, conspiracy theories, and lengthy untranslated quotes from what they presumed to be ancient Hebrew. The gist of it, as far as they could make out, was that the author of the blog, George Steiner, was obsessed with finding the Ark and had become convinced that Professor Hale knew where it was. A typical portion ran:

"Professor Hale and his elitist cronies 'Keepers' are SUPRESSING the real TRUTH about the Ark. Time and again he has avoided answering the questions he knows he can answer!!! Just last week he gave a 'lecture' at the Richmond Public Library and I confronted him about the TRUTH! Did he admit he knew where the Ark was??? Not at ALL!!! He keeps up his obfuscations, deflections and DOWNRIGHT LIES!!!! Is this an academic? No, this is a SNAKE OIL SALESMAN!!!"

"That's a lot of all caps and exclamation points," Daniel quipped.

"A true scholar, to be sure," Remi said wryly. "What's a snake oil salesman?"

"A con man. There used to be people who went from town to town selling bottles of medicine they claimed would cure everything. Said they were made from exotic ingredients like elephant tusks and snake oil. Really they were just a mixture of alcohol with a bit of opium mixed in. Made you feel good but didn't actually cure anything."

"I wonder if George Steiner is his real name."

"His bio on the blog says he graduated from University of North Carolina-Chapel Hill with a degree in archaeology. Let's see if that's true," Daniel said, opening up an FBI address database. "You learned how to use this yet?"

"The database?" Remi asked. "I've practiced a bit."

"It's like Yell on steroids," Daniel turned the laptop to her. She tapped away for a moment and brought up several name matches. Cross-checking with Chapel Hill graduates, she found a match in Ashland, Virginia. A quick check showed them the town was a short drive north of Richmond and that Steiner taught at a nearby community college.

"Let's go," Daniel said. "With any luck, you'll be back to your training program tomorrow."

"You really think it will be that easy?" Remi asked. She looked disappointed.

"Probably not. But maybe he's another piece to the puzzle. I hope so. We sure don't have a clear picture yet."

CHAPTER FIVE

When Remi thought of small-town America, she pictured a place like Ashland, Virginia. As they pulled off the highway and onto the four-lane road passing through town, a sign adorned with an American flag announced that the town had a population of "8,031 and counting!" Apparently, this vast metropolis was experiencing a growth spurt. Modest two-story homes with luxuriant lawns flanked the road, interspersed with patches of thick forest.

Remi opened the window and let the warm air and rich smell of foliage wash over her. She had been depressed all day, and the sensation eased her feelings somewhat.

Daniel checked the GPS and turned off at a sign pointing to downtown.

Downtown turned out to be a two-lane road divided by a railway track. They passed a railway station with a large Amtrak sign, then a string of little shops in nineteenth-century brick buildings. A clothing store and a place for horseback riding supplies. A café and an ice cream shop. People strolled casually along, looking far more relaxed than those she saw in D.C.

Downtown was gone in the blink of an eye. Daniel turned off onto a residential street. This neighborhood was less prosperous, with one-story prefab homes and smaller lots. It still looked pleasant. A man was out mowing his lawn, and as they passed, Remi caught a whiff of cut grass. A pack of kids shot past on their bicycles, reminding Remi that it was a Saturday. She had been so embroiled in her training, her breakup, and now the case, that she had lost track. On one front lawn some parents had set up an inflatable kiddy pool and a few small children splashed and squealed.

Life goes on, she mused. *Even amid death and heartbreak.*

Like many Parisians, Remi had country cousins, and when growing up she spent holidays in a village amid rolling hills and vineyards. A medieval castle and church stood not far off, one of her early influences. Centuries old cottage industries created local cheeses and wines, and she and her cousins would take their bikes along back roads to explore hidden hamlets or the old Roman bridge that still spanned a stream where local kids swam and attempted to fish.

It had been an idyllic time, at least looking back from the cares and responsibilities of adulthood, cut short all too quickly by her father's unexpected death. Money had grown tight, and holidays in the countryside became fewer and further between.

But she could go back to living in a small town if she wanted. Her pay scale for the FBI was decent enough, and she had savings from her academic career. Perhaps she should find a small town somewhere around D.C. The commute would be a downside, but it might be worth it.

A little house in a small town where I live all alone?

Her mood turned dark again.

"Almost there," Daniel said.

"Good. Did you check for gun ownership?"

"Of course. There's no record that he owns a gun. That doesn't mean he doesn't have one. Virginia doesn't require citizens to register firearms."

"Always assume a suspect is armed and dangerous."

Daniel shot her a smile. That cheered her up a bit. "Sounds like you're repeating something from class. I think you learned that in the field, though."

"I'm glad I can finally carry something better than my pepper spray," Remi replied.

"Oh, I hope you still carry some pepper spray. How many serial killers and priests have you sprayed now?"

"I think I'm getting a bad reputation in the Vatican," Remi thought, flushing.

That wasn't said entirely in jest. She knew the Vatican was on the trail of the cryptex, as was the Society of Devout Students, a religious organization tracing its roots back to the time of Jesus and devoted to protecting the highly secret Gospel of Longinus. While neither organization had what she had—a code she had found thanks to a map inside the cryptex, a code that she and a Canadian colleague were trying to break—both had enough resources at their command that they might discover what the code led to without its help. They both ran a vast network of informants and owned massive libraries dating back centuries. If they put large teams of scholars on the job, they might find the prize before she did.

And here she was training for the FBI and tracking down a murderer.

Plus, the Vatican had the cryptex. The crazed killer who had tried to steal it had figured out the code to open it. If the Vatican had gotten him to talk, or figured out the code themselves, then they would have found the map. It wouldn't have taken long for them to find the church where a hidden niche had contained a statuette within which the code was hidden, a statuette Remi had stolen.

The Society of Devout Students already knew what she had done, and if the Vatican found that out too, she would have two serious rivals instead of just one.

Remi suppressed a shudder. Would the Vatican resort to violence? She really had no idea. All her ideas about the Church and its teachings had been turned upside down in the past year. They wanted the key to the cryptex, and they wanted it badly.

But why? Did they know something about what the cryptex led to that she didn't?

And what about the Society of Devout Students? While she felt sure they wouldn't resort to violence, they knew a great deal about the Church's hidden past, and she had gotten a glimpse at just how large and well-connected they were.

She'd have to take care, and she'd have to hurry.

But how to do that when on a case?

"Here we go," Daniel said.

They stopped in front of a modest prefab home behind a small lawn that needed cutting. An older model Hyundai in the driveway suggested that Steiner was home. Next door, a man was playing basketball with his ten-year-old son.

I hope Steiner doesn't have a gun, Remi thought, remembering the countless articles she had read about American law enforcement getting into shootouts where innocent bystanders got killed.

Daniel turned to her. "Look, you've been a huge help on the past three cases, but I need to talk with you about something."

I know what's coming.

Daniel went on. "You're too impulsive. I've talked to you about this before. You can't go running off on your own. Previously I chalked it up to you being a civilian consultant. Now you're a trainee agent. You can't pull that anymore. It was unacceptable then and it's twice as unacceptable now. You need to stick with me unless there's an overriding reason to split up. Also, as a trainee agent assigned to a full agent, technically I'm in charge."

Remi shifted uncomfortably in her seat.

Daniel snorted. "Yeah, yeah, I know you don't like that. Don't worry, I'm not going to throw my weight around, as long as you act professionally. You're new at this, *very* new at this. You have the knowledge we need, but not the law enforcement skills or discipline. That will come with time. So stay alert, stay cool, and don't go running off on your own. Got it?"

Remi bridled against this lecture. Although it was said in a firm tone, it was not said in an unkind one. And she knew that everything Daniel said was for her own good, and his.

Still, she didn't like being told what to do.

That's unprofessional, she told herself. *Yes, you know far more about art and archaeology than he does, but he's the more experienced agent, and he is responsible for you.*

Remi had heard rumors among the agents that Daniel had been demoted. She didn't know why that had happened, but he had been transferred from a key position at the Behavioral Affairs Unit to the new Antiquities Division. Most people would see that as a step down. If something happened to a trainee agent on his watch, it might end his career.

"All right," she forced herself to say, understanding and agreeing in her mind but still objecting in her heart. "I'll follow your directives."

"No need for the long face," Daniel said, giving her a playful punch in the shoulder, "I'm sure you'll still get to demonstrate your genius."

They got out of the car and headed up the narrow, tiled path to Steiner's front door. Remi let out a slow breath and tried to relax. This was just a routine call on a potential suspect, after all.

Hopefully.

Just as they were about to step onto the narrow porch, the front door opened.

Daniel and Remi paused. Remi's hand strayed toward the inside of her suit for her shoulder holster.

Don't be impulsive, she reminded herself.

The man standing in front of them did not look like the crazy voice from the fringe who had written that blog post. He was a tidy, relatively fit man in his late thirties wearing casual clothes. A cigarette dangled from his lips and an American flag was emblazoned across his t-shirt.

Except for the lack of muscle on the arms, he looked more like a warehouse worker than a community college professor.

"It's about time you got here," he said in a slow Southern drawl.

"Mr. George Steiner?" Daniel asked as they mounted the porch. They pulled out their IDs and identified themselves. Remi cursed herself because she took out her ID with her right hand, which was her gun hand. She hurried to put it back in her pocket to leave that hand free.

At least Remi remembered to take half a step to the right and keep just out of reach of the suspect. That way both she and Daniel put him at the apex of a triangle, and he couldn't immediately lash out at both of them. Remi hoped that all this would soon come naturally.

It better, or it might get the both of them into serious trouble.

"That's me," the man said. "Read the blog?"

"Yes, we have. Why do you ask?"

Steiner chuckled. "Hale's murder was in the *Times-Dispatch*."

"Do you find that amusing?" Remi asked.

"Ironic. He spent his entire career protecting a secret and that secret killed him."

"And how is that, Mr. Steiner?" Daniel asked.

Remi remembered to look him over. He was wearing a tight t-shirt and slacks, plus a pair of slippers. She could see no obvious place to hide a gun except tucked into his belt at the small of his back, which she could not see. She kept an eye on his hands.

You should have done all this when he first opened the door. God, I have so much to learn!

"Hale and his so-called group of scholars have been hiding important truths all their careers."

"Such as?" Daniel prompted.

Steiner cocked his head and looked at him. "You know."

Pause. Remi kept his eyes on him.

"I give you consent to come into my house," Steiner said. "I also want to inform you that I have a loaded .30-06 rifle in the bedroom."

"Thank you, Mr. Steiner," Remi said. She tried to remember what to do in such a case and came up a blank. As long as he didn't try to go into the bedroom, she supposed it would be all right.

Unless he was telling them about one gun to lull them into complacency about the possibility that he had another.

Steiner turned and went into the house. Remi looked at the back of his shirt and pants and didn't see anything obviously hidden there.

They entered a living room smelling heavily of cigarette smoke. Remi felt like she was back in France, which had not succumbed to the anti-smoking craze like America had. A ratty old sofa stood against one wall. At its end was curled up a tabby cat that ignored them. In front of it was a coffee table with an ashtray heaped with cigarette butts next to several books. A television was on the wall opposite, and the rest of the walls were filled with bookshelves. A quick scan revealed a focus on theology, Biblical archaeology, and Middle Eastern and Medieval European history. The books mostly looked used. A community college teacher's salary was not the best, and Remi imagined him patiently collecting the precious collection through eBay, hunting through used bookstores and library sales.

"Take a seat," Steiner said, sitting down next to the cat. With one hand he put the cigarette to his lips and took a drag, while stroking the cat with the other. He did not look like a man worried about being charged with murder.

Remi and Daniel did not take a seat. Instead, they stood slightly apart in the middle of the room.

"Would you mind telling us your whereabouts last night?" Daniel asked.

"Teaching a night course for adults called 'Great Men and Women of the Bible.' Moses, Aaron, King David. Night courses are pretty popular, and the college pays extra to teach them. Not much extra, the cheap bastards. I'll give you the number of my boss so you can double check."

I should have known it wouldn't be this easy, Remi thought.

"You don't seem surprised Professor Hale was murdered," Daniel said.

Remi scanned the bookshelves. They were shelved by topic, and within those topics shelved alphabetically. She found both her books on the cryptex and medieval codes. Had Steiner noticed the name on her ID badge and made the connection? If so, he wasn't showing it.

"Why would I be surprised?" Steiner replied. "He was covering up an important truth, and there are people who will kill for the truth."

"And what truth would that be?" Remi asked, thinking she knew the answer.

She was right.

"The location of the Ark of the Covenant. He's part of a secret, international cabal of scholars who know the truth and have kept it secret for centuries to further their own purposes. They call themselves the Keepers."

Six months ago, Remi and Daniel would have laughed. After what they had learned about the cryptex, the Association of Devout Students, and the Vatican secret police, nothing sounded too strange anymore.

"Isn't the Ark supposed to be in a cathedral in Ethiopia?" Remi asked.

"Ha! That's what they want you to believe. It's just a fake. Don't you know every Ethiopian Orthodox Church has a replica of the Ark in the sanctum sanctorum? They admit they're fakes. Symbols. Nothing wrong with that. Except the one in the Church of Mary of Zion in Axum is supposed to be the real one. As if they'd admit that! It would get stolen. Hell, some Italian TV crew tried to break in once, and they weren't the only ones. No, if the Ethiopians have it, it's hidden somewhere else. And they probably don't have it."

"Why do you say that?" Remi asked.

"Because everyone says they have it, so it's obviously a smoke screen to hide its real location."

Remi didn't follow the logic, but logic didn't seem to be this man's strong suit. Because of the nature of her research, she had met far too many people like George Steiner. Well-read but ignorant. So wrapped up in their own little theories they couldn't see clearly. Remi couldn't count the number of times she had been cornered at conferences and endured breathless lectures about some fringe researcher's precious theory. This man had no better idea about the location of the Ark of the Covenant than anyone else.

In fact, it probably didn't even exist anymore, if it had ever existed in the first place.

But that hadn't stopped someone from killing for it.

And she had a feeling that whoever it was—and it almost certainly wasn't the man sitting before her—he or she would kill again.

And Steiner, couldn't, or wouldn't get them any closer to finding the true killer.

CHAPTER SIX

Jerusalem, Israel
Two days later ...

Professor Yitzhak Cohen packed his briefcase and turned out the lights in his office, suppressing a yawn. He had stayed late at the Hebrew University in Jerusalem, working hard on correspondence with some of his colleagues. The murder of Professor Hale had put them all on edge.

Of course, he hadn't used his office computer. He had used a laptop he had bought for cash from a dodgy dealer in Gaza, loaded up with Tor through a VPN and communicating via Telegram. His two boys thought he was computer illiterate. How they would be surprised.

You had to be computer literate if you wanted to dodge the Israeli government. If they had any idea the Ark really existed, they'd do anything to get it, and governments could not be trusted.

Sending up a brief prayer in Hebrew for a safe journey home, he switched off the lights in his office, locked the door, and walked with his secure laptop and some papers in a briefcase out of the nearly abandoned History Department building on the Hebrew University campus.

The night was warm, and few people were on campus. The students and many of the faculty were probably enjoying a beer in one of the many cafés on HaNaviim Street. The only people he saw were a few lone figures like him, or the guards in Kevlar and carrying Galils.

Cohen grimaced. When Hale had last visited him, he had said, "I'll never get used to campus security carrying assault rifles."

Hale was lucky to live in a country where terrorism was so far away that such precautions weren't needed, but now Hale was dead. He and his colleagues had racked their brains trying to figure out who had killed him. Suspects had been suggested and ruled out, until finally they had to admit they had no idea who it might have been.

All they could agree on was that Hale would not be the last.

If only he knew why Hale had said he had visited Israel but never dropped in on campus. Had he really come here? If so, why keep it a secret from his fellow Keepers? And if he didn't come to Israel, where did he go?

Cohen checked the heavy Webley revolver at his belt, an heirloom from his grandfather, who had been a freedom fighter struggling for the independence of Israel. Grandfather had gotten this gun off a British officer he had killed, back when the British still ruled over what was then called the Palestine Mandate and the British still thought they had an empire.

Compared to the assault rifles the university guards carried, the Webley looked like the antique it was; but being a historian and the wrong side of sixty, Cohen was accustomed to old things. When he was younger, many of the old freedom fighters still strolled the streets with bolt action rifles slung over their shoulders. They had used them to fight the British, then the Palestinians, and then the neighboring Arab nations, and they saw no reason why not to take them along on an evening stroll or a visit to the cinema.

Neither did Cohen. The revolver's .45 caliber bullets packed a good punch, and his obligatory military training and intermittent practice since then made him a decent shot even at his age. Being able to protect the Jewish nation was the duty of every Israeli man and woman.

Cohen got to his car in the fenced-in lot, drove to the gate where he was waved through by another armed guard, and drove out into the night.

As was his habit, Yitzhak Cohen took the long drive home so he could go down Sultan Suleiman Street past the glorious walls of the Old City built by that famous Ottoman ruler. At night it was all lit up, the old stone walls with their crenellated tops, the arched gates at regular intervals, and beyond, on a hill rising above the Old City, the Temple Mount and its later addition, the Dome of the Rock.

While Cohen would much rather see the Solomon's Temple still standing atop the Mount, he could not help but admire the intricately decorated blue and green tile walls and golden dome of the mosque that had been built there in the Umayyad Caliphate. It was quite the irony that in Judaism's most sacred city, the most recognizable landmark was an Islamic one.

That always made Cohen smile. Although an ardent Zionist who would have gladly given his life to protect the Jewish nation, he wanted all of the people living in this holy land to get along.

If only more people felt that way.

The armored car and squad of soldiers in front of the Damascus Gate told him that would never be the case. There had been a car bombing in the parking lot opposite, where the newer, more modern city started. Old hatreds in a new neighborhood. Thank God no one had been killed, although five people had gone to the hospital, including a pregnant woman. The kind of story that only lasts a day in Israeli papers, it being all too common, and wouldn't even make it into the international press.

He took a turn at that street, Nablus Street, passing the parking lot on his left and a youth hostel on the right, a group of young Europeans just coming out, eager to sightsee or enjoy the nightlife, probably unaware of the bombing just two days before. It had already been cleared up without a trace. The emergency services were good at that.

But who was going to clear up this mess with Hale? That was the real question. Hale had not been an obvious target. While he was one of America's leading Biblical scholars, he was Christian, not Jewish, and not even all that devout of one. His interest in the Ark had been more historical than spiritual, but he had been accepted into the organization for his academic brilliance and his discretion.

Despite that discretion, someone had learned what he was up to and killed him.

Why? To get the location of the Ark? Cohen doubted Hale would have revealed it. He had a will of iron and had taken the Oath. More likely, he had refused to give the killer what he wanted and paid for his bravery with his life.

Even though Hale had not been Jewish, he and a few associates in the local area had gotten together to say a Kaddish. He had deserved it, and God in His infinite wisdom would understand.

Cohen drove another couple of minutes into a quiet neighborhood of closely packed houses, parking on the street since the homes here had no room for driveways. That's something else Hale had never gotten used to, how small of a space most non-Americans lived in. Israel was a small nation packed between larger, mostly hostile ones. Living close to your neighbors didn't make you feel crowded, it made you feel safe.

Even so, Cohen scanned the street before he unlocked the car. A couple walked away from him in the distance. Closer by, a fit, middle-aged man came around the nearest corner. Cohen studied him for a second. He looked and dressed like an American and walked with the confidence and sense of direction of someone who was not a tourist. Probably one of those American West Bank settlers who gave the government so many headaches.

Harmless to him, at least.

Or so he thought.

As he got out of his car, the stranger ducked around and before Cohen could react, had pulled the Webley out of Cohen's holster and stuck it in the small of his back.

"Never make assumptions," the man said. He had an American accent. "You were looking for Palestinians, but a Palestinian wouldn't want what I want."

"You're the man who killed Hale," Cohen's voice wavered.

"And I'll kill you if you don't cooperate. Back in the car."

Cohen gave his house a long look. The lights were on. A shadow passed by one of the upstairs curtains, too tall to be his wife, Rachel. One of his sons then. Shlomo or Asher. Good boys. They'd take care of Rachel. His eyes welled up.

Goodbye.

With a heavy heart, Cohen got back into his vehicle. The killer slid into the passenger's seat.

"Where are we going?" Cohen asked. Not that it mattered.

"Go up Megadim Street to Mount Herzl."

"You're going to kill me at the gates to Yad Vashem?" That was the Holocaust Memorial.

"No need to go up to the top. Stop at the Jewish Soldiers in the Polish Army memorial a little lower down."

"Right next to the military cemetery? How appropriate," Cohen muttered, driving slowly down the street. His home dwindled in the rearview mirror.

"I'm not going to kill you if you give me what I want."

But I'm not going to give you what you want. I'm going to wait for the right moment, and then I'm going to beat the living daylights out of you, get Grandfather's gun back, and shoot you and damn the consequences.

They drove out onto the main street. The walls of the Old City came into view again, and up ahead stood the Damascus Gate. The soldiers and the armored car were still in sight.

I could ram into that armored car. We'd probably be knocked out and it wouldn't even dent the fender. Then the soldiers would rush in and ...

"Don't even think about trying anything funny," his kidnapper snapped. "We know where you live."

We.

All thoughts of fighting this man vanished at the implied threat to his family.

Cohen gripped the wheel and drove for Mount Herzl. His captor sat silent, keeping an eye on Cohen's every move. They passed the Old City, leaving its medieval walls behind, and took the main road through a fashionable shopping district, where boutiques and cafés were still full of life, then through a residential neighborhood. Mount Herzl stood not far ahead, Yad Vashem at the top. Even from this distance he could see the glass and concrete construction, looking a bit like the Ark of Noah, its prow sticking out over the steep slope.

At last, Cohen couldn't bear the tension anymore.

"What are you going to do with it?"

His captor did not need to ask what Cohen meant.

"Such an artifact will house the greatest power."

"Power," Cohen grunted. "Power corrupts, and absolute power corrupts absolutely. That building up there will teach you that, although I doubt you've ever been."

"I won't be corrupted. I'm pure."

"Sure you are."

They began to ascend the slopes of Mount Herzl, darkened olive groves to either side. Cohen drove slowly, trying to think of what to do. He could not see a way out of this, not with this man's colleagues watching over his family.

At a bend in the road was a wide patch of gravel. His captor told him to park there. No other cars were about.

Cohen did as he was told.

"Now get out. We're going to take a walk."

Cohen sent up a prayer to God, not for deliverance, because he knew he was beyond deliverance, but for the safety of his family.

Please, Lord, keep my voice level. Make him believe me. One of your Commandments is that Thou Shalt Not Bear False Witness. Surely it doesn't count in this case, and if it does, let the sin be on me and not my wife and boys.

Cohen walked into the olive grove, his captor just behind. Through the trees he could see the Holocaust Museum above, and below he could see the Old City all lit up. This was a popular spot for walks, and he hoped someone might see the man he knew was planning to kill him. Perhaps justice would be served before he got his filthy hands on the holy artifact.

"This is far enough," the American said.

Cohen stopped, took a deep breath, and turned to him.

"Don't hurt my family," he said, his voice cracking.

"I won't if you give me what I want. This isn't personal."

Says the man who's about to put a bullet in my brain. How can that not be personal?

Cohen tried to speak, but his words choked off. All the clever lies he had been rehearsing on the drive over now vanished from his mind.

"P-please, my family …," Cohen forced himself to stop. He would not beg with this criminal.

"The Ark, Professor Cohen. Where is the Ark? And don't tell me you don't know. You're a Keeper. You are one of the inner circle. You know."

This man has done his homework more diligently than most of my students.

"The Valley of the Kings," Cohen said.

That seemed to catch the man off guard. Even in the dim light filtering through the olive trees, Cohen could see his consternation.

"The Valley of the Kings? You expect me to believe the Jews would give the Ark to the Egyptians?"

"It's not just Jews in our organization, you know that. We—"

"The Jews run it, though."

"No. Anyone devoted to protecting the truth is welcome."

"Ha! You aren't protecting the truth, you're hiding it." He raised his gun. "Now tell me where the Ark really is."

"In the Valley of the Kings. Tomb KV 30. That's an unfinished and undecorated tomb that is closed to visitors. It's locked with a heavy gate, with a sign warning that it's unstable. That's to keep out curiosity seekers." Cohen saw the man was about to speak so he went on. "When

Sadat and Begin made peace at Camp David, Jimmy Carter made them seal the deal with a powerful vow. He was one of us. He got Begin to sign off on shipping the Ark from its previous hiding place to the Valley of the Kings. In return, the Egyptian got peace and became the second largest recipient of U.S. foreign aid, second only to Israel. The U.S. also agreed to keep out of Egyptian politics unless an Islamist regime tried to come in, something the Egyptian army always feared. The U.S. kept out of the Arab Spring, but when Morsi and the Muslim Brotherhood won the elections, they helped al-Sisi and his army cronies seize power. It was all part of the deal. Muslim Brotherhood rule would have meant eventual war with Israel, but as it stands, they are still at peace and the U.S. aid keeps rolling in."

Cohen paused, out of breath and astonished at his own creativity.

"And the Islamists never stole it?" the American asked, doubt lacing his voice.

"You think the Egyptian generals would share the location of the Ark with the Muslim Brotherhood? Only a few know, and they know it's in their best interest to keep it secret. If the Islamists got the Ark, it would mean war, a war Egypt would lose like all the others they've fought with us."

"So it's been in Tomb KV 30 since the Seventies?"

"Hidden in plain sight. All the records show that it's an empty, undecorated tomb found in the nineteenth century. No reason to go down there. The later records also say that it's deteriorated and become unstable. That's not true. It's been solid for thousands of years and will remain so for thousands more."

The man's gun did not waver. "How do I know you're telling the truth?"

"Billions of dollars in U.S. foreign aid every year. Why else would they give that to some minor power just because it decided, after losing three wars, to stop causing trouble to one of America's allies?"

It sounded convincing to Cohen. He held his breath, hoping the stranger would believe it.

"All right," the American said. "You just bought the lives of your family."

Cohen let out a gust of air. To his surprise, the man put away the revolver.

And pulled out a hammer. Cohen trembled.

"Y-you're going to kill me with that?"

“Security is so tight you can’t even smuggle a knife into this country. And a gun would attract attention.” The man raised the hammer.

“Wait.”

Cohen turned away before he saw if he waited or not.

Through the olive trees, he could just make out a portion of the Dome of the Rock, illuminated in the Jerusalem night. The large outcropping of pale brown stone stood out above the Old City, the brilliantly beautiful mosque atop it.

But Professor Yitzhak Cohen did not see the mosque, and he did not see the medieval walls.

He saw, in his mind’s eye so clearly that he could almost pretend it was real, the great Temple of Solomon standing atop the Temple Mount. He could see the city of Jerusalem as it was in the time of King Solomon. He could see the Pharisees in a long procession bringing the Ark of the Covenant into the Holy of Holies.

And that made him feel peace, for a brief moment, before the hammer came down and his life ended in blinding pain.

CHAPTER SEVEN

Washington, D.C.
The next day ...

Remi sat in front of a computer at her temporary office in FBI headquarters, just down the hall from where Daniel had his office. She would have liked to have shared an office, but after his reassignment, her partner had been stuck in a cramped little place with a tiny window, reinforcing the impression that the move to the Antiquities Division had been a demotion.

She was busy going through what was informally called "background work," the dull and slow but often productive job of finding out as much as possible about the victim and circumstances of his death.

So far, she hadn't come up with much. Professor Hale had an illustrious career in Biblical Studies. The only odd thing about him was that he had no strong religious convictions. Most people in the field came out of seminaries or at the very least were avid members of a church or synagogue. This was less true in Biblical Archaeology, Remi had learned, which had a deep divide between those who conducted excavations in Israel and the rest of the Levant in order to prove the Bible to be literally true, and those who simply wanted to find out more about the region's past.

And of course, these two fields attracted many fringe thinkers, even more than her own field. The Internet was awash in poorly written articles taking unlikely and unconvincing positions on every aspect of Biblical Studies.

Remi smiled. It looked like her new job wouldn't entirely get her away from academia. Indeed, being an academic was what qualified her.

Remi felt a brief welling up of pain at the thought of the old life she had left behind—the safety and security of the library, the respect of her colleagues, and most of all the loss of Cyril.

As quickly as the feeling arose, she suppressed it. She had a case to deal with. Someone had been murdered, and more people might be in danger. Her own troubles paled in comparison.

That sense of perspective made her feel better. At least a little.

Starting with Steiner's disjointed ramblings, she followed a series of links through a whole subculture of fringe theorists who thought various items mentioned in the Bible still existed, hidden around the globe by various sinister organizations.

Where they were hidden and who were hiding them depended on the conspiracy theorist. Some said the Freemasons had them. Others thought they had been stolen by the Chinese or the Russians as part of their plot for world domination. One blog claimed the Hare Krishna had stolen them in order to undermine Judeo-Christian religion. That was the least convincing theory, but definitely her favorite.

The majority said the Catholic Church had them stored in the Vatican. One added it was in a vault 666 feet below St. Peters, because of course it would be 666 feet. This sort of nonsense made Remi feel like her brain was melting out her ears.

As ridiculous as most of these theories sounded, and they were ridiculous, Remi couldn't entirely dismiss their core idea. The cryptex had turned out to be true, after all. Assuming objects such as the Ark had ever existed in the first place, wouldn't it make sense that people would do their best to protect and preserve it, keeping it hidden away from those who might steal or destroy it?

One thing was for sure—these idiots would never find it. Most of their energies seemed devoted to sniping at one another in online forums.

Daniel was busy in the other office checking with Hale's numerous international contacts for leads. The prime one, Professor Cohen of Hebrew University, he had emailed a couple of hours after the interviews of the faculty at University of Virginia. He had gotten an out of office reply.

That struck Remi as odd. She thought that with smartphones and the availability of email everywhere, an out of office reply had gone as out of fashion as CDs.

Speaking of email, she was expecting an important one.

Her gaze turned to her office door, which she always left half open. No one was in the hallway, and she had situated her desk so that her screen faced away from the door.

She checked her email and perked up to see that John MacDonald had emailed her. John was a Canadian researcher at the University of Toronto and the world's leading expert on ancient and medieval cryptography, more knowledgeable than even Remi herself.

The subject line was only one innocuous word: "Research."

Her heart beat a little faster. That one word held so much potential.

Checking the doorway again, she opened John's email.

"Hello Remi. I've been working on the code and it's a tough one. I haven't been able to break it yet, but I'm getting closer. As you suspected, it is a new type of code unlike those commonly used in that period. I've tried various decrypting methods for the most common, and less common, code types and eliminated them as possibilities.

"Now that I've ascertained that it is not any known code type, I'm bearing down on the code itself. Those pointers you gave me should help, and I'm working with the presumption that it translates into Latin. If that's the case, I might have a breakthrough in the next few days. Exciting stuff!

"It would be easier to work on this in person. Would it be possible to get a week or so off from Georgetown? I already talked with the department head, and he's found office space for you.

"Also, once we do crack the code, I bet it will point to another geographic location like the map inside the cryptex. Once we have that, I'd love to come along and see what it reveals.

"Look forward to seeing you!

"John"

Remi sat back and reread the last few lines. She and John had a brief affair a few years ago, before her relationship with Cyril. Being a gentleman, he had backed off when she had started getting serious with Cyril, and he was one of the few of her colleagues who actually knew she had been seeing him.

Had he heard somehow that they had broken up? She couldn't see how, but the academic grapevine was as efficient as it was ravenous for new material. The way he closed his email made it sound like he had heard and was opening the door for a possible rekindling of their old relationship.

Remi felt flattered … and uninterested. Still reeling from the breakup with Cyril, she was not ready to dive into another romantic entanglement.

Or perhaps he hadn't heard. Apparently he hadn't heard she had left Georgetown. But still, the tone certainly left the proverbial door open.

On top of that, John had offered to help out in the investigation in a more active way. While she certainly would give him equal credit on any publications—not to do so would be unprofessional, not to mention a poor show of friendship—she did not want him along on the hunt. This was her quest, and hers alone.

Luckily John wasn't a demanding man. If she deflected the offer, he'd only flash his kind smile and accept the situation. He had been far more easygoing than Cyril. Perhaps, she thought wryly, that's why she had found him less interesting.

A knock on her door made her look up.

Daniel stood in the doorway. Remi changed the tab on her browser from her email to the background research she had been conducting. She felt a stab of guilt over hiding her cryptex quest from her partner. She had gotten her first major lead when she had opened up the cryptex after they captured the serial killer who had been hunting for it. Daniel didn't know she had done that. It had been an illegal act, handling a museum artifact in that way, and that had kept her from telling him. Now that lie by omission had turned into a secret that had endured for months and had involved several other lies.

All thought of that fled when Daniel spoke.

"I just talked to Hebrew University because Professor Cohen still hasn't answered my emails. Now I know why. He got murdered last night."

"What?" Remi cried, sitting up in her chair.

"Beaten to death with a blunt object just outside Jerusalem."

"The man Professor Edward Hale went to see recently, and then lied about seeing more recently, has just been murdered?"

"Yup."

Daniel tapped his thumb against his thigh three times. Remi had noticed this unusual gesture before. He seemed to do it when he was on the verge of finding something out.

Remi stood. "We need to go there."

"To Jerusalem? I'm not sure I can get travel authorization. The Israeli cops must be pretty good considering everything they have to handle, so we can—"

"No. We have to go there."

"By the time we get there, the local police might have already solved this."

"Good. Then we can question the suspect."

Daniel smiled. "I knew you were going to say something like that. I'll talk to Assistant Director Ochiai. The Antiquities Division deals a lot with Israeli authorities. Maybe we can fast track a collaboration."

"Oh, right." Remi had forgotten that if an agent travels overseas, the biggest hurdle isn't getting approval from one's superiors, but to get approval from the other nation. Such a security-conscious country may think twice about allowing two federal agents to investigate a murder of one of its citizens on its own soil.

"I'll get to work on it," Daniel said.

"Right."

Daniel left. Remi switched the tab of her browser back to her email and sent a message to John.

"Thanks! I'm eager to see what you come up with." She paused, fingers poised over her keyboard, unsure what to write next. A part of the truth seemed fair. "I want to let you know that I've left academia and am currently training to be an FBI agent." She paused again, realizing how crazy that sounded, then wrote, "No, this is not a joke. I did some civilian consulting work for their new Antiquities Division. You've already heard about me consulting over the cryptex case. That was the first of three cases and they offered me a job."

She paused again. Should she tell him about Cyril? No, that might seem like an invitation. He'd be sure to hear sooner rather than later, and if she didn't mention it, then perhaps he'd understand she wasn't interested.

Plus, it hurt too much to talk about. Other than a couple of friends back home, she hadn't told anyone. Not even Daniel.

She finished the email by writing, "Please keep this information private. I'm sure people will hear soon, but I'm in the middle of a case right now and I don't want to deal with a flood of questions. I might be heading to Israel soon. Good luck cracking the code. I'm so grateful for your help and if we do publish, you will get your share of the credit. It would make quite a book! Regards, Remi."

Regards? A bit too formal? She deleted that, thought for a moment, then replaced it with "thanks again."

Letting out a breath of relief, she switched back to her background research for the case, promising herself that she would focus on this and this only until the perpetrator was caught.

She was an agent now, and she needed to do her job.

Remi didn't get to do much of it, because only a few minutes later, Daniel was back.

"You must have dug up the Long Lost Holy Key of Unlocking Travel Funds, because the assistant director just approved our trip to Jerusalem. I've booked a flight for tonight. Go home and pack."

Remi was up and leaving the office before he had even finished his sentence.

CHAPTER EIGHT

Remi had endured far too many transatlantic flights, and she had always coped by burying herself in research. Losing oneself in the stories and mysteries of the past was an excellent way to blot out the cramped conditions, stifling air, and bad food.

Now she had an even better motive—to solve a murder.

Although she had another mystery as well. When Daniel had met her at the airport to take a flight to Jerusalem's Ben Gurion Airport, he had seemed distracted, even a bit pale and shaken. He had barely said two words to her as they went through security—an extra-long chore since they were boarding a flight with El Al, Israel's national airline—and waiting in the boarding area. He kept texting and checking his phone every three seconds.

Remi decided not to pry. It was none of her business, and she knew that once the hunt was on in Israel, he would be ready.

Once they were settled into their seats and had taken off, Daniel surprised her by pulling out his phone again. Although he didn't have coverage, he appeared to be reading and rereading some long message.

With an abrupt movement, almost like he was snapping himself awake, he put the phone away and turned to her.

"We should try to get some sleep. I don't want to be chasing murderers with jetlag like last time. But first let's go through some things."

"All right." Daniel was all business again, she noticed.

"First off, I haven't received Hale's travel and credit card information yet. I got a judge to give me the warrant, but the companies haven't gotten back to me. We should have that information by the time we land. Also, there's a local detective waiting for us at the other end. David Levy. Speaks good English. He'll be our guide and our weapon arm, since we didn't get permission for us to carry our pieces. How's the research going?"

Remi shrugged, glancing out the window at the sunset over the Atlantic. "I wish I could say I got some leads, but I didn't. There's a whole online subculture of people who think the Ark has been hidden away. Most think the Catholic Church is hiding it."

"Ah, our old friends! Do you think they do have it?"

Remi shrugged again. "Impossible to say. The problem is, ancient traditions vary as to what happened to it. One account, in Second Maccabees, says God warned the prophet Jeremiah that the Babylonians were about to invade, and told him to go to Mount Nebo."

"Where's that?"

"In Jordan. It's the mountain where God showed Moses the Promised Land. It overlooks the River Jordan and what's now the West Bank. When Jeremiah went there with the Ark, God revealed a cave where he hid it. Some of Jeremiah's followers tried to mark the path to the cave but couldn't find it. Jeremiah scolded them, saying the spot would remain hidden until God finally gathers his people again and shows mercy on them."

"So did that happen? The Babylonian invasion led to the Captivity, right?"

"That's right. And the Israelites were eventually let go. It's unclear if the hiding place was revealed once they returned to Israel."

"So what are the options?"

"The only church that actually claims to have the Ark is the Ethiopian Orthodox Church. Ethiopia was one of the first nations to adopt Christianity, and before that had a large Jewish population. The people are a mix of Semitic and African."

"I didn't know that. They do look a bit different than most Africans. Good food too." Daniel patted his stomach.

"I've never tried Ethiopian food."

"Really? They have restaurants all over D.C. Great stuff. Unlike anything you've ever tried. A bunch of different gloppy types of meat and vegetable recipes put on top of a big circle of spongey bread. Spicy but not blow-your-head-off spicy. I'll take you out once all this is over."

Remi smiled. That could be fun.

Daniel quickly brought her back to the matter at hand. "So why do the Ethiopians have it?"

"According to their traditions, their royal dynasty was founded by Menelik, who was the son of King Solomon and the Queen of Sheba. God told Menelik to take the Ark to Ethiopia with him and left a fake one in the Temple."

"And Solomon didn't notice?"

"Apparently not."

"Kind of a raw deal for King Solomon."

The man across the aisle shot them an irritated look. Remi lowered her voice.

"We have to be careful with our words. We're going to a country where religious beliefs run deep, and disagreements often turn violent."

"Right," Daniel said, also lowering his voice. "Go on."

"So according to Ethiopian tradition, the Ark was placed in a church in a city called Axum. It was their ancient capital. The Ethiopian Orthodox Church still claims to have it there."

"So why would the killer go after someone in Israel?"

"Who knows? Perhaps Steiner was partially correct, that Hale and Cohen were members of some organization protecting the Ark."

"You don't think that's literally true, do you?"

"Not yet," Remi said, glancing out the window again. It was now dark, the jet speeding eastwards away from the setting sun. "No, I don't think so. But perhaps Cohen and Hale thought they were protecting some secret knowledge and the killer went after them for it."

"You mentioned there are other theories as to where it is?"

"Many. Too many. Everywhere from the United States to Zimbabwe. Hardly any say it's still in Israel, although some eccentric English gentleman led a secret expedition to look for it there a hundred years ago."

"Maybe he found it and it's in some English country estate."

Remi shook her head. "With so many stories, and so few clues, that guess is as good as any. I hope we can get some more solid leads once we get to Israel."

"Let's get some sleep," Daniel suggested. "I have a feeling we'll need it."

* * *

Remi awoke to the sound of singing and clapping. Rubbing her eyes, she looked around. Many of the passengers were singing a happy song in Hebrew and clapping in time with the tune. An open window blind in the row in front of her told her it was daylight. Asleep beside her, his head almost on her shoulder, Daniel stirred, stretched, and opened his eyes.

"What's going on?" he mumbled.

The man across the aisle stopped singing and leaned over, smiling. "The pilot just announced we're in Israeli airspace. We're celebrating!"

He leaned back and rejoined the chorus.

Remi, sitting at the window seat, opened her blind and blinked in the brilliant daylight. Far below, she could see the bright blue Mediterranean meet the shore, a thin curl of white surf just visible. Beyond stretched brown desert mottled by patches of green farmland.

Looking at the landscape below, she felt a strange sensation. Perhaps it was the obvious joy of the Jewish passengers, perhaps it was because she had never been to Israel and had read so much about it, or maybe it was the old Catholic schoolgirl coming out in her, but she felt a stirring in her heart.

So much history had happened here, and supposedly miracles too. As a child she had been only a moderate believer. The nuns had been of a more liberal cast and had told their students that some Bible stories such as Noah's Ark were parables, not literally true. Despite this, they did drill into the class that the theology behind the Bible was the important thing, that the Israelites had been the first of God's chosen people before the coming of Jesus opened up salvation to the whole world.

Remi had accepted this, but not the rules that came with it. The nuns' strict lectures about premarital sex had been ignored in favor of her teenage desires, for example. She had also not "comported herself with modesty and silence as a young lady should." Despite these lapses, she had believed in the core values of honesty, love, and fairness to others. They made sense, with or without the religious trappings.

Remi hadn't thought about these things for a long time, strange considering that she had spent so much of her career studying the medieval Catholic church. She had even devoted a large amount of her energies to finding a lost Catholic artifact.

Somehow she had compartmentalized her earlier religious beliefs, lukewarm as they were, and her field of study. Yet now, coming to the Holy Land, she was wondering if that had been a good idea.

* * *

Two hours later, Remi sat in the back of a car speeding down the highway towards the Old City of Jerusalem. At the wheel sat David

Levy, a Jerusalem homicide detective, a trim but muscular man in his fifties dressed in slacks, a polo shirt, and wearing a blue and white yarmulke on his head. His good English and friendly demeanor had put her instantly at ease.

"I'll take you straight to the murder site. Not much to see there but I know you'll want to get a feel for it. From there we'll go to his office. Do you need a coffee? I can stop somewhere."

"Later," Remi said. "Let's see the murder scene first."

She looked out over the hills around Jerusalem, terraced for farming and orchards centuries, perhaps millennia ago. Not far off she could see the walls of the Old City, and beyond that the Dome of the Rock, and her heart did a little flip flop to see what she had seen in pictures so many times before.

"First time to Jerusalem, eh?" David said, his blue eyes twinkling as he looked at her in the rearview mirror.

"Yes. How could you tell?"

"The way you're staring. Same with your partner. Newcomers always stare like that. I hope you get some time for sightseeing. There's no other country like Israel. Me, I was born here, on a kibbutz. Many of my friends were born outside of Israel. England. Russia. America. They moved here and never looked back. For a Jew, and a lot of Christians too, there's no other place in the world to live."

Remi suspected a lot of Muslims felt the same way, but she decided not to bring that up. They had two murders to solve, and she did not want to get bogged down in political discussions.

"What has your team discovered so far?" Daniel asked.

"Not much, I'm afraid. Cohen was a respected professor with no known enemies. His car was found in a neighborhood near the Old City, well away from where he lived. It had been wiped of prints. We found matching tire tracks at a pull off point near the body. It appears whoever killed him forced him to drive to that spot, killed him there, and then drove back to town in Cohen's car."

"That would make sense if he had just come from the United States," Remi said. "He wouldn't have a car of his own and might not want to risk renting one."

David nodded and then looked at Daniel. "You mentioned in your email that the killer might believe Cohen and the victim in America were hiding the location of the Ark of the Covenant. I questioned his wife and two teenaged sons about that. While Cohen had always shown a great interest in holy artifacts, he had never mentioned actually knowing where any of them are."

"Neither did Professor Hale," Daniel said. "So either our killer is a nutcase who is killing off people for completely fantastical reasons, or those two professors are keeping their secrets close to their chest."

"Surely the Ark couldn't be around after all these years," David scoffed. "It disappeared in the time of the Babylonian invasion in 587 BC. They destroyed the Temple, and there's no record of it being put in the Second Temple after it got rebuilt. It was long gone by then. It probably got burned up by the invaders."

"What about the account in Second Maccabees?" Remi asked.

"That's not an accepted book in the Tanakh," David said. When he saw the blank look on Daniel's face he explained. "That's the Jewish canon that includes the Torah, the Nevi'im, and the Ketuvim. That doesn't mean Second Maccabees is wrong, but it isn't the word of God. It's just history, and as we all know around here, history is debatable. There's actually nothing clear in the Tanakh about what happened to the Ark. The rabbis have been discussing it forever."

"What's the consensus?" Remi asked.

"Consensus? Ha! We have a saying in Israel. If you have three Jews, you have five opinions. Just look at our politics. Some rabbis say the Babylonians stole it. Others say it was hidden near the Temple Mount or Mount Nebo. Others say it got burned when the First Temple burned. No one knows for sure."

"What do you think?" Remi asked.

David waved a hand in the air. "I don't know what to think. If I was a gambling man, I'd bet a small amount of money—not a large amount, mind you—that it got destroyed in the Temple or carried off to Babylon. Look what the Romans did to the Second Temple. That's just how our history works. People are always taking from us. Here's Mount Herzl. You know who Theodor Herzl was? We call him the founding father of modern Zionism. Died before he could ever see Israeli statehood. Pity. He's buried here."

They were winding up the mountain now, which was really more of a tall hill. David pointed out the Holocaust Museum up at the summit and, through the olive groves, the white headstones of the military cemetery to their left.

"The pull off is just here, near the Jewish Soldiers in the Polish Army memorial. We'll park right where Professor Cohen was forced to park."

As they pulled off on a wide gravel area at a curve in the road, Remi felt a little shiver go through her body. She wondered what Cohen must have thought at that moment.

They got out of the car. The air was hot, with the Middle Eastern sun beating down on them. Remi felt grateful for the shade of the olive grove once they stepped into it.

The hillside was rock with a thin covering of grass. They only walked about fifty meters before they came to a spot sectioned off by police tape. There was nothing to see except a bloodstain on a patch of grass. David pulled out his phone and brought up some pictures. Remi steeled herself for an ugly sight.

"A groundskeeper found him at a little before six yesterday morning. The coroner estimates time of death to have been at around eight o'clock the previous evening. Severe blunt trauma to the back of the head."

He showed them a photo. Remi sucked air through gritted teeth. It showed an older man lying face down on the grass, the back of his skull mashed to a pulp, blood, chips of bone, and brains matting his gray hair.

Daniel studied the picture. "Odd that he hit him from behind. Maybe Cohen tried to run, but the position of the body suggests he was standing before getting hit."

Remi looking in the direction Professor Cohen had been facing, which gave her an excuse not to look at that awful photo again.

Through the trees she could get a good, if somewhat obstructed, view of the Old City.

"He was looking at the Temple Mount," she said, "where Solomon's Temple used to be. The original home to the Ark."

"Maybe," Daniel agreed. "Or maybe he was looking at something else in the Old City. If they really are hiding the Ark, wouldn't it make sense to keep it close to home?"

"Perhaps," Remi conceded.

"You two aren't seriously considering the possibility that it still exists, are you?" David asked.

Daniel shot Remi a wry glance. "In our line of work, we don't exclude the possibility of anything."

Remi returned his smile.

"I don't think we'll find much more here," she said. "Let's go see his office. That's where he did his research, and so that's where we'll find any leads."

CHAPTER NINE

Remi looked around the office of Professor Yitzhak Cohen and didn't see anything of immediate interest, certainly nothing signifying where the Ark of the Covenant had been hiding for the last few thousand years.

She had been in hundreds of academic offices, and they all looked pretty much the same. Generally too small thanks to a lack of funding to whatever department owned them, this was no exception. The bookshelf was overstuffed, the antique wooden desk with a desktop PC took up much of the rest of the space, and the walls were relatively spare. There was a Hebrew calendar, an old photo of a much younger Yitzhak Cohen in an Israeli tank regiment, and a more recent one of him with his family.

Remi gazed at it for a moment. A smiling Yitzhak was leaning in a little toward a stout woman about his age, wearing a headscarf as many Orthodox women did. Just in front, two boys in their late teens, lanky and pimply, grinned at the camera. Both had yarmulkes on their heads like their father, although she suspected the starched dress shirts they wore for the picture were not a daily habit.

The smiles looked customary, though. This looked like a family that smiled a lot together.

No more.

Steeling herself, she took another look around the room. There had to be something here. Perhaps on the bookshelf? The books were mostly in Hebrew.

"What are these?" she asked David, who was standing nearby. Daniel was out in the hallway checking messages on his phone.

The Israeli detective stepped over to the bookshelf and scanned the titles.

"The Torah … commentaries on the Torah … several old issues of a journal on Biblical studies in no particular order … a few books on early excavations during the British Mandate … studies and commentaries on the Christian Old Testament … more of the same …"

David kept looking at the titles, squatting down to study the bottom shelves. Since he stopped recounting what he found, Remi assumed he wasn't finding anything new.

"Check for bookmarks," Remi told him, "and check for any papers or receipts stuck between or behind the books."

"All right."

Remi blinked. She had just given a homicide detective an order and he obeyed.

But why wouldn't he? She was one of the lead investigators on this case for the FBI.

This new persona she wore was taking some getting used to.

Daniel spoke from where he stood in the hallway.

"Got Hale's flight records. Credit cards are still taking some time. Turns out that second trip he took wasn't to Israel at all."

"Really? Where did he go?"

"Egypt. Richmond to London then a connecting flight to Cairo. Stayed a week."

"Interesting. I wonder what the credit cards will reveal."

"We should have those by tomorrow. It's still nighttime in the States, you know."

"Don't remind me. I've been trying to ignore jetlag since we landed."

"I'm not sure we'll get much from the credit cards anyway. I got the bank records. He withdrew two thousand dollars the day before flying to Egypt."

"Is that enough to stay in Egypt for a week and not use a credit card?" Remi asked. She presumed Egypt was cheaper than Europe, but she had never been there.

"It is," David said, rummaging through Cohen's bookshelf. "If you avoid the five-star hotels and the fancy restaurants, it's quite cheap."

"It's safe for Israelis to travel in Egypt?" Remi asked, surprised.

"It isn't safe for Israelis to travel to the local supermarket, so why limit ourselves?"

"So he might not have used his credit cards at all," Remi mused. "Covering his tracks."

"Probably," Daniel agreed. "He didn't make a big withdrawal before his trip to Israel."

Remi looked around the office again, unsure what to do next.

When investigating a room or any other location, look for anomalies.

That's what her instructors always said.

The desk!

Remi had noted it but hadn't thought anything of it at first. It was an antique, nineteenth-century German if she was right in her identification. Perhaps a family heirloom. While she had seen many academics spruce up their offices with more personal items, she had never seen one bring in an antique desk. Everyone just used the ones the institution put in.

She moved over to the desk and sat in the chair behind it. She had been planning to search the desk anyway, but now it took on a greater significance.

There were two drawers on either side of the leg space. One had a lock, but the key was in it. She checked this first and found nothing but correspondence in Hebrew. David saw what she was doing and began to go through it.

"Circulars and bills from various academic journals," he said.

Another drawer revealed a collection of office supplies such as printer paper, a stapler, and paper clips. The third drawer had a heap of correspondence in both English and Hebrew that David started going through.

The fourth drawer was entirely empty. Odd considering how full the other drawers were.

"I wonder what could have been in here," she said.

David glanced over. "Probably his laptop."

"Laptop?"

"His wife said his laptop is missing. He often took it to work."

"Even though he has a desktop?" Remi asked.

The homicide detective could only shrug.

Daniel looked up from his phone. "If he was carrying a laptop around, the killer might have thought it contained important material like the books he stole in Richmond."

"And now we can't know what was on it, or what the books were," Remi grumbled.

She leaned back in the seat. Something about this desk tickled a faint memory in the back of her mind. Someone had shown her a desk like this, long ago. But who? And that brought up a question—how had she known it was nineteenth century German? She was hardly an expert in antiques, and certainly not such recent ones. Dwelling as she did in the Middle Ages, the nineteenth century was so recent as to almost be science fiction.

Someone must have told her.

When? Where? Oh! She saw a desk like this in Maurice's antique shop.

When she was a little girl, she loved antique shops. Her parents couldn't afford to buy anything in them, and probably wouldn't even if they could have, but she always dragged them to any one they passed. In a city like Paris, that was all the time.

There was something about those shops that attracted her. The smell of old wood and aging paper, the elegant gilt designs on Empire furniture, the sedate *tick tick* of antique clocks. The cumulative effect felt almost hypnotic. She would wander the aisles, wondering about the people who had owned objects older even than her grandparents (which was really, really old) and what the world was like when these old things were new.

Her favorite shop was Maurice's. Maurice was a smiling, stooped old man who smelled of clove cigarettes and owned a narrow storefront on the street between her apartment and school. The shop stretched far back and was so cluttered with things that you couldn't see the end. It felt like stepping into another world, like when the children entered the big old wardrobe in *The Lion, the Witch, and the Wardrobe*. On the way home from school, she'd tug on the hand of whichever parent was with her that day and plead to go inside.

One time, when she was about ten, she came in with her father, who had the day off. Maurice put a finger to his lips and whispered, "I have something secret to show you."

Maurice was a bit of a showman and tiptoed through the narrow aisle between the heaped up antiques. Remi giggled and tiptoed behind him. Even her father played along.

He brought her to a desk, exactly like the desk she was currently sitting at.

"There's something inside," Maurice whispered.

Excited, Remi peeked into one drawer and found it empty. She checked the next drawer and found that one empty too. She checked drawer after drawer. Nothing.

She looked up at Maurice curiously, wondering if the kind old man was playing a trick on her.

“Open the upper left drawer and the upper right drawer and tell me if you see a difference,” he told her.

She did as she was told. A soft “ah!” from her father told her he had seen something.

“Don’t tell me!” Remi warned. She liked to figure things out for herself.

She stared at the open drawers for a moment, first looking at one and then the other. Suddenly, she snapped her fingers.

“The left one is a bit more narrow!”

“Excellent!” Maurice cried. “You have a good eye. You could be a policeman like your father. Why do you think one is more narrow?”

“A secret compartment?”

Maurice smiled. “Maybe. See if you can find one.”

She had. And now, more than twenty-five years later, she could again.

Because this desk was identical to the one Maurice had shown her. She would bet that it had been made by the same workshop.

She opened all the drawers. In this model, it was the righthand upper drawer that was a bit narrower.

Placing her hands on the inner sides of the drawer, she pushed outwards.

Nothing happened. The sides of the drawer didn’t budge.

Daniel and David looked at her curiously.

Flushing a bit, and knowing she looked a bit foolish, she tried again, harder this time.

The sides snapped apart, and a thin drawer above the leg space popped out.

“Whoa!” the Israeli cried.

“What the—?” Daniel added.

Remi smiled. “The benefits of being obsessed with history from an early age.”

Inside the drawer was a single piece of notepaper, folded in half. Remi pulled it out and opened it.

Written in tidy handwriting was, “31/52/16.375 35/26/38.201”

“What could this mean?” Remi wondered.

The three of them stared at it a moment.

“Hey, it could be coordinates,” Daniel said. “Latitude and Longitude.”

"Coordinates?" David asked. "But it would be marked in degrees and minutes and seconds. This has slashes between the numbers."

"A simple way to disguise what it is," Daniel said.

"And the last numbers go out to several decimal places," David said. "That's far too precise. It would get the location down to a couple of meters."

They all looked at each other a moment, the significance of what he just said sinking in.

Daniel pulled out his phone. "I'll check on Google Maps."

The Israeli detective pulled out his own phone. "Let me. Google Maps is set at a poor resolution for Israel. Our government has an understanding with the company. But I have access to an Israeli government alternative map."

"Sounds good."

David tapped away on his phone. "I'll assume that the first set of numbers is for north latitude and the second set for east longitude. That would put it inside Israel, I think. Let's see, 31°52′16.375″ North by 35°26′38.201″ East." His eyes bugged. "Jericho. A point on a strip of souvenir shops by the entrance, to be precise."

Remi stood, her mouth hanging open in wonder. "Jericho, where the Israelites circled the city with the Ark and the walls came tumbling down. It was one of the greatest demonstrations of the Ark's power. But why is it pointing us to a souvenir shop?"

"Only one way to find out," the homicide detective said. "Let's go. But I warn you, Jericho is in the West Bank. Inside the Palestinian Authority. I'm bringing my assault rifle."

CHAPTER TEN

Daniel barely noticed the bare brown hills of the West Bank, or the numerous checkpoints they had to pass, both of the Israeli government and the Palestinian Authority. David Levy's police ID got them through with a minimum of questioning on the army's part, although the Palestinians checked and rechecked Daniel and Remi's FBI IDs, calling in to their headquarters. Even so, they didn't give David's Galil assault rifle a second glance. They were used to that sort of thing. A pair of FBI agents, on the other hand, was unusual.

Finally, they were let through, and they drove along a dusty highway past a few small, poor-looking towns of concrete buildings and some lush areas of farmland where ground water was tapped to turn bleak desert into emerald oases.

But Daniel had trouble paying attention to any of these things. His eyes were gritty, his muscles cramped, his entire body tired despite the coffee David had picked up for them, and most of all he was stressed to the max.

Veronica, his ex-wife, had emailed him just as he had headed for the D.C. airport.

"Daniel,

"I've been doing a lot of thinking, and I realize I was in the wrong. I shouldn't have been so jealous of your career. A couple of your coworkers have been keeping me filled in on your new division and the cases you've been doing, and I can see it's really important work. I was always proud of you fighting crime. I didn't tell you that enough.

"You got too obsessed over it, though. It's not healthy for you. I'd see you toss and turn night after night and wear yourself to exhaustion on one case after another. I didn't react to it right, though. I should have been more understanding to help you through it instead of taking it as you rejecting and ignoring me.

"You're a driven man. In your line of work, you have to be.

"I want to try again. This time let's keep the communication open and really try to make it work.

"LOVE,

“Veronica”

Daniel put away his phone and looked out over the empty landscape. How was he supposed to react to a message like that? She had insisted on getting divorced just a couple of months ago, and here she comes saying all the things she should have said before their breakup?

Well, some of the things.

Because Veronica wanted a baby, and he couldn’t give her one.

That had been a major thing dividing them.

Low sperm count. That’s what the doctor said. No idea why. No sign of disease or malformation. His glands just didn’t work.

Daniel had gotten stuck in his head that he shot blanks because of what Uncle Roy had done to him as a kid. He knew that didn’t make sense, but he couldn’t shake the feeling. Of course, the doctor probably could have reassured him on that score, but Daniel had never had the guts to tell him. Or Veronica. Or anyone except his mother, who hadn’t believed him.

David spoke, taking him away from all the confusion and nasty memories.

“The low mound we’ll soon see up ahead is Tel Jericho. Tel means ‘hill.’ Some towns in the Middle East were inhabited for so long, with later generations building on the foundations of earlier ones, that the people ended up living on hills, literally hills of history.”

“How long was Jericho inhabited?” Daniel asked, grateful for the distraction.

“Ten thousand years. They built a big tower and a town wall even before they invented agriculture. And people have been living there more or less constantly ever since. You see, there’s a spring nearby that’s been flowing since ancient times. And if you take a look around you, you can see how important a spring would be.”

“I bet,” Daniel said. They came over the crest of a hill and saw a small town surrounded by farmland. In the desert haze beyond, he spotted a mound overlooking the town, ringed by palm trees. It looked much like the bare hills of the Judean Desert they had just passed through except he could make out ruined walls and buildings atop it.

“Is that it?” Remi asked, peeking between the two men up front.

“Yes, and the modern town of Jericho. As you can see, the spring still feeds the land around it like it did at the time of Joshua.”

Daniel tried to remember who Joshua was. Was he the guy who blew down the walls of Jericho? He had never been religious, and his mother certainly hadn't raised him with any of that.

It didn't matter. He had Remi to rely on for that sort of knowledge. While he missed his old partner, Remi Laurent was certainly the most qualified for working with him in the Antiquities Division.

Just ahead of town, they came to yet another roadblock, manned by several Palestinian police in light blue camouflage uniforms, toting assault rifles and wearing helmets and Kevlar vests. They were deep in Palestinian territory now, well east of Jerusalem, which stood right on the border.

In fact, looking at the GPS, they had almost reached the River Jordan, the borderline with the country of the same name. All that in an hour's drive. Daniel shook his head in wonder. So much history and politics crammed into such a small space.

They had to wait as a truck ahead of them, piled high with fruit, was checked. One soldier or cop (Daniel wasn't sure) examined the driver's papers while another made a slow circuit around the truck with a mirror stuck on the end of a pole, searching the undercarriage for bombs. After a minute they waved the truck through, and it was their turn.

"I'm going to tell them we're here investigating a report of artifact theft from the site," David told them as he pulled up to the checkpoint. "We'll have to make a show of checking out the site before we can go to that shop. Don't worry. The site is only about ten acres, so it won't take long."

"All right," Daniel said, suppressing a yawn. Jetlag was catching up to him.

David presented his papers to the lead officer, a middle-aged man with hard eyes and flecks of gray in his black hair under his black beret, and started speaking to him in Arabic. Like before, Daniel and Remi handed over their IDs. Another soldier peered through the window at them while these were taken away to a nearby booth. Someone got on a cell phone.

They waited, fidgeting. It felt tense here. The checkpoints on the highway had seemed routine, even the one at the border to the Palestinian Territory, but the mood here was noticeably different. The soldiers looked alert, on edge. On a nearby roof, Daniel noted a heavy machine gun behind a heap of sandbags.

The officer who took their papers got on the radio, moving far enough away that David couldn't hear what he was saying. David asked the nearest soldier a question and got a curt reply in return.

After a minute, the officer came back, returning the documents.

"I come with you," he said in heavily accented English, opening the back door. One of the guards handed him an assault rifle, even though he already had a pistol in a holster on his belt. Remi moved over.

"Why?" Daniel asked.

"No problem," the officer said, getting in. "Security."

David asked him something in Arabic. The officer made a dismissive click of the tongue and said something back to him. He kept the assault rifle between his knees, the barrel pointing at the roof.

"Let's go," David said, starting the car. He did not look happy.

They went down the main street toward the ancient Tel, passing a row of clothing and electronics shops and a few fruit and vegetable stalls set up on the sidewalk. Palestinian men and boys walked the streets, looking curiously at the officer sitting with the foreigners. Not many women were in sight, and all of them wore headscarves or full face covering.

"So what's your name?" Daniel asked the man in back in an attempt to break the ice.

"Mohammed."

His ice did not look broken.

The officer pointed to a side street and said something to David in Arabic, who objected and was cut off by a sharp word from the officer.

"What's going on?" Remi asked.

"He's taking us on a detour," David said. "He won't say why."

Daniel turned in his seat and studied the officer. Mohammed did not look particularly tense or alert, although he did appear to be in a foul mood. He also didn't look all that menacing, despite the guns. Daniel got the feeling that could change in a heartbeat if they rubbed him the wrong way.

David turned where he was told to turn and took them down a side street that had more potholes than asphalt. The blocky concrete houses had small yards out of sight behind tall walls of bare concrete. A couple of tall apartment buildings stood to either side, washing hanging out the windows.

Now they received even more stares. Daniel got the impression not many outsiders ever left the main road.

The officer told David to go left, and they passed down another street even more pitted than the last.

"See how poor we live," Mohammed said.

"Be more like us and you won't have to," David grumbled.

"It is you who make us this way!"

"Hey!" Daniel shouted. Both men jerked and stared at him. "Can we go to the site now?"

Silence settled for a tense moment.

David turned the car around and headed back to the main road. The Palestinian officer, fuming in the back seat, made no objection. Daniel felt like slapping them both. They were on a murder investigation and these two were screaming about who hit who first? They were acting like a pair of kids.

Why did he have to listen this this? Didn't he have enough to deal with?

Plus, he still hadn't figured out what to say to Veronica. She would email him a bombshell just as he was boarding an international flight. So typical of her.

He sat there frowning as much as the other two men in the car until they made it to the parking lot in front of the mound of earth that marked one of the world's earliest cities.

They got out. It was now early afternoon and the sun beat down on them, making Daniel feel sluggish. He needed sleep. Not even the dangers of his situation could keep him awake for much longer, and that worried him. Because as he grew more tired, he grew less aware, and that could spell disaster.

Besides their own car, only a couple of other cars were in the parking lot, as well as a tour bus. A Palestinian soldier or police officer (Daniel still couldn't tell the difference) stood guard beside it. He saluted when the officer climbed out of David's car.

They strolled over to the site, which had a fenced-off path running through it for visitors. A trio of red cable cars ran along a thick cable over the site, which struck Daniel as a tasteless way to ruin the historic atmosphere. Out of the corner of his eye, Daniel saw the row of souvenir shops off to the left. They'd get there soon enough. First, they had to play along with the pretense that they were investigating a supposed illegal excavation.

They walked up the path, Daniel and the Israeli homicide detective in front, the Palestinian officer close behind, and Remi trailing a bit behind him. A group of Orthodox Jewish men wearing black hats and heavy black coats despite the heat, long ringlets to either side of their faces, passed by them, looking at the site with fascinated expressions and speaking eagerly in Hebrew.

The little crowd passed them by. David was explaining the various phases of the site, pointing out the thick city wall and the wide round tower older than the pyramids and the second oldest tower in the world.

Daniel listened with only half an ear. He was growing impatient to get to that shop and see why Professor Cohen had coordinates for it hidden. But how to shake this officer? Mohammed didn't look like he planned on leaving them alone.

Glancing back at the officer, he discovered he wasn't the only one being impatient.

Remi had disappeared.

There she goes again. I knew she would ignore my warning not to go off into danger alone.

CHAPTER ELEVEN

Remi felt jetlagged, tired, jittery from too much coffee, and hungry. For some reason that made it so she couldn't stop thinking about Cyril breaking up with her.

And the only way to stop thinking about that, she had found, was to get on with the case. Not walk around an admittedly fascinating archaeological site pretending to look for pits dug by looters, but to actually get on with the case.

So she had taken advantage of Mohammed being distracted by Daniel and David's conversation to slip away and hurry back to the line of souvenir shops.

Of course, Daniel had instructed her not to go off alone like on their previous cases, but it was broad daylight and all she was going to do was go visit a shop. It wasn't like they were in a darkened museum with a serial killer on the loose. That Palestinian officer wouldn't do anything more than shout at her.

She had already figured out the exact shop from the coordinates hidden in Professor Cohen's desk, so it was only a matter of going there.

Remi passed a couple of little shops selling the usual assortment of postcards, refrigerator magnets, and plastic figurines of people from the Bible until she came to the right place.

And it was a very different sort of place from the souvenir shops to either side.

She found herself in front of a narrow stall lined with floor to ceiling bookshelves to either side. Many of the books appeared to be Jewish religious books in Hebrew. She also saw religious commentary in various languages. Two tables in front held tourist guides and Bibles.

Far in the back, so deep in shadow compared with the searing desert sunlight that at first Remi didn't see him, sat an old man in slacks and dress shirt. He had a lean but smiling face framed by a long gray beard. A yarmulke on his head did not quite cover a large bald spot. Remi wondered how it stayed on.

“Welcome to Jericho,” he said in English. He had a New York accent. While Remi hadn’t learned to identify all the many types of American accents, the one from New York City was so distinctive that she knew it.

“Hello,” she said. Now that she was here, she wasn’t quite sure how to proceed.

She stepped inside the shop. Away from the sun, it felt ten degrees cooler, although still hot. A fan did its best to circulate the air.

“Are you looking for something in particular?” the man asked.

“Oh, just browsing.” She decided she wanted to feel out this man a bit before springing the question. “Are you from New York?”

He touched his heart. “I have lived in Israel all my life, although I was born and raised in New York. You have a scholarly air to you. French? Are you an archaeologist?”

“Yes, I’m French.” Remi found her heart beating fast. Even so, she decided she better hurry this up. She didn’t know how long she could elude the Palestinian police. In a lower voice she said, “I am an associate of Professor Cohen’s.”

The smile remained on the old man’s face, but his eyes grew calculating.

“Ah, a scholar! I knew it. You can always tell. I suppose you found the site fascinating.”

“It’s quite impressive.”

“So much history! I don’t live here, of course. I live on a kibbutz about twenty miles from here.”

“Do you know Professor Cohen?”

Pause. “Yes. Such a shame what happened. The world is a bad place.”

“I’m searching for the same thing he was.”

“Knowledge? Good. You’ve come to the right place. If you were a colleague of his, then you might be interested in this section over here. Old Testament commentary. The only testament for me. New Testament is over there. I even carry the Koran in Arabic and English. You’d be surprised at how many Palestinians we get here. It’s not a holy place in their religion but they like the history. The local schools come.”

“I’m more interested in the Ark of the Covenant.”

Again that smile. Again that calculation in the eyes. He stood. Remi hesitated, unsure what to do.

He strode over to a section of his bookshelves.

"An intriguing subject. And not for the faint of heart. Or for the weak of faith. Did you know the Philistines captured the Ark? Most people don't remember that story. Here's a commentary on it. The Israelites were in the process of conquering the Holy Land after crossing the River Jordan not far east of here and blowing down Jericho's walls. Things got harder after that. They got badly defeated by the Philistines, and the next time they came up against them they brought the Ark onto the battlefield in order to have God's power on their side. That was hubris, though. God allowed them to be defeated and the Ark captured."

"I remember the nuns teaching me that."

"Do you remember what happened next?"

"I … I think so. The Philistines put it in one of their temples."

"To the god Dagon, yes."

"That's right. And the statue of the god prostrated itself before the Ark."

"Exactly! Do you remember what happened next?"

"The Philistines were plagued with boils."

"Boils? Ha! The nuns were being polite. If you look at the ancient Hebrew word, it is actually the word for a particular type of boil. Hemorrhoids. That's right. God gave the Philistines a bad case of the piles!"

Despite the situation, Remi cracked a smile.

She glanced over her shoulder and in the distance saw Mohammed at the entrance to the archaeological site, looking around. No doubt looking for her.

Remi grew serious again.

She pulled out her FBI identification and showed it to the bookseller. His face took on a look of weary amusement.

"We believe Professor Cohen was murdered by someone looking for the Ark of the Covenant. The killer felt that Cohen, and a Professor Hale of the University of Richmond in the United States, both had clues to where the Ark might be hidden. I'm not saying he's right, but if you know anything, anything at all about the killer or where he might be heading next, it's your duty to tell me. Otherwise, someone else might get killed, and soon."

Remi paused, startled at the tone of authority she had managed to put into her words.

She immediately undermined that authority by nervously glancing over her shoulder at the Palestinian officer, who was now walking in her direction, Daniel and David trailing behind. Remi realized that they only had one obvious place to look, since the entire parking lot could be seen from the site entrance. Thus she had to have gone to the souvenir stands. The officer did not appear to have seen her yet. But she had less than a minute before he got close enough to spot her inside the relative darkness of the bookstall.

Remi turned back to the book seller and saw him looking at the approaching men.

"To answer your question," he said. "I don't know where the Ark is precisely, or even if it still exists. I know only that our secret teachings say it resides where kings lay."

"What does that mean?"

The old man shrugged. "God is not required to spell out everything for you. Remember when Moses spoke with the burning bush, knowing it was God, and asked Him what He was? God said, 'I am what I am.' Scholars and lay folk have been pondering that for four thousand years." He let out an amused chuckle. "Those are the kind of answers you can expect from the Almighty."

"Where kings lay?"

An idea sparked in her mind, but angry words in Arabic, followed by David speaking in a conciliatory tone in the same language, made her turn.

They were out of sight, but she could hear their footsteps approaching.

They're walking along the stalls, looking in each one.

The old man must have realized this too, because he stepped over to another shelf, plucked out a book, and handed it to her.

"I am so glad you visited my shop," he said in a loud, clear voice. "Do so again if you ever decide to visit Jericho and learn more about your religion. The Holy Land is the best place for that."

"Thank you," she replied in a similar tone. "Your bookstore is the best I've seen."

A flicker of shadow on the opposite wall alerted Remi to the officer's presence. She turned, holding the book, and saw him staring at her with naked suspicion.

"Why you leave?" he demanded.

"Daniel Walker is the expert on archaeology, so I left him to examine the site. I decided to question the shopkeepers to see if they had seen anyone suspicious. I also picked up a book." She lifted it up to show him.

It was only then that she looked at the title.

1001 Yiddish Jokes. Remi flushed.

The officer's eyes narrowed. It was a common mistake to assume someone who spoke your language in only a broken fashion was stupid. This man was anything but.

He proved that by stepping into the bookstall and switching to fluent Hebrew in order to interrogate the bookseller.

The old man replied in a calm and measured fashion. While Remi couldn't understand a word, she could tell the officer was getting nowhere.

Daniel and David came up to her. Daniel did not look happy. In fact, if they had been anywhere else, she knew she'd get a lecture.

"What the hell do you think you're doing?" Daniel asked in a quiet voice, almost drowned out by the officer's loud, demanding questions.

"I know. I'm sorry. But I think I might have found out everything we need to know," she whispered.

Assuming what he told me wasn't one of the jokes in this book.

At last, the officer gave up.

He turned to the pair of Americans and one Israeli.

"Time to go," he said. It did not sound like a suggestion.

It didn't matter. She had gotten what she had come for. The bookseller had said the Ark was "where kings lay." That would have meant nothing to her if she didn't know to where Professor Hale had made his last, secret, trip.

Egypt.

And where did kings lie in Egypt?

In the Valley of the Kings.

But why did Cohen have coordinates to this man's bookstall? Couldn't Cohen remember a bookstall at a famous archaeological site easily enough? The paper must have been for someone else. But who? And why not just have the coordinates lead to the Valley of the Kings? Did the book dealer act as some sort of a judge, testing out people sniffing after the Ark and leading them to the Valley of the Kings if they passed muster?

Too many questions, and these weren't even the biggest ones.

What of the killer? The kindly old man at Jericho certainly wouldn't have sent Cohen's murderer there. He would have called the police.

So the killer hadn't shown up there. Did he know to go to the Valley of the Kings at all?

Remi had to assume he did. The killer might have gotten the information out of Cohen before he killed him, or he might have found it out by other means.

Plus, it was the only lead they had. A thin trail in a very thin case.

Hopefully it would have to lead somewhere; otherwise that trail will have grown entirely cold.

Daniel was going to have to make another call to the assistant director for travel funds.

CHAPTER TWELVE

Remi awoke, sluggish and disoriented, just as the Egyptair plane touched down in Luxor. She and Daniel had spent a frustrating afternoon waiting for the FBI office to open in the U.S., then waiting to get travel approval and booking a flight.

It was now the afternoon of the next day, and Remi was still trying to catch up on sleep. She had "crashed," as the Americans so aptly put it, the previous afternoon, and then had an unproductive evening doing background research on the case that yielded no solid leads, followed by a tossing and turning night while her mind fretted over Cyril and her body insisted it was daytime.

At least she got some sleep on the plane. Exhaustion had finally dragged her under, and her body was content once again that it was nighttime in Washington, D.C.

There was a direct flight from Jerusalem to Luxor, home to the Valley of the Kings, the Valley of the Queens, and the spectacular temple of Karnak, the largest temple in the world. Many tourists, David Levy had told her as he saw them off at Ben Gurion airport, skipped Cairo and the nearby pyramids entirely and headed straight for the south of Egypt.

It seemed a shame to miss the pyramids, but she had a feeling she'd be missing a lot of sightseeing. She had never been to Israel or Egypt before, and now she was breezing through both countries in search of a killer.

A killer who may have already struck again.

She yawned and stretched, hoping Egyptian coffee would be more effective against jetlag than Israeli coffee.

"So what's the name of the policeman who's going to meet us?" she asked.

"Don't yawn, it's contagious." Daniel yawned to prove his point. "His name is Amir Karara. He's an old friend of David Levy's from a few years back when they were collaborating on tracking ISIS smuggling routes in the Sinai."

"So Karara is a soldier?"

"Levy told me that in Egypt, the line between soldier and policeman gets a bit blurred. It's better just to call them security forces."

Amir met them at the gate, flanked by two members of airport security. He was a man of early middle age with a dusting of gray in his close-cropped black beard and crow's feet on the tan skin around his brown eyes. He wore a suit that did nothing to hide a well-developed physique. Remi's training kicked in and she noticed a bulge under the left side of his jacket that hinted at a shoulder holster. The pair of airport security men carried their guns on their belts.

In their hands, they carried Remi and Daniel's luggage.

"Welcome to Egypt," Amir said, shaking their hands as the other departing passengers streamed by and stared. "I wish I could show you my country under happier circumstances. How is David? Did he take you to the Armenian quarter for dinner?"

"No, we didn't have much time for socializing," Remi said.

"There is a whole quarter in Jerusalem's Old City where the Armenians fled after the Turks genocided them. Their cuisine is excellent. Almost as good as Egyptian."

Remi found his mistake of using the nonexistent word "genocided" to be somehow more forceful than proper English.

Daniel smiled. "Well, hopefully we'll grab the suspect today and have some time to hang out with the mummies."

"We have a fine museum full of them," the Egyptian officer replied, clapping Daniel on the shoulder.

They passed through a throng of tourists waiting at the luggage carousel and out a pair of sliding glass doors into a searing sun. Amir lit a cigarette. The airport security men followed with the bags.

"The Valley of the Kings is less than an hour's drive," Amir told them. "We just have to pass through Luxor—the modern city—cross the bridge and drive out into the desert."

"Thank you for locking it down like we requested," Remi said.

Amir made a face like his cigarette had suddenly lost all its nicotine. "I couldn't."

"What do you mean you couldn't?" Daniel said, trying and failing to keep the heat from his words.

"This is Egypt, and things work differently here. At times they do not work at all. You see, the army is in charge of the businesses around here, and much of the land and is heavily invested in the cruise boats. They do not want a disruption in visitors."

"Did you tell them a murderer is on the loose?" Daniel asked.

"I told them. I gave them the evidence. But they say, 'two Americans and an Israeli think another American took a trip to Egypt and now a killer will strike in the Valley of the Kings?' And then they laughed. You don't want to hear a general laugh, my friend. It is not a nice laugh."

Remi glanced at the two airport security men.

"Do not worry," Amir Karara said, "I picked them because they have no English."

We are in a very different world, Remi told herself. *Take care.*

They were crossing the parking lot now, the sun beating down. They got to a late model Lexus and Amir opened the trunk. The airport men put the bags in the trunk, shook their hands, and headed for the terminal. Like in the West Bank, Remi ended up in back while the two men rode up front. This nettled her, but this wasn't the time to make a stand. The investigation was more important.

"As I was saying," Amir went on as they got in the car, "Thousands of tourists go to the Valley of the Kings every day. That means a lot of money. Plus, if tourists come all the way here to see it and it is closed, they get a bad view of Egypt. So the generals reject my plan. Also, when you see it, you will realize how difficult it would be to catch the killer in such a place."

"I don't see how we can catch him while it's open," Daniel grumbled.

"I have an idea," Amir said. "While many of the tombs are open to visiting, some are closed and are sealed off behind steel gates. Your killer would be looking in one of those tombs. The public ones obviously don't hold the Ark."

"That makes sense," Remi said. "Why are some tombs sealed?"

Remi felt in over her head. While she had read a fair amount about Egyptology, it wasn't her field of expertise. Not even close.

"The rock in some of them is unstable. Others were never finished and have nothing to see. So the government sealed them off to keep people out. I think your killer will come in the daytime, look around like a regular tourist, and then return at night to try to enter one of the closed tombs."

Remi nodded. This man seemed to know what he was doing. David Levy had been right to recommend him.

They sped along a dusty highway past open desert, the green line of vegetation that hugged the Nile visible in the distance.

"I have positioned plainclothes policemen at the parking lot, shortly past the entrance, and further up the valley," Amir said, lighting another cigarette from the butt of the first. "Most visitors do not come alone, so a lone man would stand out. I suspect the killer will sense this and try to attach himself to one of the tour groups. We hope to spot him if he does."

"That sounds like an excellent idea," Remi said. "Other than the fact that he is a white male in good physical condition and in his middle age, we have no description of him."

"We've made investigations on less," Amir said. "When David and I worked on the border, we used informants in the Gaza Strip to tell us about smuggling tunnels under the border. The Palestinian police would watch, using Israeli infrared equipment, and wait until the terrorists entered the tunnel to go to the Egyptian side. We were there waiting for them."

"Did you capture a lot that way?" Daniel asked.

Amir laughed. "The ISIS do not like to be captured. They prefer to martyr themselves. We helped them with this."

"I'm impressed that the Egyptians, Israelis, and Palestinians all cooperated," Remi said, remembering David and Mohammed snapping at each other in Jericho.

"In this part of the world, people only cooperate when there is a greater enemy, and there is no greater enemy than ISIS. They are sick people. They twist Islam. I will martyr as many as volunteer."

Amir took a left and passed through an ugly modern city of concrete with trash-strewn streets full of honking traffic before crossing over a bridge, the placid waters of the Nile flowing slowly beneath them.

Remi's breath caught. While her heart had always been tied to the European Middle Ages and Renaissance, there was no denying the dramatic pull of the grandeur and centuries of stability the Egyptians had created. She was also grateful for how it caught the imagination of young people. She couldn't count the number of history undergraduates who had joined the department after early exposure to mummies and statues of ancient Egyptian deities.

They passed over the bridge and into an agricultural area. Men and boys in long djellabas, looking like Victorian figures in nightshirts, worked the fields with simple equipment. Beside the road, a boy of about ten trotted along on a donkey, perched precariously atop a huge load of straw. He smiled and waved as they passed.

"Look! The Colossi of Memnon!" Daniel said.

By the side of the road rose two towering stone statues of seated pharaohs that must have been sixty feet tall. Although badly weathered, their faces worn away, they still exuded a sense of power. Daniel and Remi stared openmouthed as they passed. Amir obliged their sense of wonder by slowing down.

"You been to Egypt before?" Amir asked.

"I wish," Daniel whispered.

That caught Remi by surprise. He often disparaged historical sites and had even once said that he hated stained glass, one of the oddest things she had ever heard anyone say. When a case took them to Italy, he had spent much of the time in a foul mood and pretended he had never been there even though he showed some local knowledge and even a bit of Italian.

Now, however, he was just as fascinated as anyone would be.

How strange this man is.

They passed the two statues and the last of the cultivated area, the green cutting off almost immediately into brown gritty soil as soon as the irrigation stopped. It was remarkable. Rich farmland turned into desert within a few steps. She realized Egypt couldn't last a day without the Nile.

They took a right onto another dusty desert highway and followed a chain of rough mountains to their left. An imposing temple with giant columns appeared on their right, Daniel craning his neck to see, and then they spotted a sign up ahead for the Valley of the Kings.

Amir turned and headed toward the mountains, ending up at a large, sunbaked parking lot filled with tour buses. A wide valley rose before them, narrowing as it moved up into the mountains. They could not see the end, because it split in two, both valleys curving out of sight.

As soon as they parked and got out of the car, Remi understood why those generals Amir had complained about didn't want to shut the Valley of the Kings.

The place was mobbed. Tour buses were lined up in long rows, and private taxis brought pairs and trios of wealthier travelers to the site.

They had to fight through crowds gathering in front of Egyptian guides who called out to their charges information about the burials here.

"Not as atmospheric as I hoped," Daniel said.

"The crowd gets thinner the further up you go," Amir said. "It gets too hot for them and most run back to their hotels for a beer. Hold on."

The security official moved over to a skinny older Egyptian in a patched gray djellaba and a white turban. He carried a bunch of cheap necklaces in both hands. More hung from his forearms and at least thirty hung from his neck. Amir spoke to the necklace seller for a while, paid him for a necklace of gaudy black beads, and then Amir returned.

"Here you go," Amir said, draping the string of beads around Remi's head. She fingered them. They were made of some sort of stone, although they looked like plastic.

"Oh, you didn't need to," Remi said. How they'd laugh in Paris if she wore *this* thing to a party!

"They are awful, aren't they?" Amir said with a smile. "I don't know why foreigners buy these things. I bought them in case our man was watching. The bead seller is an informant. He says our men are following three people, all well-built middle-aged men traveling alone. They are watching them."

"Three?" Remi said, looking through the crowd. "I'm surprised it isn't three hundred."

"He might have been clever and joined a tour group before arriving. Or the neighbor of that American professor might have gotten his description wrong. You know how often that happens."

Remi bit her lip, scanning the crowd. The killer was here somewhere, she felt sure of it.

But how to find him?

She had an idea.

"Take us to KV 30," she told him.

CHAPTER THIRTEEN

"Why did you want to come to this particular tomb?" Amir asked Remi after a long, hot climb up most of the length of the valley.

As their Egyptian colleague predicted, there were far fewer tourists up here. Remi understood why. She was sweltering and had already downed most of the large bottle of water she had bought for an inflated price at the valley entrance. A line of bedraggled-looking Germans was waiting to get into the nearby tomb of Seti II.

"Because it's the largest of the locked tombs," Remi said. "It has several rooms but because there are no decorations it's not open to the public. The sources I looked at say it's also unstable, but someone who believes in conspiracy theories would think that's just a smokescreen. They would feel such a large tomb would be a good place to hide the Ark and perhaps protect it with a sealed door or something."

"All the closed tombs have heavy steel bars across them," Amir said. "I don't see how this man can think to break in."

"Logic isn't these peoples' strong suit," Daniel said, looking miserable in his black suit. He, too, carried a nearly empty bottle of water. "But they sure can be resourceful. We've dealt with some pretty tough characters who managed to commit some serious crimes before we tracked them down."

"The tomb lies in that little side valley," Remi said, pointing to a narrower cleft in the tan stone that curved away out of sight. Unlike many other side branches, this one did not have any signs to tombs. Rough, steep slopes towered to either side, and further up jagged peaks of stone, painfully bright in the sun, cut into a blue sky washed almost white.

"We'll be conspicuous going in there," Daniel said, taking another slug of his water.

"No more conspicuous than our man," Amir said, still looking sharp and at ease in his suit.

"Let's go," Remi said.

Daniel took out his phone and started taking pictures like the tourists. Remi held the map, both to find the tomb and also blend in. Amir kept a sharp eye out.

The winding little side valley with its steep sides didn't have much of a trail at the bottom, just a faint path littered with stones that had eroded down from above.

Here and there they came across pale potsherds from vessels broken thousands of years before. An archaeologist who worked on Roman sites in France had once told her that pottery was so common in some ancient cultures that excavators didn't bother collecting it all.

"There's nowhere to store it," she had said, "and most of it is all the same anyway. Once it's given you the date of the site, the vast majority of pieces are of no value."

Remi pondered the bits of jugs and dishes as they walked among them, wondering how many centuries or millennia old these vessels were and who had used them.

They passed a couple of sealed tombs, their entrances looking like the entrances to medieval dungeons with their thick steel bars and stygian darkness beyond. Weathered signs announced the numbers to each tomb.

The path curved and soon they were out of sight of the main path. The sounds of the distant crowd vanished, and all they heard was a faint breeze moaning down the ravine. A lone buzzard circled high overhead. Remi had the impression that they had gone back in time three thousand years.

"There," Amir said, pointing to a tomb up the left side of the valley. A sign said "KV 30" in faded paint, but they couldn't see an entrance, only a declivity beyond a low hump in the rock.

Frowning, Amir hurried up the skittering slope, followed closely by Remi and Daniel. They got up to the lip of the hole and looked down.

Just below them was a steel grill, laid horizontally over a nearly vertical shaft. Remi could just make out some dangerous-looking steps leading down precipitously down into the darkness.

"The chain and padlock are intact," Amir pointed out.

"Too bad," Daniel said, chuckling. "If he had picked the lock, he might have saved us a lot of work by falling down those stairs and breaking a leg."

Amir scanned the hilltops.

"I can post a man up there with a pair of binoculars to watch. He'll get a view of this tomb and one or two others."

"That might help," Remi said, feeling disappointed that they hadn't found the killer already inside.

That's just you being impatient, she told herself. *You can't expect this fellow to simply present himself to you. More likely he'll scout out the area and return at night.*

They picked their way down the slope to the faint trail on the bottom of the side valley, only to find someone waiting for them.

He was a thin Egyptian man, with darker skin than Amir and who stood very erect in a white suit. He had a learned air about him and watched their descent with detached patience.

"Hello, Professor Salah," Amir called, waving. Once they made it to him, Amir turned to the two FBI agents. "Professor Salah runs the Luxor Museum. This is Agent Walker and Agent Laurent of the American Federal Bureau of Investigations."

"Pleased to finally meet you," Professor Salah said, shaking their hands. He spoke English with a cultured accent probably developed in an English boarding school.

"Finally?" Remi asked.

Professor Salah smiled. "A colleague in Jericho told me of your investigation."

Remi blinked, her heart beating faster.

The old bookseller. He must mean the old bookseller.

He's one of those guarding the Ark.

She decided to "cut to the chase," as Americans liked to say.

"Our bookseller friend said the Ark could be found where kings lie. Based on that and some other evidence, I took that to mean the Valley of the Kings."

Professor Salah smiled. "We are instructed to say that. It isn't here."

Remi felt a crushing disappointment. Until this moment, she hadn't realized that she had really hoped to find the Ark of the Covenant.

Finding the cryptex and a secret society guarding the Gospel of Longinus has made you overly optimistic. Stop being a treasure hunter. You're an FBI agent now.

"But the killer probably thinks it's here," she pointed out.

"I certainly hope so," the museum director said. "Then we can catch him and stop this madness."

Remi cocked her head. "Hunting for the Ark is madness?"

Professor Salah only smiled.

"Hunting for it here certainly is."

Amir gaped at him. "Professor, are you saying this thing is real?"

"I said nothing of the kind. But if it was, do you think the Jews would give it to us for safekeeping, after we invaded them three times?"

Amir chuckled. "No, it doesn't make sense, but perhaps that's why they would, because no one would suspect."

"That is the exact psychology we use to fool people. Such an unbelievable location immediately becomes more believable when coming from one of us."

"And who are you?" Remi asked.

The museum curator gave another smile. "I am Professor Redwan Salah, director and chief curator of the Archaeological Museum of Luxor."

Daniel cut in. "Professor. We're on the trail of a murderer, one who has killed two of your colleagues, apparently both members of whatever organization you're in that you're not telling us about. It would be in your own best interest to be a bit more forthcoming."

"There is nothing to be forthcoming about, my American friend," he said as they strolled back down the side valley. "We are merely a loose-knit group of scholars from around the world who are interested in the same subject. We hide no great secrets, have no hidden agenda. We are, to quote my teenaged son 'a bunch of boring old men buried in books.'"

Remi and Daniel exchanged glances. They had heard this sort of blithe dismissal before, and it had hidden a far more interesting truth.

* * *

The Lion of Judah watched from the entrance to the tomb of Seti II as the curator of the Luxor Museum walked out of the side valley with a burly Egyptian man who looked like a cop and a Western man and woman. His heart beat fast and he felt a chill despite the cold.

They're after me. Somehow they've tracked me all the way here. Who are those Westerners? CIA? NSA? Illuminati?

Whoever they are, they know I'm close.

But they don't know who I am; otherwise they would have nabbed me at the airport.

The German tourists streamed around him, talking excitedly about the beautiful painted walls of one of the valley's biggest and best-preserved tombs. He moved along with them, just like he had moved up the valley with them. As the two Egyptians and two Westerners moved along—the guy looked American but the woman seemed European—he fell in beside an older woman in a huge sunhat.

"Remarkable preservation, isn't it?" he said in German, increasing the volume a bit for the cops' benefit, and hers. He'd spoken with her before, and she was as deaf as a post.

"Oh yes," she bellowed back. "The figure of the goddess Nut on the ceiling of the burial chamber was especially fine. The wings were so graceful. And did you see the ancient Greek graffiti near the entrance?"

"Yes, and some Latin examples too. I suppose the tomb had been plundered for centuries by then."

"It's a shame so much from the past is lost," the German woman said.

The police were passing them now, walking more quickly downhill than the slow moving, older group of Germans. The American scanned the crowd.

The Lion of Judah could not help but goad him, "Oh yes, so much has been lost, but perhaps less than we think."

The American didn't react. He obviously didn't speak German.

The Lion of Judah did, and fluently, thanks to several years duty on a base in Germany.

Just like good old Professor Hale. It pained him to kill a fellow serviceman, really pained him. But Hale brought it upon himself for hiding the truth from the world.

The group of two Egyptians and two Westerners moved on ahead. The Lion of Judah smiled. He was safe for the moment.

Except he couldn't take a look at KV 30, so close and yet so far. Not with the police on the alert. For all he knew, they might have left a guard hidden in the valley or watching from atop the cliffs.

Even so, that museum curator, who he knew for a fact was one of the Keepers, seemed remarkably relaxed about it all. Yes, just now his laughter came echoing up the valley. This was a joke for him! Was KV 30 another false lead? Had Cohen lied to him?

Now that he thought about it, the Lion of Judah realized the old Israeli had seemed a bit too eager to convince him. At the time he had chalked that up to fear for his family's safety. Now he wasn't so sure. Over the course of years of research, the Lion of Judah had come across rumors before of the Ark's hiding place being in the Valley of the Kings. Nothing substantive, just the usual hints and suppositions this field of study was filled with. But when he held a Keeper at gunpoint, threatening his family with harm at the hands of nonexistent collaborators, he had been entranced at the tale Cohen had spilled out. It had all flowed so easily, and with such a convincing backstory, that the Lion of Judah had swallowed it whole.

And he shouldn't have. When chasing up those earlier rumors, the Lion of Judah had made a study of the Valley of the Kings, and the nearby Valley of the Queens too, just in case the rumors were a partial smokescreen. He had found geological evidence that the rock layers that made up the side valley where KV 30 was located had serious faults. Cohen had claimed that those geological reports were made up but there were several of them, over decades of time, and from English, American, and German research teams. Could they all have been faked?

The Lion of Judah realized he had been had.

Chances were, the Ark wasn't anywhere near the Valley of the Kings.

The Keepers kept it from the public not only by hiding it, but by obscuring its hiding place with a complex web of lies.

But he'd find out the truth.

If he had to wring it out of that smug museum director's neck.

CHAPTER FOURTEEN

The Lion of Judah studied the Archaeological Museum of Luxor carefully from the broad pedestrian avenue running along the Nile. At this early evening hour, with the sun having set past the Western Desert, the traditional abode of the ancient Egyptian dead, and the darkness gathering in town, there were few lights on in the imposing stone building. Visitinh hours had ended two hours before, and now only a couple of the lights in the upstairs offices remained lit.

One of those was the office of Museum Director Redwan Salah.

The Lion of Judah had done his homework. After the Valley of the Kings, he had visited the museum, and there on the wall was a list of the offices, right where anyone could see it. A quick peek behind a door marked "Staff Only, No Visitors Allowed" in English confirmed the pattern of the numbering on the upper floor and from that it had been easy to deduce the exact location of Salah's window.

Salah was there, ripe for interrogation.

The only question was, how to get to him?

The esplanade on which he stood was crowded with locals and tourists, all enjoying the universal pleasure of an evening stroll. The museum stood right next to it, and beyond it was one of the main streets for vehicle traffic.

This wouldn't be like cornering Hale in his home or plucking Cohen off a quiet residential street.

He wished he knew where Salah lived, but there were limits to his ability to gather intelligence. Without any knowledge of Arabic, he couldn't look it up, and Salah drove to and from work. Even if he could steal a car and follow him, the traffic downtown was so bad he'd have to stay right behind him or risk losing him. The museum director would immediately know he was being followed.

So how to handle this?

He saw no way to sneak in. The façade would be fairly easy to climb, constructed of big stone blocks with raised centers, making deep seams between them. But he'd be plainly visible going up. The front doors on the west side overlooking the esplanade were shut and guarded by two armed guards, an entrance on the north end opened onto a parking lot and loading dock, also guarded by a pair of soldiers, and the service entrance on the south end also had an armed guard. Only one.

There was nothing to do but deal with that guard.

He strolled past the service entrance. The guard—some bored, lanky kid with a poor attempt at a moustache doing his required government service and probably wishing he was back in his village—stood by the door. The Lion of Judah could take this guy.

But the first rule of war was to never underestimate your enemy. He had underestimated Cohen's ability to make a convincing story under pressure. He wasn't going to make the same mistake again. This soldier might have been a bored kid, but he was a bored kid with military training and a youth spent in manual labor. He also wore a Kevlar vest, steel helmet, and carried a Kalashnikov.

Plus, the street was busy.

He'd have to play it smart and get the kid out of sight somehow.

Then an idea struck him—he'd play it smart by playing it dumb.

He turned the corner, wasted five minutes strolling along the main street with all its honking traffic and smells of roasting meat coming from the restaurants, then turned back around. The kid, assuming he had noticed him at all, wouldn't remember him now. Another couple of dozen people would have walked past, and probably at least a couple of them tourists.

The Lion of Judah walked along the sidewalk closest to the museum staff entrance, turned into the short walkway leading to it and nodded to the guard as he went to the door.

"No, mister! Museum closed."

The kid stepped out from his sentry post and moved for him. Having been raised to respect his elders, and no doubt instructed to be polite to foreigners, he did not cut him off or level his gun.

The gun was sloped, however. Guards never slung their weapons in this country. Not when there was an active cell of ISIS in the Sinai Peninsula and Islamic Brotherhood cells all over the country.

That was to his advantage, though. Who would think this smiling tourist gentleman would be a threat?

The Lion of Judah stopped with his hand on the door, putting on his best Confused Tourist face. He did not open the door, just turned the knob enough to tell it was unlocked.

"No, mister," the kid said again. The Lion of Judah wondered if that was the extent of his English.

"I have an appointment with Professor Salah."

The kid blinked. "You a friend Professor Salah?"

Turns out this kid knows a bit more English than I thought.

"Yes," he said slowly. "I am a good friend of Professor Salah. He is expecting me."

The kid brightened. "Oh yes. He tell me you come. One minute please." He pulled out a cell phone.

Uh oh.

The Lion of Judah smiled, nodded politely, and walked through the door.

"Wait, mister! I call."

Too late. He had already stepped through the door. The kid followed, cut him off before he had taken three steps down the hallway, and held up his phone for emphasis. He was probably thinking the boss's friends were pretty dumb.

The Lion of Judah glanced past him down the hall. It was a long corridor with a marble floor and a row of closed doors to either side. No lights shone beneath any of the doors. Good.

The main problem was that if the staff entrance was unlocked, that meant there were still staff inside, staff who could come down the hall at any moment.

He'd have to risk it. As the kid was distracted punching a number into his phone, the Lion of Judah gave him a hard karate punch to the solar plexus.

The kid cried out, dropped his phone, and fell to one knee.

The Lion of Judah circled around him. The kid fumbled to get his gun in position. Just as his thumb went to the safety, the Lion of Judah hit him hard on the back of the neck, just below where the helmet protected his head.

A direct hit. Almost. The Lion of Judah hissed in pain as he scuffed his knuckles on the rim of the helmet. His fist hit the nerve center, though, and the kid went down like the sacks of oats he probably hefted back on the farm. He landed on the ground with a thud and did not move.

Wincing in pain, the Lion of Judah shook his hand and blew on the red sores as they oozed blood. A quick glance down the hallway showed he had not been spotted. He tested the nearest door, found it locked, and tested the next one.

It opened into an unlit office. He dragged the kid into it, checked he was breathing all right, and shut the door on him. Then he tried the door to the office opposite, found it to be unlocked, and put the Kalashnikov in there. While he was tempted to keep the gun, he'd be more than a little conspicuous going through the museum with it. If he went unarmed, he could try to bluff, saying the kid had let him through.

He walked down the hall and passed through, opening a door he knew from his previous reconnaissance had a sign saying "Staff Only" on the other side. He listened for a moment and, not hearing anything, opened it a crack.

It opened onto the darkened main galley of the museum. Stone statues of pharaohs and animal-headed gods and goddesses stood on plinths amid glass cases filled with amulets and painted mummy cartonnage, bronze statuettes and items of daily life. Only a couple of dim lights burned—one over the door through which he peeked, and the distant illumination filtering in through a large open doorway leading to the next gallery.

No one was in sight.

The Lion of Judah jogged down the length of the gallery, knowing he was on camera. There was a camera at the staff entrance too, which is why he had to get the kid inside. He doubted anyone was sitting at the camera bank monitoring them. There was no need with armed guards at the staff entrance and the main entrance. Still, they'd be recording. He kept his head hunched low to hide his face under the brim of his baseball cap and he would ditch his clothes before leaving Luxor. Still, there was no hiding his general features.

The enemies of the truth would start closing in.

It didn't matter. They could send a whole army if they wanted to, as long as he found the Ark.

Because then he could reveal the True Ten Commandments. Then he would have the power.

At the end of the gallery, he came to the entrance of another, with glass cases along each wall and a row of stone sarcophagi running down the center. The light was clearer now, and through a large open doorway at the other end of the gallery he could see the main entranceway and broad marble steps leading up, softly illuminated with a few lights.

Moving to the doorway, he hid behind a statue of the hawk-headed god Horus and peered out. He could see the locked main doors to his left, imposing portals of black iron, another set of dimly lit galleries leading off opposite him, and to his right the flight of stairs.

Two Egyptian men appeared on the stairs, both dressed in Western fashion. One held a folder and they chatted amiably in Arabic. Neither were the man he hunted.

The Lion of Judah crouched behind the statue, peeking out through the narrow space between it and the wall. If they turned this way, they would probably see him. Could he knock out both? Neither looked terribly fit. Office workers or academics. But could he take them both out before they raised the alarm?

Probably not.

The Lion of Judah remained motionless in the shadows, waiting for them to pass, but the footsteps and voices receded.

He took another peek and let out a silent breath of relief. They headed down the other wing, to the side door opposite of the one he had entered. There, another guard stood on duty. On that side stood the employee parking lot. He had specifically chosen the door on the other side of the museum than the parking lot because it was less likely to have people passing to and fro.

They passed out of sight. The Lion of Judah slipped out of his hiding place and hurried up the steps. It wouldn't be long before someone found that kid he had knocked out. He needed to get learn the truth and get out of here.

At the top floor he came to more public galleries. It was better lit up here, and he heard the faint sounds of distant conversation. Keeping low to hide himself behind sarcophagi and display cases as much as possible, he hurried to the north wing of the museum, where he knew the director had his office.

At the end of the gallery, he eased open a Staff Only door and passed down a lit hallway flanked by offices. He saw light coming from under one or two.

The Lion of Judah grimaced. Too many people. This could all go wrong.

At last, he came to the director's door. Hoping he was alone, he opened it, darted inside, and shut it behind him.

Salah was just rising, startled from behind a large desk, when the Lion of Judah bounded across the room and hit him hard with a right cross. Salah tumbled to the ground, knocking over an Egyptian flag and tilting a framed photo of the Egyptian president Abdel Fattah al-Sisi.

The Lion of Judah rounded the desk and straddled the prone man. He held one hand to Salah's throat and held the other up in a poised fist.

"Where is the Ark?" he demanded.

"In the Valley of the Kings."

The Lion of Judah hit him. Not too hard. Just hard enough to hurt. He could easily knock this man out but that would achieve nothing.

"Where is the Ark?"

"KV 30."

The Lion of Judah pulled a knife from the back of his belt, where he had wrapped it in cloth and hidden it beneath his shirt. Like in Israel, he couldn't bring in any weapons, so he had stolen a butcher knife from the kitchen at his hotel. Good enough.

He held it against Salah's throat and pressed a little. Blood welled up around the blade.

Professor Redwan Salah did not show fear, only resignation. He began to recite something in Arabic. After a moment the Lion of Judah recognized it as the *shahadah*, the Islamic expression of faith.

The Lion of Judah waited until he had finished.

"Yes, you will die. I won't lie to you. You've seen my face and you can't be allowed to help the police stop me. But if you want to protect your family from the vengeance of my colleagues, you will tell me where you have hidden the Ark."

Salah's eyes widened a moment. "M-my family is innocent."

"Many innocent people are sacrificed in the course of history. They don't have to be among them. All you have to do is tell me the location of the Ark of the Covenant."

To his surprise, Salah frowned.

"Isn't it obvious?" he said, contempt dripping from his words.

"What do you mean?" the Lion of Judah demanded.

"*We* didn't hide it anywhere. Promise me you won't hurt my wife and children."

"I won't if you can convince me of the truth."

"It's all a smoke screen. The Keepers don't have the secret. Our secret is that there is no secret. We've been spreading rumors for generations to mislead people from what's right under their noses."

The Lion of Judah blinked. "You mean … ?"

"It's in Axum, just like the Ethiopians always said it was. Just like it's written in the *Kebra Negast*."

The Lion of Judah pressed the knife a little harder. Salah hissed in pain.

"It couldn't be!" the Lion of Judah growled.

"Of course it is. And who better to guard it? The Land of Israel has been overrun a dozen times since the days of Solomon. And Egypt? You think our corrupt government could keep a secret like this? The Ethiopians may be poor, they may be in a remote corner of Africa, but that's to their advantage. When they say they have the world's holiest treasure, no one believes them. Their poverty is their greatest disguise."

The Lion of Judah looked him in the eyes, trying to find deceit. But in them he saw only fright and contempt.

Just then the door to the office opened, and on instinct the Lion of Judah cut into the museum director's neck.

CHAPTER FIFTEEN

Remi sensed there was trouble the moment she saw the guard wasn't at his post.

Professor Salah had told them to visit him at his office after hours, coming in via the staff entrance. He would discuss the Ark with them over dinner. They were supposed to mention his name to the guard, who would be expecting them, and the guard would call up.

But the guard was missing.

She glanced at Daniel, who instinctively put his hand inside his jacket to where he usually wore his shoulder holster.

But of course, it wasn't there.

"We need to get in there," Remi said.

"Right. I'm calling Amir."

The Egyptian officer was still at the Valley of the Kings organizing the night watchmen.

He pulled out his phone and moved through the side door along with Remi. She had no idea where Salah's office was, and the corridor they found themselves in was dark and quiet. There was no one to ask.

Then something the museum director had said came back to her.

"Mention my name to the guard and he'll call upstairs."

"His office is upstairs somewhere," Remi whispered.

Daniel only nodded.

They passed to the end of the corridor and through a door to find themselves in a darkened exhibition hall. Hurrying through this and the one beyond it, they came to the main hall with a stairway leading up.

Here they stopped, listening. They heard nothing.

Daniel, still with the phone to his ear, raised a hand.

"Amir, thanks for picking up." Remi realized the man's phone must have been ringing the entire time. She pressed her head close to Daniel's phone so she could hear.

"Sorry for not answering sooner," Amir said. "I was in that side valley and wanted to get out to get better reception. What's going on?"

Remi glanced upstairs. The killer could be up there right now. In fact, he probably was.

She moved off, heading for the stairs.

A snap of the fingers made her turn around. Daniel was on the phone, explaining the situation to Amir and gesturing angrily for her to get back to his side.

Remi gaped. Did he just snap his fingers at her, like some nouveau riche Englishman to a Parisian waiter?

It took some effort to remind herself that he was the senior agent on this case, and that he had been specifically told by the Assistant Director to keep her in line.

Still, her hands balled into fists, and she simmered until he got off the phone.

"He's calling the museum guards right now," Daniel said as he passed her and headed for the stairs. "Then he's going to call the Luxor police department. Let's get up there. Stay behind me."

Behind him???

They ascended the broad marble staircase three steps at a time. As they got to the first landing, they heard a distant shout upstairs, followed by some words in Arabic.

Remi didn't understand a word, but the man's shock and fear was obvious.

They ran up the second flight of steps. There was a cry, and a door slammed.

They came upon a poorly lit gallery. The sound of running feet to their right. They hurried along past displays of ancient Egyptian artifacts. Daniel's phone rang. He ignored it.

A door opened at the far end of the gallery, framing a lit hallway. A dark figure came out of it, shouting something in Arabic and waving his arms. He came straight down the center of the gallery, shouting the same word over and over again.

"Halt!" Daniel shouted, cutting him off.

The man stopped short. He was a thin, small Egyptian man with a badly receding hairline and spectacles.

"Who are you?" he demanded in heavily accented English, backing off as he did so.

"Where is Professor Salah?" Remi asked.

The man pointed back to the lit hallway with a trembling finger. At the far end they could see an open door and a couple of Egyptian men staring inside.

Daniel and Remi ran for the hallway, the Egyptian running alongside.

"Who are you?" he asked again.

The two men in the hallway started crying out in anguish. With the man they had bumped into still demanding to know what was going on, and Daniel demanding to know the same thing from him, no one heard when Remi herself cried out.

She had seen something move in the shadows.

It had been in the corner of her eye, and only for an instant, but it was enough to make her stop and back away, her gaze darting over that part of the room, trying to locate what she had seen for a brief moment.

Another cry from the hallway. A figure burst out of one of the closed office doors. She caught a brief glimpse of a white male before the newcomer hit a light switch, plunging the hallway into shadow lit only by the light of a couple of open office doors.

"Halt!" Daniel shouted again, rushing for the now darkened hallway.

Remi moved a bit to the side, trying to keep an eye on the confusion in the hallway while scanning the gallery. She jerked as her back hit something, only to whirl around and see it was a statue of a giant, crocodile-headed god towering over her in the gloom.

A soft sound in the shadows. She saw a dark shape flit from behind one display case to disappear behind another.

"Daniel! Over here!" she shouted.

He gave no indication that he heard. The hallway was filled with shouts and the sound of a scuffle.

Could there be two killers? Remi darted away from the crocodile-headed god and hid behind a goddess with a cat's head. Crouching low behind its plinth, she peered into the dark.

There! The shadow was moving along the far end of the gallery. In the few seconds she had taken her eye off of it in order to change position, it had moved like the wind almost out of the room.

No time for sneaking now, she ran after it, keeping as many statues and other displays between herself and the mystery figure as possible, hoping that would cover her advance.

She was halfway down the length of the gallery when the figure of a man briefly appeared in the open doorway before entering the room where the stairs led down.

Remi picked up speed, not wanting to lose the fleeing figure. They had gotten so close on so little evidence, she didn't think they'd get another chance.

Making it to the doorway, she peeked around the corner. A few weeks before, she would have run straight in, but she'd learned enough about situational awareness to know that doing that was a good way to get ambushed, and that her overabundance of enthusiasm on previous missions should by all rights have led to her serious injury or death.

She saw the figure rush for the stairs, then stop as the sounds of shouts and the stomp of booted feet echoed up from below. Amir had warned the guards.

The figure darted off in the other direction, disappearing into the next gallery. She had only seen him from behind, but he looked like a well-built white male, neither old nor young.

Remi ran at full speed in pursuit. She didn't try to shout down to the guards. They probably didn't speak sufficient English and she didn't want to warn her quarry that she was after him.

When she got to the doorway to the next gallery, again she stopped and peeked carefully around the corner.

The man had disappeared.

Not that she could see much. No lights were on in this room, and the windows had their blinds down, so only a little illumination from the streetlights seeped through at the edges.

Cursing silently to herself, she slipped into the room and ducked behind a giant sarcophagus. Briefly she wondered if it was still occupied.

This interesting academic question soon got discarded when she saw the shadow move off toward the far exit. She could not tell if the man had seen her or not or was only spooked by the approach of the guards.

All she could tell was that he was well ahead of her.

He seemed to know the building, moving with a confidence she would not expect from someone breaking in for the first time.

He must have scouted out the museum beforehand, perhaps several times.

Shouts and running feet from the staircase, plus fainter shouts from where someone had switched the lights off near Salah's office, covered her footsteps as she moved after the intruder. That all seemed distant now as she focused on the pursuit, a pursuit she knew she had to do alone.

Just her and the killer.

All the warnings Daniel had given her had vanished from her mind. Even her own personal safety took second place. All that mattered was catching her prey.

They came to another gallery, this one overlooking a small internal courtyard. A narrow flight of steps led down. The man was already halfway down them. Remi realized she had no hope of catching him now.

My personal trainer is right. I do need to work up some more speed.

She got to the railing and made a quick assessment. From the dim light of some skylights and the light given off from a refrigerated display case at a little café set amid potted ferns, she saw the only exit was just to her right, next to a large statue of a pharaoh that stood almost to the height of the walkway on which she stood.

And that gave her an idea.

She moved over to the statue just as the man made it to the base of the stairs. Remi still wasn't sure if he had noticed her or not. He didn't seem to have looked her direction at any time.

Swinging her legs over the railing, she gripped the smooth stone and set her feet on the other side. The man angled across the courtyard, almost beneath her.

She jumped, landing on the pharaoh's smooth shoulder. She wavered, feet slipping, arms cartwheeling, and half-fell, half-jumped onto the fugitive passing below.

The impact was harder than she expected. Although she landed straight on his back, her chest slammed into the man's head, knocking the wind out of her as he fell with her on top of him. They ended up on a heap on the floor.

For a moment neither moved. Just groaned.

It isn't like in the movies.

How many times had she said the same to her students about the Middle Ages? She should have known better.

Remi gathered the strength to roll off him. The man got to his hands and knees, clearly stunned. She fumbled for the handcuffs on her belt, wishing for the hundredth time that she had her service pistol.

Just as she got the handcuffs off her belt, the man turned to her. She stared …

… and gasped.

She recognized this man.

CHAPTER SIXTEEN

"What are you doing here?" Remi asked.

It was Father De Sanctis, one of the Association of Devout Students, an ancient order dating back to the beginnings of the Catholic Church and dedicated to defending the secrets of the Gospel of Longinus. She had helped arrest a killer who had been targeting members one by one, trying to get at the gospel itself.

"Monitoring you," he said, staggering to his feet.

"Stop right there, you are under arrest," Remi said.

Father De Sanctis smiled. "Am I? You have no authority here. And what have I done that's illegal?"

"You killed the museum director."

"No. That was a young man stronger than I am. I had a brief glimpse of him coming out of the director's office. Through connections I knew that you were to meet with Salah, and I came here to find out what you were up to. How does he fit into the hunt for the cryptex? Why did that man kill him? My Arabic is a bit rusty, but I understood that much."

Looking at the older but still fit Italian, Remi realized he didn't fit the witness description at all.

But the man she had seen Daniel go after certainly did.

She should get back up there and help him, but first she needed to straighten out what was going on here.

"This isn't about the cryptex. The man we're hunting is …," *watch yourself, Remi,* "trading in stolen antiquities."

Remi felt guilty saying even half a lie to a priest, but she wasn't about to let him in on details of an FBI investigation. Then the horrible truth of what he had just said came down on her.

"Wait. You think I'm after the cryptex and you followed me all the way to Egypt?"

Again, that smile. Father De Sanctis rotated one of his arms, massaging the shoulder with his other hand. "Ouch. Landing on me really hurt. I'm not sure if it's better or worse than getting pepper sprayed."

"If you don't want to keep getting hurt, stop following me."

"You and I both know that's not going to happen."

Remi took a step closer to him. "I could arrest you for obstruction of justice and for breaking and entering."

"You don't have the authority here, and even if you did, you wouldn't."

"And why wouldn't I?" Remi demanded.

"Because I would press charges for your theft of the cryptex clue from one of our churches."

Remi blinked.

"You have no proof of that." She wished her voice sounded a bit more forceful.

"Don't we?"

"And you wouldn't make that public because it would reveal your existence."

"Wouldn't we?"

Remi paused.

Father De Sanctis's smile broadened. "Both the Association of Devout Students and your have skirted at the edges of the law. We have both done so because we thought under the circumstances it was the right thing to do. And we both rely on secrecy in order to achieve our ends. I suggest we continue with such a practice. Now don't you have a murderer to catch?"

Remi glanced back up the stairs. She moved for them, spun and pointed at the priest.

"This isn't over."

"Not by any stretch of the imagination." Father De Sanctis turned and disappeared into the shadows.

Remi hurried back to the museum director's office. Her chest hurt from where she had hit Father De Sanctis on the back of the head, making each breath sting. She knew she must be developing a horrible bruise.

But what hurt more was the knowledge that Association of Devout Students was watching her closely enough to know she had come here. They had even sent one of their members to break into the Luxor Museum to eavesdrop on their meeting with Professor Salah. She hadn't made any progress on hunting down the cryptex. The special training program and now this case had taken up all her time.

The Association of Devout Students hadn't been so preoccupied.

Did they know she was training to be an agent now? Did they know she had left Georgetown? Perhaps they knew everything about her. They had known she was going to Egypt, after all, and yet they didn't know what for.

So they didn't have a contact in the FBI. They did, however, have her general movements under surveillance.

That was frightening enough.

But, she reasoned as she jogged through the darkened gallery, trying to ignore the pain she felt with every inhalation, they couldn't be too far along in their search. If they had found the next step to the cryptex puzzle, they wouldn't be following her. Indeed, if they had any clear idea where it might be, they wouldn't have come all the way to Egypt in the hopes that she'd come across a clue.

Whatever reassurance she felt at that vanished as she got to the hallway with Salah's office and saw the crowd of people there.

One of the armed guards stood at the end of the hall, talking excitedly on the phone. The others were nowhere to be seen. Neither was Daniel. No doubt they were still pursuing the intruder. An academic-looking man in a suit came staggering out of the office at the end, shaking and despondent, blood on his hands.

He looked up at Remi, and in a wavering voice said,

"I … I tried to save him. Nothing will stop the bleeding."

Remi cut past him and into the office.

Professor Salah lay on the floor. Two of his colleagues knelt by him. One was praying in Arabic and moving a string of beads between his fingers. Another was holding a handkerchief up to a deep throat wound. From the large pool of blood all around the museum director, a pool both other men were kneeling in, the man's efforts weren't doing any good.

Remi approached, wanting to see but not wanting to intrude. Her heart clenched. He seemed like such a nice person, a scholar and no doubt a family man, like someone she might have worked with in her days in academia. And now he had been brutally attacked by the man she was trying to catch.

Trying and failing.

To her surprise, Salah's eyes still had some life in them. They turned to look at her, his head remaining motionless.

He mouthed some words. The man trying to staunch the wound whispered something to him in Arabic.

Salah mouthed something again and made a feeble attempt to motion to her. His two colleagues looked up, noticing her for the first time.

Salah tried to speak again, only managing to produce a faint gurgle.

Remi took a final two steps to get by his side and crouched down. He whispered something but she couldn't catch it. She had to get closer.

She knelt in the pool of blood, feeling it soak through the fabric of her trousers. Bending closer to Salah's mouth, she heard him try again.

At first all that came out was a strangled, wet cough. Remi winced as she felt a fine spray of blood hit her cheek.

But she did not move.

Then he managed to speak.

"Ethiopia."

"Ethiopia? He's going to Ethiopia?" Remi asked.

Salah closed his eyes for a moment, then opened them and looked at her.

"Yes?" Remi asked.

His eyelids fluttered, hooded, and the spark left his eyes and he stopped focusing.

Professor Redwan Salah, director and chief curator of the Archaeological Museum of Luxor, was dead.

* * *

Daniel trudged up the stairs of the museum, one of the guards following quietly behind. When the intruder had switched the lights off in the office hallway, confusion reigned. Daniel had tried to grab him, only to get grabbed by a confused museum worker. In the ensuing struggle, Daniel had torn himself free but not before the intruder had booked it down the hall.

Daniel had rushed down these very same steps after him. When he saw two of the guards coming up the stairs, guns drawn, he thought it was all over, but the guy had some more tricks up his sleeve.

The guy shouted, "he's up there!" while pointing behind him. That made the guards pause for a moment. They didn't know who this foreigner was, and his panic sure looked genuine. They turned away their guns and tried to ask something.

That's all the killer needed. He had leapt the last few steps separating them and, in a move that would have done credit to any professional wrestler, slammed feet first into one of the guards.

The guard went down for the count, followed by his colleague a moment later courtesy of a right hook.

And the killer kept on running.

Daniel kept after him, even though he felt sure all he'd earn was a good ass kicking. He really, really wished he had been allowed to carry a gun on this trip.

To his surprise, the killer didn't turn to face him, only picked up speed.

Daniel chased him down the long corridor to the staff entrance and out into the night. The killer led him on a zigzag path through Luxor, Daniel getting more and more out of breath and further behind, until at last he lost him in some back street of shuttered shops and towering apartment blocks.

And now Daniel was back at the scene of the crime, with nothing to show for his trouble. He pulled out his phone and called Amir Karara.

"Hello, my friend," the security official said. "I am in my car headed for Luxor. I will be there in ten minutes."

"We lost him," Daniel said between heavy gulps of air. "Got a good look at him, though. About six one. Dressed in a green polo shirt and tan slacks. Fit. Muscular and broad-shouldered but not overly bulky. Late forties or early fifties. Close-cropped dirty blond hair. Not sure of the eye color but I think they're hazel. Good fighter. Right-handed. I noticed his right hand was bleeding on the knuckles."

"We will send an alert to all police stations and hotels. We will get him, my friend."

Daniel wished he could feel so optimistic.

Just as he hung up, his phone buzzed again.

A message from Veronica.

"For God's sake, not now!"

"What, sir?" the museum guard asked.

"Nothing," Daniel mumbled, putting his phone back in his pocket.

He came to the office hallway, where a grim-faced little knot of Salah's coworkers stood outside his office door. He didn't need to ask. He'd seen that look far too many times before.

Remi stepped out of the office, pale and with a stricken look on her face. She had a bit of blood on her left cheek, and circles of blood on her knees.

Daniel rushed up to her. "You hurt?"

Remi shook her head. "It's … his blood."

"Where did you go? You disappeared. Of course, running after that guy I might have missed, but it seemed—"

"I was after someone else."

"Someone else?"

Her eyes darted around the others gathered in the hallway. "Not here."

Daniel nodded to upper gallery of the museum. "Let's go talk over there. The guards can handle the situation here. Amir and the cops will be here any minute."

They walked out into the shadowy gallery, stopping at a large stone sarcophagus. Remi leaned against it, looking utterly spent.

"I saw someone in here," she whispered.

"Who?"

"I chased him and caught him in the inner courtyard. It was … Father De Sanctis."

"Father De Sanctis? The guy we found hiding inside a burnt-out church? What the hell was he doing here?"

Remi paused. Even in the half light, her features betrayed the struggle going on in her mind.

"Following me."

"Why would he follow you? We solved that case."

She hung her head. "The Association of Devout Students thinks I'm hunting for the cryptex."

"The cryptex? But you don't have it." Something clicked. "But you have an idea where it is." Something else clicked. "You opened it! In the couple of minutes that you were left alone in the High Museum, you unlocked it. The Association knows that somehow. You've been keeping that from me since Atlanta?"

His partner grimaced. "I couldn't resist. Inside was a map that led me to a church where I found a code that I'm still trying to break. I should have told you, but I couldn't. But now that the association is interfering with this case, I had to come clean. I know I broke the law. I wasn't an agent then but that's no excuse. If you want to report me to the assistant director, I understand. I won't hold it against you."

Daniel stared at her a moment, trying to process what he just heard. Then he chuckled, the chuckle growing louder and longer before turning into a full-on belly laugh.

Maybe it was the stress of the evening, maybe it was the ridiculousness of the whole situation, but he found it hilarious.

Then he remembered a man was dead and cut it off short.

Remi stared at him, looking like she wanted to be anywhere else.

"Are you going to tell the assistant director?" she asked.

"What? No! So you took a little peek when confronted with the culmination of your life's work. Who could resist that temptation? And technically it was part of the investigation. Also, since the cryptex was hidden inside another artifact its ownership was in doubt. I don't think the museum could have pressed charges. Anyway, it's all in the past. Having the Association of Devout Students on our tail does complicate things, though." He scratched his chin, thinking, then shook his head. "It doesn't matter. Did you drill into De Sanctis's head that this has nothing to do with the cryptex?"

"I think so."

"Good."

"I suppose I should have detained him, but I came back to help you. And … I got something from Salah before he died."

"Really? What?"

"He only said one word. Ethiopia."

"That's where the Ark is supposed to be."

"Exactly. George Steiner was convinced it wasn't there, mainly because everyone said it was."

"Typical logic of a conspiracy theorist."

"Exactly. But maybe it was a double lie. Maybe having the Ethiopians proclaim it's there is a way to convince people it isn't."

"This is making my head hurt."

"Mine too. I'm not sure if Salah was naming Ethiopia because that's where it is or that's where he told the killer it is. Either way, we need to get there."

"Go to Ethiopia? Um, Remi, I don't know if you've been keeping up with current events, but there's a civil war there right now. I don't really understand what it's all about. Some tribal thing. The north had split off from the south. Axum is right close to the border."

"He'll take advantage of the chaos to grab the Ark, probably killing some priests to get it."

“Good point. Assuming he can even make it there.”

“He can. Look how resourceful he’s proven to be so far.”

“True enough,” Daniel replied, thinking about how the guy knocked out a soldier, snuck through the museum right to Salah’s office unseen, killed him, and then fought his way past two more soldiers and Daniel himself.

“Yeah,” Daniel sighed. “Yeah, he probably will get to Ethiopia. I don’t see Assistant Director Ochiai giving us travel permission to go there, though. Two U.S. law enforcement officers tracking someone through a warzone? That could cause an international incident.”

Remi put a hand on his arm. “Ask her. Make her understand.”

Daniel looked at her.

What I understand is that if I don’t get the travel permission, you’ll probably disappear, and the next thing we’ll hear about you is that you’re in an Ethiopian jail.

Daniel sent their boss a long email explaining the situation and requesting permission to continue the hunt to Ethiopia. Even as he wrote it, he could see how ridiculous the request sounded. There was no way Ochiai would say yes.

And she didn’t. She didn’t say anything. Until late into the Egyptian night, well through the morning in D.C. local time, she didn’t even acknowledge receipt of the email.

He had expected a curt no. Or a long no in which Assistant Director Ochiai asked why he was wasting her time with such an insane travel request. What he didn’t expect was silence.

What was going on?

CHAPTER SEVENTEEN

Daniel got a text early the next morning, the middle of the night in D.C., with the instruction to go to a certain address in downtown Luxor where a representative of the U.S. government would meet them. He was specifically instructed to identify himself only by name and not by his bureau affiliation. Remi was to come but under no circumstances should they bring along any Egyptians.

That surprised him. There was no U.S. consulate in Luxor. He'd checked.

The final line of the text read, "Once you have memorized the address, delete this message. Do not write down the address. Commit it to memory."

Utterly confused, they took a taxi to an address just down the street. If the FBI wanted to be so cloak and dagger, Daniel wouldn't even give the taxi driver any clue as to where they were going.

The address was a fashionable apartment complex overlooking the Nile. A bit of irrigation had made a lush garden between the building and the river, and a few Egyptian families relaxed on park benches as their children laughed and chased each other around. Daniel and Remi went to the front door and pressed the call button for the correct apartment. Within moments they were buzzed in.

Upstairs, they were greeted by a trim American in his forties wearing office casual who gave them a firm handshake and ushered them into a large, clean apartment.

Once the door was closed, their contact said, "I'm Wilson Snowcroft, CIA."

Daniel and Remi looked at each other.

"The CIA is getting involved in the case?" Daniel asked.

"Not as such. We're just offering a secure line to D.C. and helping insert you into the mission area."

Snowcroft took them through a spacious living room with a fantastic view of the Nile, with an ancient temple visible on the far riverbank, and into a Spartan office. Daniel noted there were no papers on the desk and got the impression that it had been cleaned up before their arrival. A desktop computer took up part of the space.

"Both of you can sit here. I just need to set up the connection."

"Why are we getting a secured line?" Remi asked.

"Perhaps your D.C. contact can explain that to you. I was just instructed to provide it."

Snowcroft brought up a program Daniel didn't recognize, opened Tor and a VPN, and made the connection.

All they saw was a black screen.

"When your conversation is over, the other party will terminate the call. You don't have to do anything. Just come get me."

Snowcroft left the office, closing the heavy door with a soundproofing thud.

Daniel and Remi exchanged glances again.

"Why all the cloak and dagger?" Daniel asked. He found himself whispering.

"Does this happen often?" Remi whispered back.

"This has never happened."

The screen came on, showing not Assistant Director Ochiai, as they had expected, but Deputy Director Burton, her immediate superior. He was a tough old Vietnam veteran in his seventies, and not someone to be trifled with. From what little Daniel could see of the background, he could tell Deputy Director Burton wasn't in his office.

"Good evening, Agent Walker and Trainee Agent Laurent, or I should say good morning for you. We've discussed your travel request and have decided to approve it pending your consent. As you are no doubt aware, there is a civil war going on in Ethiopia at the moment. The Tigrayans who control the north, including the city of Axum, have broken away from the Oromo and Asmara dominated government. The front line has moved back and forth constantly in recent months and Axum has changed hands twice. Currently it is in the hands of the Tigrayans and their provisional government. The front line is only fifty miles to the south, however, and the Ethiopian government air force occasionally launches airstrikes in the area."

Daniel shifted in his seat. He'd read about this last night. He'd also read about unconfirmed reports of massacres and ethnic cleansing on both sides. The FBI was actually going to send two of its agents into this, and one of them only a trainee? And the CIA was going to help them do it?

Deputy Director Burton went on.

"Agent Snowcroft can arrange for you to fly to Djibouti, a small nation on the Red Sea. From there you will meet Lucas Mekonnen, an Ethiopian-American who will help you get overland into the portion of northern Ethiopia controlled by the Tigrayan faction. He can assist you while you are in country, but he is not a U.S. government agent, and I must stress that he is under no obligation to do so."

"Wait. He's not a government agent?" Daniel asked. "Then what is he?"

The corner of Burton's mouth twitched, a barely perceptible movement. Daniel suspected he wasn't even aware he was doing it.

"More of a freelancer. But he comes with the highest recommendation."

From whom? Daniel decided not to ask. He had the feeling he wouldn't get an answer.

Deputy Director Burton leaned forward a little. "This is a highly dangerous region of the world. Djibouti has a U.S. embassy and a CIA station, but after you cross the border, you will be operating beyond our authority. Other than Mr. Mekonnen, you can expect no help while you are in the region. I cannot in good conscience let you go without your consent. If you wish to return to the United States now, it will not be held against you. The suspect has probably headed to Axum as you believe. He will face the same dangers you would and may get arrested or killed. We can continue to monitor the situation from D.C. There is no need for you to pursue this personally unless you both agree to do so."

Daniel was stunned. He had never been given this option before. Then again, he had never been sent into a war-torn region before. Deputy Director Burton hadn't mentioned that the Ethiopian or Tigrayan provisional government had been informed. Daniel guessed not. This had turned from an international police investigation into a spy mission.

That was out of Daniel's league. It was out of Remi's league too.

The FBI was showing a lot of faith in their abilities, faith he himself didn't share. If the bureau wanted to give them a promotion, they could do it without endangering their lives.

He turned to Remi, and saw she looked as doubtful as he felt.

And that really got him worried. She should be going full guns for the chance to track the killer to Ethiopia or the Republic of Tigray or whatever region Axum was in this month. Instead, she looked hesitant.

He looked back at Burton, sitting in some private soundproof room like they were and talking over a secure CIA line, and wondered what was really going on. The FBI had no authority to operate in a foreign state without that government's consent. Yet the deputy director was allowing them to do just that.

He must have gotten approval from the head of the FBI himself, and the head of the FBI would probably have had to get approval from the White House.

Wait. The president *wants us to go to Ethiopia?*

Something seriously strange was going on here.

Burton sat there, impassive, awaiting a decision.

Daniel stared at that craggy old poker face and wondered.

He wondered why the FBI cared so much about some lunatic hunting the Ark of the Covenant.

He wondered why they had been given permission to follow him.

And most of all, he wondered why they specifically were being allowed to go. If it was so damn important, why not send someone more qualified?

And he knew for a fact that he wouldn't get any answers to those questions if he declined and asked to be brought back to D.C. Even if he did go, he might not learn any of the answers. But he might.

At last, Daniel spoke.

"I'm willing to go if Trainee Agent Laurent is willing."

He put a slight emphasis on the word "trainee," wondering if that would make the deputy director think twice.

"So what is your decision, Trainee Agent Laurent?" Burton asked.

Guess not, Daniel thought.

"I'll go," Remi said.

To investigate the murders or investigate the motives of the FBI? Daniel asked silently. *Because I want to get to the bottom of both.*

* * *

If Daniel thought the sun of southern Egypt made him feel like he was in a sauna, the late afternoon heat of Djibouti City, the capital of Djibouti, felt like a steam room. It had to be at least a hundred degrees and the humidity coming off the Red Sea was near one hundred percent. Even though he had switched into loose safari clothes and a broad-brimmed hat, he could feel the sweat break out almost the instant he walked down the stairs from the plane onto the tarmac. Remi, similarly attired, didn't look like she was having a good time either. When they entered the terminal, the air conditioning hit them like a plate glass window. Daniel hoped he didn't get pneumonia.

They passed through customs on a business visa, Snowcroft having arranged a bogus invitation from an American shipping company that used the busy port, and passed through the terminal to a teeming reception area.

Snowcroft had shown them a photo of Lucas Mekonnen and told them he'd be waiting in the airport café by the main entrance carrying a briefcase and wearing a bright blue shirt. No phone number, no guy holding up a sign with their name on it, just a place and a time and a photo they didn't get to keep.

Daniel sure hoped the guy showed, or this little mission would be dead in the water before they left the terminal.

"There's the main entrance," Remi said, pointing. Djibouti had been a French colony until 1977, and so the signs were in French as well as in Arabic.

They passed through a crowd of locals dressed in everything from Western business suits to loose robes and turbans and made it to a small collection of tables enclosed by a low railing. Behind a counter to one side, where a lit display case offered up various cakes, a man was brewing up some delicious smelling coffee.

I could use one of those.

Not far from the counter he spotted their contact sitting alone at a small table sipping from a tiny cup of coffee, a half-finished éclair in front of him. He was a short, compact man of indeterminate age, with a lean, wiry body that hinted at athleticism.

Before Daniel could say anything, Lucas Mekonnen spotted them. He stood, flinging his arms wide.

"Ah, my good friends!" he said in heavily accented English. "Welcome to Djibouti. I hope everything is going well in the main office."

"Yes, things seem to be progressing quite quickly," Daniel said, shaking his hand. His grip was strong, the hand calloused. Especially the forefinger. The trigger finger.

"I am glad. You must be tired after your long journey. Hot here, no? Not like New York. Come, I will take you to a nice restaurant so you can—how do you say in English—refresh yourselves? Come."

He led them out of the terminal, carrying Remi's suitcase, and across a wide parking lot that the sun hit like a hammer on an anvil.

Other than a busy taxi stand right next to the terminal, the parking lot was nearly empty. Even the locals didn't want to hang out in a place like this.

"I'll take you to a safe house and we'll plan our route," Mekonnen said in a low voice. "I'll give you some Ethiopian birr. You got some dollars on you, right? Good. Those are useful anywhere. I can get you over the border and to Axum, and I might be able to get you a contact there. We'll have to see. My car's right over there. If you have any messages to send, send them now. Cell phone coverage disappears pretty quick once we get out of the city."

His accent had disappeared. Now he spoke like the American that Deputy Director Burton had said he was.

Daniel's heart went cold. This was all too strange.

They got to the car, a late model Nissan. Daniel put his bag down.

"One second," he said, stepping away from the car.

He took out his phone. He had loaded up his Egyptian Sim card with plenty of points. Hopefully it would allow for a text message.

There was a new message from Etisalat, the Egyptian phone company, probably telling him the roaming rates, but since it was in Arabic, he couldn't read it.

Here goes.

He opened up Veronica's last message, the one he hadn't read the night before in the Luxor museum. He'd been dreading it.

"Daniel,

"I still haven't heard from you. I know you must be angry and upset and I don't blame you. But I need to hear what you think. Please don't shut me out.

"LOVE,

"Veronica"

Daniel sighed, wiped sweat from his brow, and typed.

"I need to think about this. I'm on a case right now. I know, I know, once again I'm putting a case before our relationship and I'm sorry. It's just this one is a bit …," Daniel paused, trying to find the right word, "… different. I'm overseas and I'm not sure I'll have cell phone coverage where I'm going. I'm …." another pause, longer this time, "… also not sure I'll be coming back. I can't explain. This case is dangerous and way beyond my skillset. I don't want to scare you. I just thought you should know. I do love you and I do think about our marriage often. Remember that.

"Love,

"Daniel."

He paused before hitting send. The message seemed so inadequate, both alarming and vague, and yet he couldn't think of something else to say.

What could he say as he stood in a sweltering parking lot in a country he had barely heard of the week before while some spy or mercenary or whatever he was waited to drive him into a warzone in search of a killer hunting a Biblical artifact?

There was nothing to say, nothing he could tell Veronica to make her understand, because he didn't understand himself.

He hit send and walked over to where Remi and Mekonnen waited by the car.

"Let's go," he sighed. "Let's get to Axum."

CHAPTER EIGHTEEN

Remi felt the hot desert air blast her face as she sat by the open window in the truck. They sped along a wide highway where trucks and cars moved at crazy speeds, weaving in and out of lanes. It seemed more like a race than a drive.

This was the main road between Djibouti and northern Ethiopia. Being a landlocked country, Mekonnen had explained, Djibouti was Ethiopia's main access to the sea. Somaliland was too underdeveloped, and Eritrea was cut off thanks to the civil war. So traffic had grown on this highway in recent months.

Traffic had grown, but its destination had shifted. In a major offensive the previous month, the Tigrayans had taken over this border area, cutting off the portions of Ethiopia under government control from access to the sea. A series of bloody counteroffensives had failed to dislodge the rebels from this strategic strip of East African desert.

And what a desolate stretch of the world! They had quickly left the modern, prosperous downtown of Djibouti City, stopping at a walled compound with a large, new house that Remi assumed was Mekonnen's. There the man served them piping hot, thick coffee in little cups, followed by spicy samosas—which they learned were a Somali as well as an Indian recipe, and then more coffee. Mekonnen disappeared for a minute and returned wearing old shoes, faded jeans, a loose top, and a battered old Aramco baseball cap before leading them to a large, battered truck with a tarpaulin hiding whatever was in back.

"The story is that you are missionaries who have paid me to drive you to Axum," he had told them. "I'm carrying a shipment of vegetable oil and wheat from India."

"Is that what you're really carrying?" Remi had asked.

"Yes."

"Well, I guess they'd need it."

"Not in a good year," their contact had said. "When Ethiopia is stable, they actually export food, but when they are in a civil war like now, a lot of fields don't get planted and the trade network breaks down. If they could just stop fighting, no Ethiopian would have to starve."

"Did you grow up in Ethiopia?" Remi had asked.

"Let's go," he had said, climbing into the cab.

They passed through a shantytown sprawl of tin shacks and traditional beehive-shaped huts made of brush and out into an open, featureless desert. For hours they drove, the desert unrolling ahead, nothing to break the monotony except the occasional outcropping of rock or the rare forlorn oasis where date palms clustered, and shepherd boys led small flocks of skinny goats to nibble on the grass and scrub.

The heat and the monotony lulled Remi into a doze. Daniel, sitting between her and Mekonnen, nudged her.

"You should drink more," he said, and handed her a bottle of mineral water from a case Mekonnen had bought on the edge of town.

Remi kicked a couple of empty water bottles rolling around the bottom of the cab. "I think I'll drink a whole ocean before we make it to Axum."

She took a long pull on the bottle.

They passed a gas station, little more than a couple of pumps, a breeze block building with a large water tank on top, and a small concrete mosque.

There were little mosques at every gas station they had seen along this highway. She supposed that in this part of the world, people took their religion seriously.

It was strange, but she'd been thinking more and more about religion in recent months. Their cases had all involved religious artifacts. It was shocking how many people would kill for them or get obsessed with their acquisition or protection. There was a whole secret world of people expressing their religion in sinister and often illegal ways.

And her own faith? She had been wondering about that. She did believe in God in a vague sort of way. While her parents hadn't spoken about religion much, they would go to Catholic services on Christmas and Easter, and there had been no question that she would go to a Church school. Other than that, religion hadn't been a part of daily life, not like the people here, or the people they dealt with on their cases.

It made Remi wonder if she was missing something. Obviously, she didn't want to end up as some obsessive like some of the people they met, but maybe she should stop skirting around religion, stop treating it like an academic subject and more as an essential part of life.

She turned to their local contact, who hadn't said anything in almost an hour.

"Lucas, if you don't mind me asking, are you Muslim or Christian?"

"I'm whatever I need to be," he said, not taking his eyes off the road.

Remi fell into silence again. There was really nothing to say to an answer like that.

Daniel spoke. "Are we carrying any weapons?"

"I have an AK under the driver's seat. Now that you asked, if you look under your seats, you'll find a present for the two of you."

Remi and Daniel looked down, and amid various bits of trash and crumbs, they saw two plastic bags. They each took one.

"Keep them out of sight of the other drivers," Lucas Mekonnen said.

They opened the bags and found each had an identical model of pistol. Remi studied hers. It was a snub-nosed automatic with a smaller caliber than the 9mm Glock she was trained in. The pistol felt light and cheaply made. She noticed a red star embossed on the well-worn grip.

"Type 77 Chinese-made service pistol," Lucas Mekonnen said. "It fires 7.62x17 rounds, pretty easy to find in these parts, and has a seven-round clip. This was standard issue for the Chinese army and police forces from the Seventies through the Nineties. Then they upgraded and sold the surplus to Africa."

Daniel pressed a button to release the magazine, jacked the slide to eject the round in the barrel, then felt inside the open slide to make sure no round remained. Remi looked on. This was standard safety procedure. When she went through it, she had to remind herself of every step. Daniel ran through it like he was tying his shoelaces.

Now that the firearm was safe, her partner looked down the barrel.

"The rifling on this is pretty worn down," he said.

"And they're crappy guns even when new," Lucas replied. "Sorry, but it's the best I could do at such short notice."

"Isn't it illegal for us to carry these?" Remi asked.

Lucas laughed like it was a stupid question, which Remi realized it was.

"First off, I'm carrying them. Not you. And I'm a citizen of Djibouti, so I'm allowed."

"We were told you were Ethiopian-American," Remi said.

"I'm whatever I need to be."

Remi stared at him. With most other men, she would have taken all this as bluster and boasting. Not with Lucas Mekonnen. This man was different.

Very different.

"Are we allowed—um, are *you* allowed—to bring these guns over the border?" Remi asked.

"I'm an Ethiopian citizen, so yes."

Remi took a moment to digest this, and then asked, "With all the ethnic tensions in Ethiopia, may I ask what ethnic group you are?"

"Tigrayan."

"So it won't be a problem," Daniel said.

Lucas grinned. "As long as you don't ask me to drive you to Addis Ababa. Not too healthy for Tigrayans in the capital right now. Vigilante groups are hunting them down there."

You just said them and not us. Are you really Tigrayan? Ad if not, can you fake it?

Daniel and Remi put their guns back under the seat.

"We weren't given any instructions about your payment," Remi said.

"That's all been taken care of."

"Do you—?"

"You ask a lot of questions."

Remi fell silent.

The road climbed through barren foothills, then started winding its way up a mountainside. The desert stretched out far below. The road climbed up and up, Lucas navigating hairpin turns at crazy speeds, other trucks and cars at times overtaking him. There was no guardrail. At one turn, Remi looked down a steep slope, the truck's tires only centimeters away, and saw a rusted old wreck of a truck.

We won't have a chance to get killed in Ethiopia if he keeps driving like this.

The air grew cooler, or at least less hot, and now that they were well away from the coastline the humidity disappeared. The temperature became almost bearable. Remi would have almost enjoyed it if she hadn't felt sure they would go flying off a cliff at any moment.

They went down a valley to where a small settlement straddled the road, herds of goats and sheep to both sides. The place was big enough for two mosques. Men and women strolling along the side of the road stared as they noticed the foreigners in the truck.

"The border is over the next line of hills," Lucas said as they climbed up the far side of the valley. "Let me do the talking. You are with the Traveling With Christ Ministry, a group a evangelicals going to the far corners of the Earth to spread the Word. You'll find a couple of Bibles in the glove compartment. Clutch them. If anyone talks to you, try to convert them. Don't worry about offending anyone. Most Tigrayans are Ethiopian Orthodox Christian. Their church is one of the oldest Christian churches in the world. They were praying to the Cross when you guys were still making sacrifices to Thor and Odin. They have no interest in converting to another brand of Christianity. They tolerate missionaries, though."

Again you refer to Tigrayans as if you're not one of them.

Remi decided not to point that out. Instead, she opened the glove compartment and pulled out two Bibles, each stamped with a logo staying "Traveling With Christ Ministry" and a silhouette of Jesus walking down the road flanked by a man and a woman.

"Is this a real organization?" Remi asked.

"Real enough."

"I'm not too up on religion," Daniel said. "I'm not sure I can play this part."

Lucas gave him a grin. "Come on. You went to college in the States, didn't you? You must have had someone try and convert you."

"I used to play hoops with a guy from Campus Crusade for Christ. He was always trying to get me to go to meetings."

"Imitate him."

"I could never imitate his three-pointers. But yeah, I know what you mean."

Lucas looked at Remi. "You good?"

"I'd be better if you looked at the road."

Lucas shrugged, dodged an oncoming car, skittered near the edge of the cliff, and evened out.

After Remi recovered from that near heart attack, she found something else to worry about. They had climbed up to the top of the next mountain and came to a flat, high plain where a few low trees clung to the rocky soil amid the shrubs.

Up ahead, they saw a line of trucks and cars parked in the road. Beyond that stood a border post. On either side of an invisible line stood two concrete structures. From one flew the green, blue, and white flag of Djibouti with its red star. She hadn't known what the Djibouti flag looked like until she landed earlier today. From the other building flew a red and yellow flag with a yellow star that she didn't recognize. She guessed it was the new flag of Tigray.

Of more immediate concern were the men and women in camouflage toting AK-47s checking each vehicle.

"Remember what I told you," Lucas Mekonnen said as he parked at the end of the line. "Don't speak unless spoken to."

"Gladly," Remi replied. While she usually didn't like some guy telling her to keep silent, she could swallow her pride considering the circumstances.

"Damn," Lucas muttered. "They've spotted us already."

Half a dozen uniformed men with small Djibouti flags embroidered onto their shoulders strolled in their direction, their assault rifles sloped. One had some stripes on his shoulder that Remi assumed signified that he was an officer.

He came to the open window on Lucas's side, but his eyes were on Daniel and Remi.

The officer asked something in Arabic. Lucas smiled and responded, handing over some tattered papers. The man gave them a cursory look and walked around to Remi's side of the cab.

He opened the door.

"Please," he said, motioning for Remi to get out.

Remi glanced at Mekonnen, who nodded.

Apparently, she didn't move fast enough for the soldiers, because she heard someone rack the bolt on their AK-47.

CHAPTER NINETEEN

At the sound of the assault rifle being primed, Remi froze. There were four of them now, arranged in a semicircle around the door on her side of the cab. The other two were still on Mekonnen's side.

Their contact said something in Arabic, hopping out. Suddenly everyone was talking at once, a flurry of words that meant nothing to her. She held up her Bible, tried to put on a smile, and climbed out of the cab.

The officer barely looked at her. Instead, he pointed to Daniel.

"You! Out!"

Daniel hurried to obey. Remi glanced in the cab and noticed that the plastic bags containing their guns were clearly visible under the seat. All the soldiers would have to do would be to get curious enough to open one.

The officer grunted and nodded his head toward the concrete building by the border. Daniel and Remi, staying close to one another, began to walk slowly toward it, the officer in front and three of the soldiers behind. Remi glanced over her shoulder, saw unsympathetic eyes, and turned to face front.

After a few steps she realized Mekonnen wasn't with them. She looked back again, and saw him still by the cab, hemmed in by the other two soldiers, smiling and gesturing.

Had they been sold out, or was he trying to defuse the situation?

The sun seared down on them. As they walked along the line of parked trucks, the drivers, squatting in the shade of their vehicles in tight little groups, stopped their conversations to stare.

"Missionaries," Daniel said, waving the Bible at the officer.

"Come," the man said waving his hand.

They got to the concrete bunker. Inside lounged a couple more men. A desk with an antiquated computer sat below a fan that did nothing but blow hot air at everyone. The man at the computer and the officer exchanged words. One of the soldiers nudged Daniel. With obvious reluctance, he entered, leaving Remi alone with three male soldiers.

A low whistle from her left made her turn. On the other side of the border, barely ten meters away, two young female Tigrayan soldiers, kitted out the same as their male counterparts, nodded at her. They looked in their late teens, their Kalashnikovs sloped. Standing casually in the brutal sun. Their cornrows were pulled back and tucked under army caps. One wore a bracelet of pink beads on her wrist.

Remi's eyes locked with one of them, and the woman nodded again, reassuring.

"Ferenja. Zeyn," the woman said.

Remi had no idea what she had just said. She wasn't even sure what language it was in, but something familiar, something universal, was in those words. They seemed to say, "If you haven't done anything wrong, we won't let the men hurt you. We're in this together."

Remi nodded back at her. Managed a smile. The pair beamed back at her, showing brilliant white teeth.

Daniel emerged from the bunker, looking pale. When Remi saw what was on the computer screen behind him, she figured she went pale too.

It was a photo of the suspect; she was sure of it. While she had only heard the witness description from Hale's neighbor and briefly seen him from a distance in poor light, it couldn't be anyone else.

The photo was a bit blurry and pixelated, as if taken at maximum magnification.

"Who's that?" Remi asked the officer as he came out.

"No problem. Your husband fine."

The officer passed them and led them back to Mekonnen's truck. The three soldiers didn't follow.

"Did you see that?" Daniel asked.

"Saw it and couldn't believe it."

"They got an A.P.B. on a white male so all they wanted to do was compare me to that picture. Damn, I wish someone here knew English."

The officer led them back to the cab. Lucas Mekonnen hopped behind the wheel and turned the ignition. The officer waved them on. Mekonnen pulled out and started to pass the parked trucks.

"Lucas, wait," Remi said. "They had a picture of the suspect we're hunting."

"None of my business," Mekonnen said, shaking his head.

"But you need to ask them who that is. If they have a name, a last known location."

"I don't have to do anything of the kind," Mekonnen said. "I was hired to get you to Axum and that's what I'm doing."

"But—"

"I don't work for you, and I don't work for the people you work for."

"All you have to do is act curious," Daniel said. "Be casual and—"

"Curious and casual don't work here."

Lucas stopped the truck on the other side of the border. The Tigrayan soldiers crowded around. Lucas produced his papers a second time and the two female soldiers came up to Remi's window.

She opened the door and dropped down to the cracked asphalt and gave them a smile.

"Thank you," she said. "You made me feel a lot safer back there."

The two women started talking. It sounded friendly, curious. One of them touched her hair. The other pulled out a cheap flip phone. The two soldiers flanked her, and they took a selfie.

Remi laughed. She had always thought selfies were silly. Any Parisian is thoroughly tired of tourists taking selfies everywhere, and Remi had been knocked on the head more than once by that worst of all modern inventions—the selfie stick.

But she could make an exception in this case.

She pulled out her phone. The women oohed and aahed at her late-model smartphone. Remi noted the battery was getting low and wondered how she would recharge it.

It didn't matter. She had no one to call here.

Remi held out the phone. The two women flanked her, leaning in close and brandishing their guns.

How in the world did I go from academia to this?

She snapped a few photos and checked them in her gallery. The women got curious and motioned to see more, so she scrolled through images of a snowstorm in D.C. the previous winter. The images of snow-covered cars and branches draped with ice got more oohs and aahs.

Then she came on a photo of Cyril, smiling in his living room, a glass of wine in his hand. Remi's heart sank.

Judging from their reaction, the women liked the look of him. One said something to the other and they both laughed. The one who spoke tickled Remi in the ribs and then made a universal gesture more appropriate for a high school boy.

Remi blushed and shook her head.

"Oooh!" The woman who had tickled her pointed to Daniel, who sat in the cab watching the scene with an amused look.

"Um, no," Remi said.

The two women chanted something, holding their Kalashnikovs high and swaying their hips.

"Hello, ladies," Daniel said with a smile.

Lucas hopped back in the cab and said something in what Remi assumed was Tigrinya. The women called back something. There was a brief exchange, with Lucas not sounding happy, and then the female soldiers playfully pushed Remi back into the truck. After she closed the door, they peered through the open window at Daniel for a minute, whispering to each other and giggling.

"Looks like you've made some friends," Daniel said, smiling back at them. "Care to introduce me?"

"They are interesting, aren't they?" Remi said as one took her hand. "An odd combination warrior and teenybopper."

"They don't look much older than teenyboppers, but wearing fatigues and toting guns, it's kind of hard to tell."

"If they're that young, maybe you shouldn't be ogling them," Remi said, feeling a bit annoyed.

"They're old enough to serve in the military," Daniel said with a shrug.

"Let's go," Lucas said, shifting into drive. "We have a long drive ahead of us. They're going to give us an escort until we get away from the border region. They say there's been some fighting."

"I thought the front was well to the south of here," Daniel said.

"The front is unstable, and there are local militias on both sides of it loyal to the other side. Keep those guns close but out of sight. We might need them."

They drove down the highway, which they could see climbed a mountain not far ahead on a series of terrifying hairpin turns.

They hadn't made it a hundred meters before an open-top jeep blew past them. At the wheel was one of Remi's new friends. The other stood in back clutching a huge machine gun mounted onto the vehicle. A couple of guys were in the Jeep too. They all waved as they passed, then cut in front of the truck and paced it as they headed for the mountains.

"There's something about women with automatic weapons," Daniel said with a sigh.

"Don't I know it," Lucas said. They bumped fists.

"That's so sexist."

Lucas wagged a finger. "*Au contraire, mon amie*. It's women's liberation, at the rate of 600 rounds per minute."

Remi noted that his French pronunciation was perfect.

"If you gentlemen are going to act like pigs, I'm going to ride with them," Remi said.

"No, you're not," Lucas replied.

The road began to climb. The landscape remained desolate—brown hills and desiccated clumps of grass. In the distance, however, she caught glimpses of narrow green valleys fed by mountain streams.

After a few kilometers and rising further up the mountainside they passed one, a narrow gorge with a stream rushing through it. Terraced farmland filled the green valley, which measured barely a kilometer wide. Further up its steep slopes, thatched-roof huts clung to the almost sheer rock like oversized mountain goats. Farmers in dirty and patched robes manned heavy wooden ploughs pulled by skinny donkeys. A line of women and children carrying baskets on their heads made their way up a thin path toward a cluster of huts.

A cooler, moist breeze blew through the window. Remi breathed deep. She hadn't smelled vegetation since she had left the United States.

"What are they growing there?" Remi asked.

"*Teff*, mostly," Lucas said. "It's a grain. Very nutritious."

"Is that what they use in *injera* bread?" Daniel asked.

"Yeah. Sounds like you've been to some Ethiopian restaurants."

"Love the stuff."

A low boom off to their left stopped the conversation. Remi looked. It sounded like thunder, and she had visions of a storm hitting and washing them off the mountainside to end up as one of the many rusting wrecks they had seen by the side of the road. But the sky looked clear.

They heard another rumble, followed quickly by a third.

"Artillery," Lucas said.

"Is it far?" Remi asked.

"A mile or so."

"Can they reach the road?"

"The fire is over that ridge. Looks like the Tigrayans are holding the ridge and the national government is shelling it from the other side. We're out of sight."

"The road isn't going to loop any closer to that show, is it?" Daniel asked.

Lucas Mekonnen's face grew grim. "As a matter of fact, it does."

CHAPTER TWENTY

Remi looked anxiously out the window as distant plumes of smoke smudged the brilliant sky. The shelling seemed closer, and much as she'd like to deny it, the road was definitely veering toward the fighting. It looked like the government was trying to take the highway to Djibouti, just like Lucas had feared.

The Jeep escorting them pulled back to come alongside Lucas's window. The soldier in the passenger's seat was shouting into a radio. The female soldier Remi had befriended back on the border, still standing and holding onto the heavy machine gun bolted to the back of the Jeep, shouted something to Lucas. There was no giggling or smiles now. She was all business. She looked twenty years older.

The soldier and Lucas traded a few words before the Jeep pulled ahead again. Lucas turned to them.

"They'll keep escorting us for the next twenty kilometers until we get out of range. Hang on. It's going to be a bumpy ride."

"Isn't there another road we could go on?" Remi asked.

"This isn't Europe. There's one road and one road only. The only other option is to walk along a goat path all the way to Axum. I figure you folks are in a bit more of a hurry than that."

"I suppose we are," Remi replied, although she had to wonder how the suspect could have possibly made it across the border when the police were looking for him and passed through this warzone. Were they endangering themselves for nothing?

Daniel must have been thinking the same thing, because he asked, "If you were going to try and sneak across this border, how would you do it?"

"Easy. Hire some Somali or Afar nomads to take you across on a camel or hire a smuggler to take you over the desert in a Land Rover."

"I take it there's not much chance of detection?"

"By the government? No. The Tigrayans are too busy fighting their government and the Djibouti security forces are too small. The biggest danger is the *shifta*."

"The shifta?"

“Bandits. They’ll intercept nomads or smugglers to steal their stuff. Steal their women too. They attack microbuses and cars on lonely stretches of highway. That Jeep full of soldiers is protecting us from bandits as much as they are from the battle.”

Remi leaned back in her seat, the hot, gritty air baking her face and the low rumble of artillery growing ever louder.

The road took a wide curve around the slope of the mountain, and suddenly the battlefield lay in full view below them.

They had risen above the Tigrayan positions and could see on the slopes below several bunkers and trenches lined with sandbags. In a few larger pits, hacked laboriously out of the rocky soil, cannons were pointing downhill to the south. As Remi watched, horrified, one about five hundred meters away fired with a loud thud. Here and there along the slope, plumes of smoke rose as government shells hit. Remi could see the government position in the distant lowlands from the flares of artillery. Sunlight gleamed off a few distant tanks.

Another shell hit, closer this time.

“Don’t worry,” Lucas shouted over the din. “The government forces won’t shell the highway. They need it intact.”

“What about stray fire?” Daniel shouted back.

“You mean like that?” Lucas pointed to a crumpled, burnt-out car by the side of the road.

A nearby explosion drowned out what Daniel said next. Remi cringed. There was nothing in her training on how to deal with an artillery bombardment. Lucas Mekonnen seemed unphased, as if driving past a battle was a daily occurrence for him, although he did speed up.

The Jeep ahead set the pace. Lucas maintained the same speed but kept well behind them. Remi supposed that was because it was obviously a military vehicle and might get targeted. Remi imagined some government officer watching them through a pair of binoculars and wondering if he should open fire on the Jeep full of soldiers or the mysterious truck driving behind it.

What if that officer thought they were carrying military supplies? Come to think of it, what if they really were carrying military supplies? Lucas had said he was carrying vegetable oil and grain, but she hadn’t checked. They certainly got accepted by the Tigrayan troops quickly enough, and she doubted they escorted every truck coming along this highway. What if they knew Lucas and had some sort of deal with him?

Another shell hit the slope below, close enough that she could feel the shockwave in her gut. Lucas hunched over the steering wheel, barely keeping his head above the dashboard to see the road. Daniel slid down in his seat too. Remi did not. The scene transfixed her. She stared as more explosions erupted all along the Tigrayan line. In the distant lowlands she could see tanks advancing, firing as they approached.

The attack seemed to be heating up.

Remi squinted. Something else was on the plain below, thin back lines that moved behind the tanks. It took her a minute to realize what they were.

Soldiers, advancing on Tigrayan positions.

This wasn't a bombardment. This was a full-scale assault.

"We need to get out of here!" she shouted.

"Working on it," Lucas said as another round hit close.

"Are they targeting the road?" Daniel asked. Remi hardly ever heard fear in his voice. She heard it now.

"Hard to tell," Lucas replied. "The army isn't known for its accuracy. Just be glad there are no government jets strafing the Tigrayan lines."

As if his words summoned them, they saw three silvery needles approaching from the southwest, flying low and fast. They resolved themselves into jet fighters.

They came at the Tigrayan position at an angle. Missiles launched from underneath their wings, trailing flames and smoke.

The missiles hit the trenches with a series of booms that shook the truck. Smoke enveloped portions of the Tigrayan line. She saw at least one bunker in flames. Still the Tigrayan guns thundered. In the valley she saw a tank, tiny in the distance, go up. It looked for all the world like a cigarette lighter sparking and failing to catch a flame.

She knew it must look far different for the crew.

Still she couldn't tear her eyes away, or even slouch in her seat to make less of a target. She simply sat and stared.

The jets roared close overhead, making the truck judder. A rhythmic thudding up ahead caught her attention. By the side of the road half a kilometer ahead sat some strange, four-barreled gun surrounded by sandbags. The crew was busy firing at the jets.

Remi poked her head out the window and saw the jets fly off, banking sharply and gaining altitude.

"Floor it!" Daniel shouted. "If those guys come around for another pass they might fire at the antiaircraft position, and the idiots put it right next to the road!"

"I'm already going as fast as this truck can go," Lucas said, gritting his teeth, knuckles white on the steering wheel.

The troops in the Jeep in front of them looked worried too. They pulled ahead, the woman at the machine gun gesturing for them to follow.

Remi craned her neck to see the jets, having to practically lie across Daniel's lap to look up out the driver's side window. As she feared, they were coming for another pass. She tried to gauge whether the truck would get by the antiaircraft emplacement before the jets could return for another run. It would be close.

She sat back up. The jets swooped down low. She no longer needed to crane her neck to see them. They looked like they were coming straight for the gun emplacement that had been firing at them.

The gun emplacement they were just passing.

That gun started firing. The woman in the Jeep ahead of them started firing her machinegun too.

The jets came closer.

Daniel was screaming, words she had never heard him say before. Lucas was shouting something in Tigrinya. He was probably swearing too.

Remi found herself swearing in French. It seemed the only logical thing to do given the circumstances.

The jets opened up, this time with machine guns, their wings sparking. Remi screamed as she saw six lines of gunshots stitch their way across the slope toward the antiaircraft gun.

Toward them.

She curled into a ball as the sound of the bullets passed. There was a bag. The truck swerved. Lucas shouted and almost lost control before straightening out.

The truck jerked, bouncing up and down and tilting a bit toward the driver's side The telltale *flap flap flap* of a flat tire told them a bullet had hit.

"You seriously don't have a flat in the middle of a battlefield!" Daniel shouted.

"I'll drive on it for a bit, but we're going to have to change it soon."

"Drive on it until we're out of here!" Remi shouted.

“Can’t. Truck’s too heavy. If I drive much more, I’ll bend the axle. You don’t want to be stranded here, do you?”

Remi glanced in the sideview mirror. The antiaircraft gun and its crew seemed unhurt, which meant the government jets would probably come around for another attempt. And here they were only a couple of hundred meters away from it, slowing down thanks to a flat tire.

“This is as far as I can go,” Lucas said. “Let’s try to get this done quickly.”

He slowed further and pulled off on a patch of level ground by the side of the road. The Jeep stopped about a hundred meters ahead, the female soldier at the machine gun reloading.

Lucas leapt out of the cab, Daniel scrambling to follow. Remi got out on her side and ran around the truck to check out the damage.

The front left tire was completely flat. A couple of bullet holes had punctured the step up to the driver’s side, coming perilously close to Lucas and even closer to the spare gas tank on the side of the vehicle. Remi had visions of lighting up in the middle of a fireball.

Other than that, she could see no damage.

Lucas grabbed a jack and a tire iron from the back of the cab. He passed the tire iron to Daniel, who rushed over to where a spare tire was secured to the side of the truck. Lucas stayed in front, positioning the jack. Remi followed Daniel. He started to frantically unbolt the spare tire, looking over his shoulder every few seconds.

Remi looked out over the battlefield. The tanks and line of infantry had made it to the bottom of the slope, still a kilometer away but close enough that she could hear the rattle of small arms fire. The Jeep had parked a hundred meters ahead of them, the young woman she had befriended at the border ready with her machine gun, the others raising their assault rifles. Two hundred meters behind was the antiaircraft emplacement with its crew busy reloading.

Two perfect targets for the government fighter planes.

And they were stuck right in between them.

The road disappeared around a curve another couple of hundred meters beyond the Jeep. It might as well have been a million.

The regular *thud thud thud* of artillery from both sides filled her ears. Daniel got the wheel detached and together they rolled it over to Lucas, who started jacking up the front of the truck. To save time, Remi started unbolting the flat tire even as he was still raising up the truck.

The staccato banging of the antiaircraft gun started again. Remi whirled around and went cold with horror.

The jets were coming around for another run.

CHAPTER TWENTY ONE

Remi forced herself to get back to work on the tire. Lucas had almost finished raising up the truck and she still had three more bolts to go on the tire. The best thing she could do to ensure her survival was to get that tire changed quickly, even if that meant turning her back on a trio of jets swooping in to kill her.

The roar of the jets grew louder. The machine gun in the Jeep opened up. Remi gritted her teeth and worked faster.

The last bolt came off. Daniel and Lucas snatched the tire and threw it to the side of the road. Within moments they had fitted the spare in its place. Remi grabbed the first nut and began to screw it on.

She heard the *rat tat tat* of the fighters' machine guns. Remi forced herself to focus on the task in front of her.

The sound of the antiaircraft gun cut off. The jets roared overhead, so low the shockwave almost blew them off their feet.

Remi got the second bolt on, then the third. She felt sure the jets would come around again. She had to get the tire secured before that.

Another bolt, and another. Finally! Lucas began lowering the jack, waving the other two back in the cab. Remi hurried to get back in the truck but couldn't resist stopping for a moment to look around her.

The battle at the bottom of the slope was a maelstrom of explosions and gunfire. The jets were circling around for another pass. Over at the antiaircraft emplacement, one man staggered around, his uniform soaked with blood. The rest of the crew lay crumpled on the ground or draped over their guns.

Feeling sick, Remi jumped into the cab. Daniel was already in. Lucas joined them a moment later and revved the engine. He pulled out, cursing as the heavy truck accelerated at a snail's pace up the sloping road. Remi ducked down to peer out the window on his side. The jets banked high in the distance, preparing for another run. The truck passed the Jeep. For a moment she locked eyes with the woman at the machine gun. She saw terror there, and determination, and then they were gone. Remi sat up and stared through the sideview mirror. The woman braced herself, aimed the machine gun and began to fire as the roar of the jets grew louder and louder.

The jets opened fire. Remi's heart clenched. Everyone in the Jeep was firing back.

Just then Lucas took the truck around the corner and the scene disappeared.

The firing continued, reached a crescendo, and slackened. The sounds of the battle began to fade as Lucas picked up speed and the road curved further to put the mountain between them and the fighting. Soon all they could hear was the distant thunder of the artillery.

Remi's eyes blurred with tears. She would never know what happened to those two bright-eyed girls.

She slumped in her seat, utterly spent.

* * *

The rest of the ten-hour drive to Axum was a nightmare of checkpoints and searches, and exhausted half-waking dreams of the young women in the Jeep getting torn apart by gunfire. Remi didn't understand this war, didn't know who was wrong or right, or even if there was a wrong or right. All she knew was that she hated it.

The road continued through mountains and valleys, leaving the desert far behind as they gained altitude and the land grew greener. At last, they got out of the rough terrain onto a high plain, driving past villages and fields. It looked like there was a lot of agriculture in these parts, but not enough. Everyone looked thin, and in some places, people looked on the verge of starvation.

"The civil war has disrupted trade," Lucas explained. "The farmers can't get fertilizer, and some foods that have to be imported don't make it in. Plus, the prices of everything have gone up. As you imagine, not many truckers want to brave the route we just went through. There are shortages of everything in Tigray. The government-controlled areas aren't much better off. Ethiopia barely works in a good year. A civil war like this just wrecks everything."

Remi looked at the rake-thin men and women working in the fields, and the listless children wandering around the dusty streets of the villages. The Tigrayan army wasn't short of weapons, so there was money somewhere. It just wasn't making it to the people.

"Do you think the government is going to retake the road?" Daniel asked.

"Hard to say. I asked at the last checkpoint, but they didn't know. The government has tried to take that road plenty of times before. It's starving them of trade. But they can't use their full force in the north because they're also facing an insurrection in the east, among the Somali peoples. The eastern section of the country is part of the Somali desert and the locals are predominantly Somali. The people there say they've never gotten a fair shake from the government and now they're taking advantage of the situation up here to make another bid for independence."

Remi shook her head. If the people in this green land were on the brink of starvation, what must it be like for the Somalis in the desert?

This whole region was being torn apart by war. Remi had dim memories of when she was a small child and the famine of Ethiopia was on television, those horrible images of starving children and bleak, cropless fields. There had been a drought then, but what would have been a food shortage became a total famine because of a civil war.

And now they were heading back to that.

* * *

It was well past nightfall when they arrived at the outskirts of Axum, the lights twinkling in the distance. They were speeding across a dusty plain, the air having cooled. Remi had the window open and felt hungry, tired, but a bit more at ease.

At least until they came to a roadblock.

The only lights were the headlights of a Jeep casting a harsh glow on the road. Remi couldn't see beyond the brightness if this Jeep had a weapon mounted on it like some she'd seen. She supposed so. There was a wooden boom blocking the road and a few men and women in uniform standing to either side. She could discern the vague shape of some other large vehicle in the darkness beyond. She thought it might be a tank. She had never been this close to one outside a museum before.

Lucas stopped the car. A couple of soldiers advanced, shining bright flashlights through the windshield. Remi covered her eyes with one hand and held up her Bible with the other. She felt relieved that she and Daniel had put the pistols back under the seat.

Lucas rolled down the window and a young officer came up to his window. The flashlight beams remained on Remi and Daniel.

Remi shifted uncomfortably in her seat. They'd been through several checkpoints that day, but this one seemed more serious. She had been half expecting Daniel to be compared with a photo of the suspect they were chasing, but that had only happened on the Djibouti side of the border. The mystery of that lingered in the back of her mind, an unanswered question that could tell them so much about what was really going on.

And after all she had been through today, she could really use some answers. Had the suspect even gotten over the border? Lucas seemed to think so, although he showed no interest in their mission other than being an escort to Axum.

Lucas and the officer talked for a minute while the officer's eyes kept straying to the two foreigners. Then the officer went around to the passenger side and opened the door.

"Welcome to the Republic of Tigray. Your driver says you are missionaries?"

The man's English was quite good, and now that she got a better look at him, she could see he was younger than she had first thought. Remi guessed he had been a university student before getting swept up in the war.

"Yes, we are with the Traveling With Christ Ministry, here to spread the good news about Jesus Christ," she replied.

The officer smiled. "We heard that news many centuries ago. Perhaps you should go among the Oromo. Half of them are Muslim."

"We go wherever the need is great," Daniel said. "With the war, many are losing hope and may stray from the right path."

Remi was impressed. Daniel had sounded sincere. That boy he used to play basketball with had obviously preached to him a lot.

"What we need is food and medicine. Does your organization provide these things?"

Remi paused. How to answer? She could give him an attractive lie, but then she wouldn't be able to back it up. And if she said no, would they be allowed to pass?

She decided to "hedge their bets," as Daniel sometimes said.

"The ministry has helped out in many places in the past, and asks its missionaries for information about the regions they travel in."

"Excellent. Tomorrow I am off duty. I will show you around Axum and you will see the situation."

Uh-oh.

Remi felt tempted to object, to say that Lucas would show them around, but realized that any hesitation on their part would look suspicious.

"That would be wonderful. Thank you," Remi replied, trying to sound enthusiastic.

"Bless you," Daniel added.

"I will come visit you at the Endubis Hotel. Stay there. It is the best in Axum and one of the only ones still open. The war has taken all the tourists away."

"So there are no other foreigners here?" Remi probed.

"Some Red Cross workers landed yesterday. A few people from other NGOs. Most pulled out. We have a great need for food and medicine. Once you see tomorrow you will be able to make a good report to your organization."

He looked over to Lucas and said something in Tigrinya. It sounded like an order. Lucas only nodded and got the truck into gear.

"You got yourself a government spy," Lucas said as they headed down the darkened road. They passed a huge tank squatting in the darkness, its gun pointing at the road.

"I don't see that we have much choice," Remi said with a sigh.

CHAPTER TWENTY TWO

Daniel cursed. To his surprise, his Egyptian SIM card worked in Ethiopia, but only enough to receive messages. When he tried to send one, he got some notification in Arabic. He didn't need to be able to read the language to know what it said.

"You are out of credit."

And he really, really needed to reply to this message.

It was, of course, from Veronica. He had a few other messages from friends and some message from his Neighborhood Watch association. He didn't bother even opening those.

"Daniel,

"What's going on? Your last message was strange. You're on some case? PLEASE be careful. You've been hurt before. Remember that nutcase who stabbed you?"

Daniel grimaced. Yes, he remembered. A serial killer he cornered in a dive bar in Wyoming. The guy jabbed him in the side before Daniel could take him down. A good beating stopped the guy from any further resistance, and a leveled gun and a screamed threat stopped the other rednecks from joining in, which they had looked seriously tempted to do. Why was it that so many people automatically took sides against the government? Those guys wouldn't have squared up to Daniel if they had seen the pictures of the women this guy had cut up and left in ditches all over the state.

Anyway, the stab wound had been more painful than dangerous. Six stitches and a bit of blood loss. His real mistake was coming home with his blood-soaked shirt instead of throwing it away at the hospital. That sure freaked out Veronica. High-flying businesswomen tend not to encounter very many stab wounds in their day-to-day work environment.

The message went on.

"You have me worried. You're in some foreign country? Why can't you contact me?"

And that was all. He had to get a reply to her. He didn't see how, though.

So typical of their marriage. Lots of emotion and no real communication.

He forced himself to put his phone away. He had a killer to catch and a warzone to survive.

And an army officer to fool. That guy was due any minute now.

Daniel thought the Endubis Hotel was surprisingly nice for a Third World nation undergoing a civil war. It was a series of bungalows around a green, shady courtyard. Other than a couple of Tigrayan engineers working on the local AM transmitter and a family of refugees whose town was on the front line, the hotel was empty. His room was Spartan but clean. He had already checked it for bugs of the electronic kind but hadn't found any.

That didn't mean they weren't under observation.

He joined Remi for breakfast at a small table in the courtyard, where an overly anxious waiter fussed over them.

"It is very good that you come to help Tigray," the waiter said. "Our hotel have no business. You tell the American people we need to win war."

Daniel felt bad for the guy. How could he tell him that the West had little knowledge and less interest in his troubles? Even Daniel didn't know much about what was going on. Who was to say the Tigray People's Liberation Front was in the right and the central government was in the wrong? Chances are both sides were partially in the wrong and partially in the right. He reminded himself to leave the waiter a large tip. Who knew how many family members depended on him?

Lucas Mekonnen hadn't joined them for breakfast. In fact, they hadn't seen their driver all morning. The mercenary or double agent or whatever the hell he was had shown no interest in helping them in their mission beyond getting them here. There hadn't even been any clear discussion about him getting them back to Djibouti. That worried Daniel. A lot.

His phone buzzed. He pulled it out, wondering if he had given his number to Lucas and forgotten. No, it was a message from Amir Karara, the investigator in Luxor.

"I have discovered that Professor Hale visited Museum Director Salah on that secret trip you mentioned. Several museum employees recall them being together at that time. No one knows what they spoke of, only that Salah and Hale were gone all of one day. Whatever they were doing, that secret died with them.

"Good luck, my friend, wherever this investigation takes you."

I never thought it would take me here.

He showed the message to Remi.

"Interesting," she said. "I wonder what it all means."

"Damned if I know," Daniel grunted. "It's another piece of the puzzle, that's for sure. Unfortunately, it doesn't fit with any of the others we have so far."

They had barely finished their eggs, bread, and coffee when the young officer from the previous evening showed up. He was still wearing his uniform, a revolver in a holster on his belt. Daniel recalled that he had claimed this was his day off.

"Greetings, my friends. I hope you slept well?"

"Yes, it's a very nice hotel," Daniel said. "The Lord has been kind to us."

Daniel had remembered to bring his Bible to the table. He had debated whether or not to bring his gun and had decided to hide it in his room.

The officer sat down. "My name is Captain Seyoum Kebede. It is fortunate that I have leave for the next three days. It gives me a chance to show you traditional Tigrayan hospitality."

Yeah, real fortunate. And last night didn't you say you only had today off? I guess you had a talk with your superiors and got reassigned from checkpoint duty.

Remi spoke up. "There was fighting on the road to Djibouti yesterday. Did the government take the road?"

"Oh, you saw the fighting? I am glad you got through safely. The government has tried many attacks and we have defeated them every time."

"So the road to Djibouti remains open?" Remi asked.

"The road to Djibouti will always remain open. You might not know this, but the government controlled that sector for much of the war, but the Afar people who live there tired of their oppression and joined forces with us."

"I see," Daniel said, although he didn't. In the little research he had managed to do on the area before coming here, he had heard the name of the Afar mentioned, but he knew nothing about them. He wondered how many tribes were in Ethiopia. How many rivalries.

"If you are done with your breakfast, allow me to take you around our beautiful city in my car."

Like we have a choice.

Daniel stood. "Just one minute. I need to go to my room and freshen up. Brush my teeth and all that."

"Me too," Remi said.

Captain Seyoum Kebede smiled. "Of course."

They headed back to their room and the officer sat down in the seat Daniel had just vacated and clapped his hands to get the attention of the waiter.

"Guns or no guns?" Remi whispered.

Daniel was surprised she was even asking. Maybe she was finally learning some moderation, or maybe she felt just as overwhelmed by the situation as he did.

Daniel thought for a moment as they passed through the garden.

"I'll bring mine. Leave yours in the room."

"That makes no sense."

"I don't want to endanger a trainee agent."

"Deputy Director Burton doesn't seem to mind."

"Yeah," Daniel grumbled. "That's been eating at me."

"You know they're going to search our rooms while we're out today. I couldn't find a good hiding place."

Daniel let out a deep sigh. "All right. Bring your gun. Lucas has his room right next to mine. I'm going to talk to him."

They split up, Daniel retrieved his pistol, hid it on his person, then went to the next room to knock on Lucas's door.

No answer.

He knocked again. Nothing.

Daniel tried the door and found it locked.

"Great," he muttered. "That's just great."

Remi joined him. "He's not here?"

"Nope."

His partner went pale.

They returned to the garden to find Captain Kebede enjoying a coffee.

"Ah! You are back. Do you like our coffee here?"

"It's delicious. The best I've ever had," Daniel admitted.

"We discovered coffee. The legend says that a shepherd boy noticed his goats eating a certain type of bean and getting very active, so he roasted some, ground it up, and made the very first cup of coffee."

"Then I owe him a lot," Daniel said. "In my line of work, we drink gallons of the stuff."

"And what is your line of work?" Captain Kebede asked, peering at him over the rim of his coffee cup.

"Preaching the word of Our Savior."

You're not going to get me that easily.

Captain Kebede drained the rest of his coffee and stood. "Come."

Reluctantly, they followed.

He led them to a battered old two-door Nissan in the parking lot. Daniel noticed Lucas's truck parked nearby, the load in the back now gone. He saw no sign of their one and only contact in the Tigray.

Where the hell is he?

They got in the car, Remi in back and him in the passenger's seat next to their mysterious host.

"It would be wonderful to pray at the Church of Our Lady Mary of Zion," Remi said.

That was where legend said the true Ark of the Covenant was kept. Daniel had read that every Ethiopian Orthodox Church had a replica, but the one here in Axum was supposed to be the real thing.

Good job, Remi. While the local law investigates us, maybe we can do a little investigation of our own.

"Certainly," Captain Kebede said, starting the engine. "We will make that our first stop."

They drove out of the hotel's parking lot and onto a quiet street. Other than the busy downtown, there wasn't much traffic in Axum. Daniel supposed with the disappearance of tourism, the decline in trade, and probably a rise in the price of gas, that was to be expected. In the distance rose brown hills, but here in the valley all was green. Eucalyptus trees lined the street, and the nicer homes and public buildings all had gardens and flowerbeds. This looked like it had been a prosperous city before the war had gutted the economy.

Up ahead, giant obelisks of gray stone rose like skyscrapers above the treetops. Some were plain, others were decorated with strange designs that were difficult to see from this distance, topped with a fan shape.

"What are those?" Daniel asked in wonder. "They're enormous."

"The monuments of the great kings of Axum," the captain said with obvious pride. "The oldest are almost two thousand years old. Each king erected one, and each tried to outdo the king before. Your hotel is named after one of the greatest kings. He traded as far as Greece and the gold coins he minted were used from the Mediterranean to India."

"We never learned about this in history class," Daniel said.

"That does not surprise me," the captain said in a quiet voice.

Captain Kebede slowed down as they passed a broad field with at least a dozen of the giant monuments. The tallest looked to be eighty feet tall. An even bigger one lay in fragments on the ground.

"Incredible," Remi said from the back seat.

"I will show you this after we pray in the church. And then after that I want to show you some of the refugee camps on the edge of town, and the public grain stores that are almost empty. Then you can call back to your organization and get us some help."

"I'll tell my director about the situation here," Daniel said, "but I can't promise he'll help."

Daniel didn't like giving this guy false hope. He didn't see a way around it, though.

I'm not sure Deputy Director Burton could do anything except kick it upstairs to some agency in D.C.; although if the government wanted to help, they already would be.

Or maybe they are. I wish I had more time to read up on this situation.

They turned a corner and parked next to a large compound of church buildings. The main building was circular with a huge dome topped by a cross. Next to it was a tall bell tower of gray stone built to resemble the ancient obelisks. A few smaller, older looking buildings stood to either side. A large courtyard lay in front of the main building and the entire compound was blocked off with an ironwork fence. A couple of soldiers, one man and one woman, stood guard at the gate.

"I am not sure I can get you in," the captain said. "They are very nervous about security. The government took Axum for a time and killed many people."

"I hope they didn't damage the Ark of the Covenant," Daniel said.

"They wouldn't dare. It is safe."

Daniel had to wonder about that. He also had to wonder if their suspect could even be here.

He'd try, though. Daniel had hunted enough obsessed killers to know that the man they hunted would get to Axum, or die trying.

They got out. The sun on the exposed street was already getting hot. A few children in tattered clothing saw them and hurried over. A curt word from Captain Kebede scattered them.

They walked over to the gate. Daniel smiled at the soldiers and clutched his Bible, making sure the big cross on the cover was visible. The soldiers looked at them curiously.

Captain Kebede and the soldiers traded a few words; then their minder turned to them.

"They say you can enter, but they apologize that it is required to search you first. I am sure you understand."

Before Daniel could think of something to say, the male guard strode up to him, the female guard went over to Remi, and they began to pat them down.

Daniel squirmed and objected, but they didn't listen.

It did not take them long to find the guns.

CHAPTER TWENTY THREE

Remi's blood went cold as the female soldier pulled the Chinese pistol Lucas had given her out from under her shirt.

She tried to sputter out an explanation but couldn't make a coherent sentence. It didn't matter. There was no explanation for why a missionary would be carrying a concealed firearm.

The male soldier found Daniel's pistol a moment later.

The guards took them, stepped back, and leveled their AK-47s. Those kids the captain had told to back off started to run.

Remi and Daniel both raised their hands.

"They're for self-protection," Remi managed to say. "We were worried about *shifta*."

Captain Kebede gave her an unreadable expression. "There are no *shifta* in the Church of Our Lady Mary of Zion."

"Sorry," Daniel said. "We have been carrying those pistols since we got to the desert west of Djibouti City. Carrying them became such as habit that we forgot we had them on us. We didn't intend to bring them into the church."

The captain snorted at this ridiculous explanation. Remi felt tempted to do the same, although to be fair to Daniel she couldn't think up a better excuse.

Captain Kebede said something to the male soldier, who handed him a walkie talkie.

Oh God, he's calling for backup. They're going to take us to some military prison and torture us.

She wondered if Cyril would ever know what happened to her, or any of her family or friends. Or would she simply vanish and remain a painful mystery to everyone who cared about her?

Captain Kebede talked into the radio and got a response from a male voice. The captain said something at length while looking at each of them up and down. Remi got the impression that he was describing them.

The conversation continued. Remi and Daniel fidgeted. The two soldiers kept their guns leveled at them, their faces emotionless.

At last, Captain Kebede gave back the radio to the guard and said, "Let's go."

"Where are you taking us?" Remi asked. She could hear her voice waver.

"To the church. You wanted to see it, didn't you?" His voice came out level. Remi tried to read the emotion behind it and found she could not.

He opened the iron gate with a creak and walked through. Remi and Daniel exchanged an uncertain look and followed. To her surprise, the two soldiers stayed at their post.

Is there a prison inside the church? That doesn't make any sense. Are we even under arrest?

Nothing has made any sense since we landed in Djibouti!

They walked across the courtyard, the sun and the tension making Remi sweat. Captain Kebede walked along with an easy stride, Remi and Daniel following a couple of paces behind. It took all of Remi's willpower not to bolt and run.

They headed for the main building with the huge dome and tall bell tower. The place looked strangely deserted. Other than them, no one was in sight. Wasn't this the holiest church in the country? Where were the crowds of the faithful?

Remi felt conspicuous. Off to their right and left stood smaller buildings. Remi's heart jumped when she recognized the Chapel of the Tablet, a modest stone building with blue stained-glass windows and a little green dome topped by a white cross. She had read about it. The Ark was supposed to be housed in there.

But their escort, or captor, led them to the main church.

"It is a great honor to be allowed in here," Captain Kebede said. "Only a few outsiders ever get to see the inside of the church. It's usually for members of the Ethiopian church only. You are very special guests."

Remi stared at him, amazed. He acted as if nothing had happened. What kind of game was he playing at?

A pair of large bronze doors stood open. A priest emerged, an older man with a deeply seamed face. He wore a heavy red robe embroidered with gold and carried a large, ornate silver cross. The cross was of an unusual type, the arms of the cross so elaborate that the whole thing almost looked like a flower made of precious metal.

Captain Kebede and the priest exchanged a few words and the old man turned to them and gave a respectful nod, which they returned. He gestured for them to enter.

They walked into a church unlike any Remi had ever seen. It was a grand circular building with a high metal dome. The entire inside wall was painted with bright colors. She saw scenes from the Bible, such as the three kings coming to honor the baby Jesus. In another scene, an adult Jesus stood in the River Jordan, the brilliant blue waters rushing by him, as John baptized him. Then there was a crucifixion scene, and next to that the Trinity sitting in glory in a golden heaven.

Remi stopped and stared. There were dozens more scenes like this. All the figures were black, with wide brown eyes that looked straight out and seemed to fix on the viewer. Compared to the art of the European Renaissance they were simple, almost cartoonish, with bright, clear colors and little shading, and yet the cumulative effect was just as stunning as any interior by Giotto or Messenta.

Ahead of them stood a golden altar atop a couple of steps of white marble. Several rows of pews stood before it.

"The priest says we can go to the front pew and pray there," Captain Kebede said. "Of course, you will pray in your own fashion, but you are welcome."

Wait, so you really aren't going to arrest us? What in the world is going on?

Daniel and Remi sat on the front pew, bowed their heads, and closed their eyes. The priest started chanting, and they could hear the captain in the pew behind them chanting in a low voice as well. The smell of frankincense suddenly filled the air. Remi opened one eye a little and saw the priest swinging a silver censer and walking back and forth in front of the altar.

Remi closed her eye again. She was supposed to be praying, after all.

When was the last time she had prayed? She tried to remember. Of course, at the school they had morning mass and they said grace before eating lunch, but Remi and most of the other girls simply went through the motions, not really feeling anything at all.

There had been times, though, when she had prayed for real. Like when her favorite grandparent had died when she was fourteen. Remi remembered lying in bed that night, crying softly, and praying to God to let her into heaven. She had done the same when her father died. His mass after the funeral was the only one that she could recall truly joining in with all her heart.

And here she was, in a strange church on the other side of the world, pretending to pray while searching for a killer trying to steal the world's holiest object.

And what about that object? Could the true Ark of the Covenant really be in that little building they had passed a minute ago? It seemed hard to believe, but then again so was the idea of an all-knowing being who created the universe, and she believed in that.

Didn't she?

Yes, she did believe in God. In a vague, distant sort of way, it was true, but she did believe. She just never really thought about God all that much.

And why not?

She was trying to save lives and protect a holy artifact, assuming it existed, so didn't that count as doing God's work? It could even be said that she was on a holy mission.

The chanting continued. Her nostrils filled with the smell of frankincense. Feeling awkward and self-conscious, she spoke directly to God for the first time in years.

If you're really up there, please help us stop this killer.

And, if it's possible, let me see the Ark of the Covenant. That might help me believe a little better in you.

Remi sat for a moment more, letting the significance of what she had just done sink in. Even though she had only thought a few short sentences to whatever higher power might be out there, it made her feel a bit better, more relaxed, more prepared for whatever might lie ahead. She knew it didn't lessen the danger she was in, but it made her feel a little less alone.

Thank you.

Oh, and please protect Daniel too. He's a good man. He seems deeply troubled, and not just about the divorce. Whatever it is he's dealing with, help him through it.

Remi let out a slow breath and opened her eyes.

She looked over at Daniel, who sat looking uneasy. Captain Kebede shifted in the seat behind them.

Remi turned and looked at him. He was smiling.

"Such a holy place always makes me feel good inside," he said. "I think even false missionaries like you must feel something."

Remi felt herself go pale. Captain Kebede chuckled.

"Shall we go to the Chapel of the Tablet now?"

Remi stared. "You mean … to see the Ark?"

"Yes."

"I thought only the priests were allowed to see it."

"On special occasions that rule can be lifted."

"Why are you helping us?" Daniel said, sounding as astonished and baffled and Remi felt.

"I've been told to."

"By who?" Daniel asked.

"Come. You'll meet him now."

The priest had stopped his chanting. He stared at Remi and Daniel for a moment and then gave them a nod. He looked grave.

I wish I knew what you knew, Remi thought.

As they walked back up the aisle toward the door, she glanced over at the scene of Christ on the cross that she had noticed before. She had seen so many scenes like this in her studies of medieval and Renaissance art, but this time it felt different.

This time, she had asked God for a huge favor, and it seemed like He had just granted it.

They went back across the sun-soaked courtyard to the small side chapel Remi had noticed before.

"The guardian of the Ark wants to meet you," Captain Kebede said. "He doesn't speak English so I will have to translate. He has been guardian for twelve years."

"I read that the guardian has to stay in that building all his life," Daniel said.

Captain Kebede nodded. "That is true. Once they take on the task, they may never let the Ark out of their sight."

Remi found her heart beating faster. She walked toward the chapel in a daze.

In a moment, she was actually going to set her eyes on the true Ark of the Covenant.

CHAPTER TWENTY FOUR

Remi could barely contain her excitement as they passed over the threshold of the Chapel of the Tablet and into the dim interior. A thin old man in a pure white robe stood just inside. The air smelled heavily of incense. Sunlight shone through the door and the blue stained glass. Other than that, and a few candles, there was no illumination. The walls were decorated with frescoes just like the main church, but these looked older, their colors faded and smudged with the residue of smoke.

The priest spoke to Captain Kebede but looked right at Remi and Daniel. The captain translated.

"The priest wishes to welcome you to the Chapel of the Tablet, and asks that when he shows you the Ark, that you do not touch it."

"Thank him for us," Remi said, her words coming out hushed.

He translated this and got a response.

"The priest says that he should thank you, since you are here to keep the Ark safe. I explained to him that you were carrying guns and pretending to be missionaries, but he does not mind. He says you had to do this in order to achieve a good aim."

Remi blinked. "Wait. How does he know why we are here?"

"He says a colleague told him that you would come."

Remi and Daniel exchanged glances.

"The bookseller at Jericho," Daniel said. "It must be."

What's going on? It seems like this organization that calls itself the Keepers is watching over us.

Then why not help us a bit more? They could have gotten us into the country, for example.

Maybe it really is only a few academics and holy men, and they have no real power. They need us.

"Tell the priest we'll do everything in our power to keep the Ark safe," Remi said. "The man who is killing to get it is white, not young but not yet old, and is muscular and athletic. We don't have much more of a description than that, I'm afraid."

Captain Kebede translated all this, and the priest motioned for them to walk further into the church. Heart thudding in her chest, she followed.

The priest led them past the altar. Through the dim, smoke-hazed air she could see a curtain of heavy red material behind it. Captain Kebede stopped before the altar. When Remi and Daniel hesitated, the priest motioned for them to follow.

The priest drew back the curtain and they passed through into a small chamber. A tiny skylight let a ray of sunlight angle down from the ceiling to shine on something Remi never thought she'd ever see in her life, something she had never even thought was more than a legend.

The Ark of the Covenant, the storage for the tablets of the Ten Commandments and the conduit that God used to speak to the Israelites.

The Ark sat on a stone plinth and was just as was described in the Book of Exodus.

It was a small, gilded box, a little over a meter in length and a little less than a meter in width and height. On each of its four corners were rings of gold through which two wooden poles were stuck so that it could be carried. The top of the lid was ornately decorated with a pair of cherubim standing on either end, and leaning toward one another as if bent in prayer. Their foreheads touched, leaving a space between their curved bodies and the top of the lid.

Remi took in a sharp breath. The Bible had mentioned that God would appear between these two cherubim, and she could see these angels created a space much like a small video screen.

A prickling sensation went all over her skin. Even if she hadn't promised not to touch it, she would have never dreamed of extending a hand toward it. the Ark didn't seem of this world, and she did not feel worthy even to be in the same room as it, let alone to sully it with her finger.

Tears welled up in her eyes.

Thank you. Thank you so much.

For a long moment the three of them stood there in silence, then the priest opened the curtain again as a signal that it was time to go. Remi walked out of the room in a daze.

Once they were in the main chapel room before the altar, Captain Kebede and the priest began to talk in Tigrinya. Remi wandered off to stare at a painting of Jesus raising Lazarus.

Daniel touched her elbow.

"It isn't real," he whispered.

"What do you mean it isn't real?" she replied, putting more heat into her words than she had intended.

"Didn't you see the gold decoration? It was machined. You could see the marks of a rotary buffer on some of the edges."

Remi blinked. "Are you sure?"

"I'm not an expert, but I've had to study a lot about old art for this job. Yeah, definitely machine tooled. The Israelites didn't have that technology."

Remi felt crushed. She hadn't noticed that. She had been so overcome with emotion she had barely even focused on it. But Daniel, being less affected, had given it a closer study, and while she was the real expert, he did know what he was talking about.

So it was an imitation, just like the ones in all the other Ethiopian Orthodox Churches.

So why did the priest tell them it was the real one? Was this some sort of trick to lead them astray?

But why do that? She and Daniel were trying to help them.

Or perhaps the priest didn't know. Perhaps he thought it really was the true Ark. He wouldn't devote his entire life to living in this building if it wasn't.

That must be the answer. But that only led to another questions.

Where was the real Ark? Because that's what the killer seemed to know far more about this than they did, and so that's where he would strike next.

Or would he try for the one they had just seen? If so, the Tigrayans had it well-guarded. Breaking in there would be far more difficult than breaking into the museum at Luxor.

In the meantime, she and Daniel had to work on the assumption that he knew that wasn't the real one and try to find out where the real one was in order to stop him from killing again.

* * *

From across the street, The Lion of Judah had watched as the two officers got escorted in to the Chapel of the Tablet. How the hell had they gotten to Tigray? The CIA agents or law enforcement officials or whatever they were had certainly showed themselves to be far more resourceful than he had given them credit for.

They were still fools, though. They probably thought they were being shown the true Ark.

He knew that one was a fake. He'd done his research.

The Lion of Judah, sitting in a Land Rover with tinted windows, smiled as that Tigrayan officer led them into the chapel.

It had been a long, hard slog getting here, and the Lion of Judah was tired. He had gotten to Djibouti and found a Somali willing to drive him across the border, no questions asked. That had been expensive, but he had gotten his money back when he killed the man and dumped him in a ravine on the Tigrayan side of the border. He got an AK-47, a 9mm pistol, and this Land Rover too.

And now he was almost to his goal.

The main church with its tall bell tower and impressive dome was almost modern, as was the Chapel of the Tablet. Both had been built by Haile Selassie in the 1950s across the street from an earlier church built in the 16th century. The Old Church had become unstable after its walls had cracked from the spiritual heat given off by the Ark.

Many people, even many Ethiopians, dismissed that as a fable. The Lion of Judah knew it to be the truth. The truths hidden inside it were too much for a building to contain.

He also knew that the Ark had never been removed from the Old Church. A careful reading of all the sacred texts in Ge'ez, the ancient liturgical language of Ethiopia that he had painstakingly studied for several years, revealed coded references that proved the Ark had never been moved. A ritual was performed to protect the church from further decay and the Ark was kept in a reinforced room behind the altar.

The Lion of Judah gazed longingly at the Old Church. Its triple-arched façade of tan-colored stone topped with battlements like a castle seemed a humble place to store the world's holiest relic, but that, and the lack of guards, made people pass it by. Visitors were also put off by a sign in various languages saying the Old Church was structurally unstable and closed until further notice.

He needed to get in there, but those two mysterious Westerners were just across the street. He should come back later.

No, he needed to do it now. They were close on his trail and there was no telling how long he could elude them.

They had just gone into the Chapel of the Tablet. They would probably be in there for at least a few minutes.

Time enough.

He checked that his knife and pistol were well hidden under the loose shirt that hung over his trousers, then got out of the Land Rover.

He had barely made it five steps before some local man cut him off.

"Hello. Welcome to Tigray. Do you need a guide?"

This had been a problem ever since Egypt and had grown ten times worse since he had gotten to the Horn of Africa. His white skin made him stand out.

"No, I don't need anything," the Lion of Judah said, not slowing his pace. Ignoring them generally worked after a while.

"I can show you good hotel. Or restaurant? And the obelisks of Axum! You must see."

"No, thank you."

"Oh sir, you cannot go into the church. It is closed."

"The priest invited me."

"Oh, you are an NGO worker! Let me introduce you to the priest, my good friend."

The Lion of Judah rounded on him, lifting up his shirt enough to show his weapons for a moment.

"I'm not an NGO worker. I'm a mercenary."

The man took a step back, turned, and walked quickly down the street.

The Lion of Judah smiled. Doing that in Israel or Egypt would have been foolhardy. The man would have made a beeline to the police. But in an unstable region like this, mercenaries were common, and feared.

He walked quickly to the entrance, hoping no one else spotted him, and didn't hesitate as he entered the church.

The signs weren't entirely lying. A latticework of steel support beams propped up the front wall, and extra pillars had been erected in various spots in the church to hold up the roof.

A pity. It marred the beauty of this place and blocked the view of the old frescoes on the walls. Dust had gathered on the floor, and to one side sat a toolbox and a stack of lumber.

The church wasn't entirely abandoned, though. He could smell incense and saw the altar at the back was carefully maintained. A curtain hung behind it, as it did in every Ethiopian Orthodox Church. The holy of holies, where the church's Ark was kept.

All fake, except for this one, hidden in plain sight.

The Lion of Judah licked his lips and wiped his sweating palms on his trousers. The journey had been so long, with so many twists and turns. The Keepers had lied to him at every stage, misdirecting him and trying to keep the True Ten Commandments for themselves.

No more. He would reveal them to the world, and everything would change.

From the dark recesses of the back of the church, a priest appeared. He was younger than most, and burly. In fact, other than the red robes and clean white turban, and the big silver cross hanging around his neck, he looked more like a soldier than a priest.

Of course. They need someone who can protect it in case a man like me comes along who knows the truth.

Careful now.

The Lion of Judah didn't waste time. He strode over to the priest or soldier or whatever he was. He cracked a grin to put the Tigrayan off his guard.

"Sorry, the church is closed."

The Lion of Judah whipped out his gun. "Not for me it isn't."

The priest raised his hands and froze. The Lion of Judah patted him down and didn't find any weapon.

"Is there anyone else here?"

"N-no."

"Come on." he shoved the priest ahead of him and headed for the altar.

"We do not have much silver, and no money."

"That's not what I'm after and you know it."

He gave the priest another shove up the steps of the altar.

"Open the curtain," the Lion of Judah ordered.

The priest hesitated. The Lion of Judah raised his gun and pointed it between the man's eyes.

"All right. All right."

The priest drew back the curtain. The Lion of Judah's eyes went wide. There it was, exactly as described in the Book of Exodus!

He moved into the little chamber, mesmerized by the sight of the true Ark of the Covenant. He did not, however, let his aim stray from the priest. He had come too far and struggled too hard to be lax now.

"Open it," he ordered.

"But—"

"OPEN IT!"

The priest grasped the heavy lid, made of wood and gilded, and pulled it aside.

The Lion of Judah took a deep breath and looked inside …

… and saw nothing.

The Ark was empty.

The Ark? No, just a box. Just another fake!

"Where's the real one?" he bellowed.

"There are no real ones. They are a symbol, something for the faithful to admire and use to connect with God."

"You're lying!"

"No, my friend. I do not know why you have come here, but you have been misled. The Ark of the Covenant was destroyed when the Babylonians destroyed the Temple in the time of King Zedekiah."

"That's a lie."

"No, my friend. It is the truth. Now be sensible and put down the gun."

The Lion of Judah glared at him. "Put down the gun? All right. I'll put down the gun."

He tucked the pistol back under his shirt and pulled out his knife.

He had just enough sense beneath his rage to know that a shot might be heard by those who hunted him.

And with a knife, he could cut and cut until he got this guy to give up the truth.

CHAPTER TWENTY FIVE

Remi sat on one of the pews in the Chapel of the Tablet, feeling gutted. For a moment, while praying, she had felt a connection to God she hadn't experienced in years. And then she had thought her prayers had been answered in an immediate and stunning way.

Only to find that the Ark was a fake.

She recalled something Sister Beatrice used to say about prayer when she was a schoolgirl.

"Remember, young ladies,"—even when they were little, Sister Beatrice always addressed them as 'young ladies'—"God is not like Santa Claus. Just because you are good doesn't mean He will give you everything you ask for."

Remi smiled. If only Sister Beatrice could see her now.

Captain Kebede and the priest had sat down on the other side of the church and were deep in conversation. Occasionally one of them glanced over to where Remi and Daniel sat. Her partner seemed uncomfortable at this, but Remi didn't worry too much. It looked like, for whatever reason, the captain had decided they weren't a threat.

But what about the priest? And the church? And Captain Kebede's superior officers? They were still two foreigners here without government permission and caught carrying weapons. She was surprised the captain and priest had believed anything they said. They certainly had no reason to.

Suddenly, a skinny young priest burst into the church, shouting and waving his hands in the air. Captain Kebede and the guardian of the Ark sprang to their feet. There was a quick exchange, and then the captain rushed over to them.

"The priest in the Old Church across the street has been murdered!"

"How? With a knife?" Remi asked.

He really made it. He really managed to sneak across a warzone to get here.

The captain looked surprised. "Yes. How did you know?"

Time to tell the truth and hope for the best.

"We are two FBI agents hunting a man who is trying to steal the Ark of the Covenant," Remi said. Daniel nodded.

Captain Kebede turned and stared at the guardian of the Chapel of the Tablet.

"So what the priest told me is true," he whispered. "I did not believe it."

Remi blinked. "Wait. He knows who we work for?"

"He is very well informed."

"By whom?" Daniel asked.

"It is not for me to know," the captain said. "Come, let us see what happened."

They hurried across the street. Some more soldiers had appeared, doubling the guard at the gate. Several more were at the Old Church across the street.

"One of the guards says a Land Rover was parked close by while we were inside the Chapel of the Tablet. A white man got out and went into the Old Church. He came out and drove off a few minutes later."

"Did the guard get any more description than that?" Remi asked.

"I am afraid not. It was from a distance, and they saw the man from behind."

It didn't matter. Remi knew who it was.

They passed a sign saying the church was closed and structurally unstable and entered through the open doors. The interior looked like a construction site. A group of soldiers and a couple of priests stood in a cluster around the altar. The curtain behind it was open. Remi, Daniel, and Captain Kebede ran up the two steps to the altar.

In a little alcove behind the curtain, a burly young priest lay on the floor. He had several slash wounds to his arms and hands, what Remi had learned were called defensive wounds from when someone tries to fend off an attacker. She had sustained a couple of those herself.

His throat was slit too, and he lay in a pool of still-wet blood.

Remi gingerly edged around the pool and peeked inside the half-open Ark sitting on its plinth.

It was empty. Even more, a fine layer of dust covering the inside had not been disturbed.

There had never been anything inside this Ark.

A priest shouted something and moved toward her. Captain Kebede said something to him, and he stopped, looking uncertain.

Remi studied the gilding on the twin cherubim and all around the box itself. She could tell right away that it had been machine tooled.

So this one was a fake too.

Remi stepped out of that horrid scene and back into the public part of the church.

Captain Kebede looked grim. They stood apart from the growing crowd of priests and soldiers and consulted.

"This has never happened in my memory," the captain said. "Such an insult must be avenged. This man needs to be brought to justice."

"We'll do our best to arrest him," Daniel said.

"Arrest him? You are not in the United States. You will arrest no one. You can help, though, and if you catch him, he must be handed over to Tigrayan authorities."

There was a pause. Daniel looked uncomfortable. Remi knew that if the killer was handed over to the local police or army, he wouldn't live a day. Like most Europeans, she was against the death penalty, thinking it was a barbaric act that didn't actually prevent crime. The United States had the death penalty, and Europe didn't, and the United States had a much higher crime rate. She did not want to hand a suspect over to some kangaroo court and executioner.

But what choice did they have? Captain Kebede was right. They had no legal authority here. In fact, they were technically criminals. They were only free on sufferance.

Daniel spoke. "Let's discuss this later. The first priority is to catch this guy."

"Agreed," Captain Kebede replied. It sounded like he only said this to placate the foreigners, and that the decision had already been made.

"It seems he knew that the Ark in the Chapel of the Tablet was a fake," Remi said. "And thought for some reason he believed that this was the real one. He must have been desperate to go after it when a couple of soldiers were standing right across the street. He would have been so conspicuous."

"Not so much. Land Rovers are common for NGOs, and we do have a few still here. The Red Cross and Save the Children. I think one or two more. But they are not common. We must call around to the hotels to find out where he might be staying. That will take time."

"I thought you said the Endubis Hotel was one of the only ones open," Daniel said.

Captain Kebede smiled. "I said that so I would know where you were. It is only empty because it is so expensive. There are many cheaper hotels filled with refugees. Those who have money stay at a hotel. Many more are in the camps outside of the city."

"We don't know if he even is staying at a hotel," Remi said.

The captain nodded. "That is a problem. But at least we have an idea where he might attack next. You said he is very knowledgeable. It seems so. The priest told me a secret. The true Ark is indeed in Axum, one of a dozen Arks in different churches and monastery chapels all around the city and the countryside nearby. One of them is the real one. The priest says that no one knows which is the real one. This is a way to protect it."

Remi wondered at this. Surely they would keep track of which one is real. And there must be experts, scholars or trained priests, who could tell if an artifact is ancient or modern, just like Daniel and she could tell.

There must be an upper layer to the church hierarchy here that knew the truth.

But they weren't revealing it. They did not trust the two foreigners, or even the young captain from their own army.

Once again, she sensed a hidden hand at work, one that only revealed itself briefly before returning to the darkened background to pull the strings.

What have we gotten ourselves involved with here?

Figure that out later. We need to catch this man before he kills again.

"Can wc inform all the twelve churches?" Remi asked.

"I just gave orders for that. There is a problem, though. Not all the priests have mobile phones. We are having to radio to nearby security units to check on them."

"Good. Let's go," Daniel said.

Captain Kebede led them out of the church and to a Jeep parked outside that had a long radio antenna sticking out the back. A soldier sat at the wheel.

"We will take this. Get in the back. Oh," Captain Kebede reached into the Jeep and handed them their pistols.

"You're letting us go armed?" Remi asked.

"Normally we would never allow this, but the priests say we need your help. Do not betray their trust."

“We’ll do everything we can to stop this man,” Remi promised.

The Jeep headed out, speeding down the nearly deserted street. Captain Kebede got on the radio that was set into the dashboard. There was a lot of chatter and he had trouble being heard. After a minute he got off and turned to look at them in the back seat.

“Many of the security forces are occupied because they have noted suspicious movements around various neighborhoods.”

“What kind of movements?” Remi asked.

“It is unclear. There has been trouble before with militia loyal to the central government. I hope it is not that again. I have heard back from four of the twelve locations. They are safe and under guard. I am still trying to get through to the others. We are going to one that has no telephone. It is up in the hills. It will be a long drive. I am thinking that because it is one of the most isolated, that is where the true Ark is kept.”

They drove through the town. Remi noticed it seemed unusually quiet. Few people were on the streets and several roadblocks were in place. The soldiers looked on edge. Captain Kebede continued to talk on the radio as the chatter grew worse. Then he let out what sounded like a curse and slapped his knee.

“There is a report that the guardian priest at a small church here in Axum has just been found unconscious. The Ark is missing!”

So the killer realized the one in the Chapel of the Tablet was a fake and immediately went to the next likely candidate, and this time he found it.

“Where could the thief have gone?” Daniel asked. “He’ll probably want to get out of the country as quickly as possible.”

“The airports,” Captain Kebede said.

“Airports?”

“There are two. Public and private. They stand next to one another. We will go there now. There is a military airport as well. He could not go there.”

Captain Kebede said something to the driver, and they turned off on another road. The driver hit the gas and they sped down a long avenue.

It was then that the first crackle of small arms fire sounded out from several places in the city.

CHAPTER TWENTY SIX

Remi sat low in the back seat of the Jeep, gripping her pistol. The gunfire grew louder, closer. They could see the control tower of the city airport just ahead, and a smaller control tower in the distance for the private airstrip.

"The security at the airport says there is fighting there," Captain Kebede said. "It is the pro-government militia. We thought we had defeated them last time, but we were wrong."

"We have to get in there!" Remi said.

"We will. Tigray cannot lose the Ark. But I cannot ask that you come with me. This is our fight, not for foreigners."

"He killed an American citizen," Daniel said. "We're going in. Just keep us clear of that militia."

"We will try."

Remi looked at Daniel and nodded. She didn't want to take sides in a fight she knew almost nothing about. Not only would that be wrong, but it would cause an international incident.

But wasn't their mere presence here threatening to cause an international incident?

Why had the FBI allowed them to come?

They sped another kilometer and ended up at a roadblock. A large, armored car with a heavy machine gun on the roof was firing across a field at some distant buildings. About twenty soldiers knelt behind the armored car or a nearby concrete barrier.

The Jeep screeched to a halt. The men at the roadblock seemed to recognize Captain Kebede and thankfully didn't point their guns in his direction.

There was a hurried conversation and then they sped off the remaining distance to the airport.

A gate in a chain link fence stood open. The nearby guardhouse was empty.

"I think they are inside," Captain Kebede said, pulling out an AK-47.

"How can they be inside if the roadblock is still manned?" Remi asked.

"They could have overwhelmed the guards at the back entrance or cut the fence and fought off the guards on the property. We must be careful. They could even be wearing the same uniforms as us."

Daniel looked at her.

"You up for this?" he asked.

"If you're asking if I'm ready or have sufficient training, absolutely not. But I'm not turning back now."

Daniel gave her a grin that warmed her heart. "Neither am I. You're a hell of a lot of fun, you know that?"

"So are you, even if you do have atrocious eating habits."

"It's part of my charm. Stay alert."

They passed through a parking lot about a third full of vehicles but entirely devoid of people. The terminal stood on the other side: a long, low building made of concrete with several large windows. The sun was too bright to see inside.

Captain Kebede hopped out, as did the other soldier, both gripping assault rifles. Remi and Daniel stayed behind them, keeping low.

Gunfire erupted from inside the terminal. The sliding glass doors opened, and a rush of civilians swarmed out, screaming. None appeared hurt. The firing continued.

Once the crowd had passed, they moved through the doors. A couple of soldiers swung their AKs at them, saw Captain Kebede's uniform, and turned back to fire down the terminal. About a hundred meters away, Remi saw several men hiding behind counters and benches and firing back. None appeared to be wearing uniforms.

A few shivering civilians lay curled on the floor between the two factions, trying to make as small of targets as possible.

Remi and Daniel ducked behind a stack of luggage as bullets smacked against the tile floor, sending fragments in all directions. Captain Kebede joined them. The driver from their Jeep darted to the side, got behind a row of chairs, and began firing at the pro-government militia.

"Now what?" Daniel asked.

"We need to move!" the captain said.

A bullet thumped through the suitcases near Remi's head, reminding her of the obvious but little-pondered fact that luggage is not bulletproof.

"Where's the runway?" Remi asked.

Captain Kebede pointed. "That way! We will go through the staff entrance."

The captain started crawling along the row of luggage, then sprang up and bolted for a counter and dove behind it. Remi and Daniel followed.

A burst of fire erupted from further down the terminal. Bullets sang past their heads and cracked the tile around their feet. They dove behind the counter, almost landing on the captain and surprised they were alive.

"Damn it!" Daniel said. "They saw you go and figured we'd come next. They were waiting for us."

Captain Kebede grinned. "Welcome to the Republic of Tigray."

"Now where do we go?" Remi shouted, barely hearing herself over the roar of gunfire as four soldiers using the counter as cover returned fire.

"That door over there," the captain said, pointing.

Remi stared. Daniel groaned.

"You mean that door past a wide stretch of open space with no cover whatsoever?" Daniel asked.

"Did you think you would live forever?" Captain Kebede asked.

"It's nice to think of it as a possibility," Daniel grumbled.

"Let's all go together so those gunmen don't get prepared," Remi suggested.

Captain Kebede nodded and shouted something to the soldiers, who all crouched behind the counter and reloaded.

"This attack on the airport just when the Ark gets stolen can't be a coincidence," Remi said.

"No, it can't," Daniel said. "We seemed to have stepped into an international conspiracy."

"Sorry," Remi said.

"For what?"

"For all the international conspiracies I keep making you step in."

Daniel laughed. "Life has definitely gotten more interesting since you showed up."

"*You* showed up in *my* life, remember?"

"Oh, right."

Captain Kebede shouted a command to the four soldiers, who rose as one and let out long bursts from their AK-47s.

Remi had gotten through enough of her firearms training to recognize cover fire when she saw it. She sprang up and sprinted for the door.

She made it halfway there before she noticed two things.

First, the door had a swipe card lock on it.

Second, the covering fire wasn't working. The pro-government militiamen were still firing at them.

A counter stood right next to the door. Remi ran for it as bullets filled the air around her.

She dove behind the counter and found it already occupied by a female airline employee, curled up in a ball and no doubt wondering if she would live to see the end of her shift.

Daniel sprang in after her. A moment later, Captain Kebede fell next to them, crying out and holding his leg. Blood soaked his camouflage pants.

Daniel dragged him in behind the meager cover.

"It is not so bad," Captain Kebede hissed as he clutched his leg.

To Remi it didn't look life threatening, but he sure wasn't going to walk anywhere.

The captain realized the same thing. He said something to the airline employee, who pulled off a key card from around her neck and handed it to Remi.

"Go, my friends," Captain Kebede said. "And may God go with you."

Remi crawled over to the door and swiped the key card without standing up. The door clicked and she pushed it open. That movement attracted several bullets to pockmark the wall just above her head. She and Daniel crawled through.

They found themselves in a long back room where conveyor belts, now switched off, brought luggage to depots outside. Not bothering to search for the door, they crawled along one of these conveyor belts and ended up in a luggage loading area looking out over the runway.

No one was around and they didn't hear any shots nearby. A Sudan Airways plane was parked on the runway. Beyond it stretched a wide, flat field with dried clumps of grass and then the runway of the private airport. Beyond that stood a hanger with several small private aircraft. They saw two men, one white and one black, loading a large crate onto the back of a twin-propeller aircraft.

"There!" Remi shouted, pointing.

"No way we're going to get there unseen."

The pair pushed the crate into the back, slammed shut the hatch, and ran around to the front of the airplane.

"We're not going to get there in time either," Daniel added.

Remi looked around and spotted a flatbed truck filled with luggage.

"Yes, we are," she said, running for it.

They clambered aboard, Remi in the driver's seat. The keys were in the ignition, and she started it up.

Grinding gears in her rush, she drove off across the tarmac. The propellers of the plane began to turn. Remi tried to pick up speed, but the truck was old and couldn't get any faster than about thirty.

They passed the Sudan Airways plane, the astonished pilot and copilot peering out at them, and they started over the field between the public and private airports. The luggage truck bumped over stones and hit ruts, the luggage on the flatbed toppling off to leave a trail behind them.

"Stick with the FBI. You'll never make it in the airline business," Daniel said.

The private aircraft started to move forward. Remi angled the truck to cut it off.

As Remi got the truck onto the tarmac, the pilot, realizing he wasn't going to get past in time, turned the plane around.

"He's going to take off in the other direction!" Daniel shouted. "Pull alongside."

Remi went after the plane. Even though the truck moved faster now that all the luggage had fallen off, the plane picked up speed and began to move ahead.

"Keep the truck steady," Daniel said, aiming his pistol.

He fired. The bullet sparked off the metal around the engine casing behind one of the propellers. For a moment nothing happened, and Remi gritted her teeth in frustration to see the plane pulling ahead, but then a stream of black smoke started coming out of the engine casing. A terrible grinding of metal on metal filled their ears.

The plane slowed. Remi began to catch up.

A loud bang announced the engine's final death. The propellers slowed to a stop, as did the plane.

Remi cut ahead and blocked it with the truck. Remi and Daniel hopped out, guns leveled. Inside the cockpit, the two men raised their hands.

"Get out!" Remi ordered.

They shut off the other engine and climbed out of the plane.

Remi stared. The white man was not the man they had been hunting.

He was at least ten years older, with a receding hairline and streaks of gray. He also had a belly while the man at the Luxor Museum had been fit.

"Who are you?" Daniel asked.

"A private citizen fleeing the fighting," he said in an Eastern European accent.

"Open up the back of the plane," Remi ordered.

"I am a private citizen. Who are you to tell me what to do?"

"I'm the one holding the gun," Remi said. "Open up the back of the plane."

They walked around to the back of the plane. In the distance they could hear the crackle of small arms fire. It seemed to be less than before.

The Eastern European man opened up the hatch while his African copilot stood there looking morose.

The large crate they had seen before sat inside.

"Pull it out," Daniel ordered.

The two men did so, placing it on the tarmac.

"Open it," Remi ordered.

They did so.

Remi peered inside …

… and then groaned in disappointment.

CHAPTER TWENTY SEVEN

Remi felt like kicking something.

The Ark inside was obviously a modern fake. The machine marks that Daniel had spotted on the Ark in the Chapel of the Tablet were evident on this one too.

Not only was this the wrong Ark, but this was the wrong thief.

But who was it?

"Let's cut a deal," the Eastern European man said. "I will reveal to you evidence that the Ethiopian government is behind this in exchange for my freedom."

"And my freedom too," his copilot said.

"Shut up," the Eastern European snapped.

"So the militia attack wasn't a coincidence, it was to cover your escape," Remi said. "It kept customs from checking your cargo."

"Yes. Let's make a deal."

"Do you know anything about a younger, fit, Western man here on the same mission?"

The Eastern European man blinked. "Someone else?"

Remi could tell from his expression that he was telling the truth.

It made sense. If they worked together, they would be fleeing together.

Damn it! Another dead end!

A forklift came speeding over the field between the two airfields, driven by an airport employee. Hanging onto the side, his wounded leg raised so it didn't bump against the vehicle, was Captain Kebede.

Daniel indicated the approaching soldier.

"If you want to make a deal, you'll have to make it with him. But I don't think he's in a deal-making mood."

Remi slumped. After all this trouble they still had no idea where their man was, or where the real Ark was.

She stared at the fake. At least it was beautiful, and perhaps historically significant. All the ones they had seen were identical. Supposedly they would be exact copies of the original, if the original existed.

So looking at this Ark was almost like looking at the real thing.

Almost, but not quite.

She noticed the sides were embossed with scenes in the Ethiopian style, facing forward with those large, expressive eyes. The Book of Exodus mentioned no scenes on the sides of the Ark, and it was quite detailed as to its construction and design. The only figures it mentioned were the twin cherubim on the top, and yet here was a relief of priests flanking the Ark with their hands raised in prayer. Behind that scene stood an Ethiopian-style church. On the other side of the Ark was a scene from the Book of Joshua of the Israelites crossing the River Jordan. The priests carrying the Ark stood in the riverbed, the water having parted, and the Israelites were crossing to the Promised Land.

These had to be later additions. The Israelites did not decorate the sides of the Ark, and they certainly wouldn't have done so in the Ethiopian style.

So not only was this a fake, but it wasn't even a faithful copy of the original.

Did that mean the real Ark never came to Axum? Or perhaps never existed in the first place?

The forklift pulled up.

"Good job, my friends!" Captain Kebede cried. "You have saved the Ark. But this man doesn't look like the man you described."

"That's because he isn't," Daniel grumbled. "He's some Eastern European, probably a mercenary who got the pro-government militia to launch an attack to cover his escape."

Captain Kebede's face twisted in anger. "They try to steal our holy object?"

He gripped his AK hard, knuckles going white. Remi could see he felt tempted to shoot the man down where he stood.

Common sense prevailed.

"We will take him in for questioning," the captain said. "And it will be a very forceful questioning."

The two prisoners paled.

"This is another fake," Remi said.

"That is a relief, but that will not save them."

Remi looked at the decoration again, noticing a detail that she had missed before. On the scene with the church above a group of priests praying before the Ark, a faint horizontal line ran below the church and above the priests and Ark.

What, at first, she had interpreted as a church standing behind the Ark could actually be interpreted as the church being above the Ark.

Remi stared at it for a second as the significance of what she had noticed sank in.

"Captain Kebede, are there tunnels underneath the Church of Our Lady Mary of Zion?"

"I don't know."

"We need to get there," Remi stated. "Now!"

Daniel came over to look at the Ark and saw what she saw.

"Whoa. Do you think he knows about this?"

"It's our only lead."

The Jeep they had arrived in came speeding up, the diver having been joined by a couple more soldiers. Remi cocked her ear and didn't hear any more firing.

The soldiers had a quick conference with Captain Kebede as one bandaged his leg. Remi stood by impatiently, itching to go. She couldn't very well tell the man to stop bandaging a bullet wound, however.

Gently they put Captain Kebede into the passenger's seat of the Jeep. Now that the adrenaline from the fighting was gone and the pain from his wound had started to set in, he looked exhausted.

"The pro-government militia has retreated," he gasped. "Let's get back to the church."

Two of the soldiers took the prisoners into custody and led them back toward the airport. Remi and Daniel hopped in the back of the Jeep and the driver hit the gas.

"The fighting might have given the real killer an opportunity to sneak into the church," Remi said.

"We will catch him," Captain Kebede muttered, slumping in the front seat.

Not you, you poor man, Remi thought. *You're going to need a stay in the hospital.*

She glanced at his bandage. Some blood had seeped through, but the bleeding didn't look too bad. He would live.

They passed through abandoned streets. A few shots rang out in the distance.

* * *

Other than a couple of checkpoints, they didn't see any Tigrayan soldiers. They must have all been hunting down the retreating militia.

They came to the gate to find both guards lying dead from gunshot wounds. The other two that had come as reinforcements just before Remi and the others had left were nowhere to be seen.

"Get in there!" Captain Kebede said with the last of his energy. He snapped an order to the driver, who grabbed his AK and ran to follow Remi and Daniel.

"Under the Chapel of the Tablet or the main church?" Daniel asked.

"I have no idea."

"You're the art expert."

"For medieval Europe!"

"Then make a wild guess!"

She headed for the Chapel of the Tablet.

At first when they got inside, they didn't see anything had changed. The curtain was closed. Remi took a peek behind it, eliciting an objection from the soldier, and found the fake Ark in place.

"Do you speak English?" Daniel asked the soldier. He got a response in Tigrinya. Remi tried him in French and Italian with the same result.

Shrugging her shoulders, Remi moved toward the side of the chapel where the priest had first appeared. She felt tempted to call out to him but decided against it. It was quiet inside the chapel. Too quiet.

They passed across the main room and through an open door. There they found a small sitting room leading off to an even smaller bedroom and a kitchen. Obviously, the living quarters for the guardian. A door at the corner of the sitting room had been forced. Beyond it, a narrow spiral staircase led down.

Remi went for it. Daniel shouldered her aside.

"Age before beauty," he said.

"I beg your pardon?"

"You're a trainee. I get into dangerous situations first," he replied.

"Oh."

The Tigrayan soldier had different ideas and cut in front of Daniel to take the lead, his assault rifle at the ready.

The spiral staircase plunged down into a cool shaft of packed, rocky earth. The old, rickety metal clattered under their footsteps, sending echoes into the unseen distance.

Once at the bottom, they found themselves in a long tunnel barely wide enough for two of them to walk side by side. If she stood on tiptoe, she could reach out and touch the arched ceiling.

The walls and ceiling were of hardpacked earth, reinforced here and there with wooden beams. The entire place gave an impression of great age.

The corridor ran straight in both directions, dimly lit by a few underpowered electric bulbs placed too far apart. A single electric cable to power them was fixed with clamps to the ceiling.

The Tigrayan soldier looked both ways down the corridor before turning to them. He pointed at himself and then one direction, pointed at them and the other direction.

Remi and Daniel nodded.

Then the soldier pulled out a crucifix hanging inside his uniform shirt. He kissed it and said something in his language, looking at them as he did so.

"God be with you too," Remi said.

The soldier nodded and jogged off the down the corridor.

They turned the other direction and followed the corridor for a time, eyes and ears alert.

They didn't get far before they saw the first of the bones.

CHAPTER TWENTY EIGHT

Remi tensed as they came up to a niche in the right-hand wall packed with bones. Long bones—those from the arms and legs—were stacked in orderly piles with the ribs and smaller bones for the fingers, toes, and spine packed in as filling. Atop this sat tidy rows of skulls. They were all packed so tightly as to make almost a solid wall of bone.

Daniel gave her a horrified look. Perhaps he had never been into any catacombs before. She had—in Paris, in Rome, in several other European cities—but this sort of place always gave her the shivers.

They passed the wall of bones, only to come across another less than a minute later. And then another. Many of the bones looked quite old. None had traces of skin or hair.

Then they came across the newer ones.

In one large annex, the size of a walk-in closet, were several shelves hacked into the dense soil. On them lay stretched out skeletons on which clung leather skin and shreds of the white and red robes that the priests wore. Embedded into the wall was an ornate silver cross. The air had a musty odor.

She had seen this before in other catacombs. Bodies would be laid out until they fully decomposed, the last sinews keeping the body together rotting away until the bones could be gathered up like a bundle of dry sticks. And packed in with those of others.

Daniel shuddered and leaned against the wall of the corridor, hanging his head.

"Are you all right?" Remi asked, putting a hand on his shoulder.

"When I was a kid, someone took me into a place like this," he gasped. "He …"

"He what?" she asked, rubbing his shoulder. She had never seen him like this before.

Daniel shook himself. Remi snatched her hand away. He stood tall, his face set with determination although sweat beaded on his brow.

"Nothing. Let's get on with it."

Remi stared in confusion as he moved past her and continued down the corridor.

She followed, sneaking glances at her partner. Whatever had overcome him at the crypt, he had now shoved side and he advanced like the fighter he was.

After another minute they came to a four-way intersection. Identical corridors ran into the distance. At regular intervals they saw niches for bones.

For a moment they paused, listening.

A distant, echoing shout sent them running down the left-hand corridor.

The shouts continued, that of a man screaming in incoherent rage. It was English, but Remi couldn't make any sense of it. A deeper, accented voice replied,

"It is not here! It was never here! You must believe that it is a legend! You—ah!"

The accented voice cut off with a cry of pain.

"FBI!" Daniel shouted. "We have the place surrounded. Drop the weapon and come out with your hands up!"

At first Remi thought Daniel foolish to be announcing their presence when they hadn't even arrived on the scene yet, but then realized that with an attack already underway, calling out to the suspect was the only chance they had to stop it in time.

Daniel's shout was answered with silence.

They kept running past the grinning skulls of dead priests and monks. There seemed to be no side passages here. Daniel was right; they did have him cut off.

Unfortunately, running down a single, narrow corridor made them perfect targets if he had a gun.

He did.

Just as the end of the corridor came into view, where it opened up into what looked like a small chapel, they saw the flash of a gunshot.

The bullet shattered a skull in one of the niches, sending fragments of bone smacking into Remi's face. Daniel and Remi threw themselves on the ground as another couple of shots came close.

Daniel and Remi both fired an answering shot, but they couldn't see if they hit the dark figure that ducked back behind the doorway.

For a moment there was silence save for the ringing in her ears. Remi felt a trickle of something damp run down her cheek. She rubbed it with the back of her hand and came away with a little smear of blood.

The skull fragments. One of the skull fragments cut me.

Remi felt bile rise up in her throat. She forced it down and aimed at the distant doorway. She was pretty sure that neither her nor Daniel's shots had come anywhere close. These old, cheap pistols had no accuracy at anything further than a few dozen meters.

And he had a hostage.

A couple more shots came from the chapel, one hitting so close to Daniel that he flinched. For a moment she thought he had been hit, but then he raised his gun and fired back.

There was a pause, the sound of flesh hitting flesh and a brief struggle. Then the American voice called out to them.

"I'm coming out with the priest. You try to stop me, and he gets it."

Two figures appeared in the doorway. In front was an older Tigrayan man in white robes spattered with bloodstains. Behind came the athletic, middle-aged American they had briefly spotted in the Luxor Museum.

The thing that struck Remi the most about him was how normal he looked. Just some regular fellow in his forties who kept in shape. She could pass him in the street and not notice him.

Except for the eyes. They were aflame with religious zeal.

She had seen that look before in some of the people they had hunted. It signaled that this man was capable of anything.

He held a gun to the priest's head. In his other hand he gripped a bloody knife.

The priest stumbled along, clutching his torn left sleeve, from which blood dripped steadily onto the dirt floor.

"All right," the killer said. "Whoever you are, you've chased me all the way here. Why? Who are you with? The Vatican? The CIA?"

"We're agents Walker and Laurent with the FBI," Daniel said. "Now let him go."

The killer snorted. "So the FBI is in on the game now too, eh? I shouldn't be surprised. Their tentacles have gotten everywhere."

"If you want to talk about it, let him go and we can talk," Remi said. Her mind raced for insights into hostage negotiations. Her course hadn't reached that module yet.

"Stay out of my way. So the Ark isn't here. The Keepers have tricked me once again, but they won't stop me. I'm going to reveal the True Ten Commandments to the world if it's the last thing I do."

Something in Remi's mind clicked.

"The True Ten Commandments? That's what you're looking for?" Remi forced herself to laugh, hoping it sounded realistic. She had never gotten any good roles in school plays. "They're not in the Ark, because the Ark was destroyed by the Babylonians when the First Temple was destroyed."

"Bullshit! That's just one of their lies!"

"There is no Ark, and there are no True Ten Commandments." *Whatever those are supposed to be.* "Did you hear my name? Laurent? Professor Remi Laurent?"

The killer stopped, studying her. "The cryptex researcher?"

God, does every lunatic and conspiracy theorist know about me? At least it might be useful.

"The same. You probably heard about me helping out on the Cryptex Killer case. It was all over the media. Didn't you ever come across the link between the cryptex and the True Ten Commandments?"

"What? It's just a Renaissance puzzle!"

"You mean to say you never read the Hansen Manuscript in Antwerp?"

The killer blinked. "No."

Of course, you haven't. I just made it up.

"It was one of the keys to lead me to the cryptex. It's how we managed to catch him before he stole it."

Daniel nodded.

"So you found it?" the killer gaped.

Resourceful, relentless, ruthless, and a rube. What a bad combination.

"The cryptex? Yes. And it led me to the secret corridors beneath the Temple Mount, the preserved back hallways of the Temple of Solomon. We had to get the head of the bureau to talk to the CIA to get Mossad's permission to go in there. All to preserve the Ark."

"The Temple Mount," the killer said, his voice almost stilled with awe. "So a portion of the original temple still exists underground."

"The Israelis started exploring it secretly after independence in 1948. The Arabs never knew, and after the Israelis took East Jerusalem in 1967, they began work in earnest. Once they had cleared and shored up as much of the old temple as they could, they brought the Ark there."

“Of course! If the Jews still had it, they would want it to be in Solomon’s Temple.”

Remi could see the priest shifting his weight and getting a determined look on his face. Or perhaps a resigned one. She worried he was about to try something. She had to defuse this situation as quickly as possible.

She shook her head, trying to look disappointed.

“It was a reproduction, although a faithful one. It didn’t include the decorations the Ethiopians added. But the rabbi who showed it to me told me it wasn’t the original. That had been lost in the Babylonian invasion.”

The man’s face turned scarlet. “No! You’re lying!”

The priest locked eyes with Remi. She could see he was summoning the courage to try something. The killer, being behind him, couldn’t see this, and Remi couldn’t reply in any way without being seen.

“It’s true,” Daniel said. “It’s a priceless artifact, made after the Israelites were released from captivity, and preserved ever since, but it isn’t the original.”

“Where are the True Ten Commandments? The real instructions from God to the Israelites, the ones the Jews have been covering up all this time?” The killer demanded, shoving the priest forward so he could advance. “You must know! Where are they?”

The priest locked eyes with Remi again raising his eyebrows slightly. Remi tried to keep her gun hand steady. Faintly behind her she could hear the sound of running feet. Probably the soldier, attracted by the sound of gunshots. When he turned the corner and the killer saw him, he might panic.

“Where are the True Ten Commandments?”

The priest’s eyes narrowed. Remi could see his lips moving in silent prayer.

“You want to know where the True Ten Commandments are?” she said, her anger and contempt rising at this obsessive fool. “Look in the Bible.”

“Liar! Those aren’t real!” The killer shoved the priest forward again, and the older man fell flat on his face. As soon as he hit the dirt he kicked out at the killer’s legs. The blow didn’t land well, and wasn’t strong, but it did make the killer lose his balance and take a moment to steady himself.

Long enough.

Remi and Daniel fired at the same moment. With startling clarity, Remi saw her bullet hit his left arm just above the elbow. The knife dripped from his hand. Daniel's bullet hit him straight in the torso.

The killer staggered back, trying to raise his gun. Daniel put another bullet into him. Remi was just squeezing the trigger for another shot when the man fell back.

The priest scrambled for them, not daring to get up in case more bullets flew. Daniel and Remi rushed past him to the killer. Daniel kicked his gun out of reach. Remi could see there was no danger. The man lay unmoving, his breathing ragged, eyes already glazing over.

"Lies. It was all lies. Now I'll never get to know the truth."

The light went out in his eyes, and he said no more.

Daniel knelt by him and checked his pulse. He looked up at her and shook his head.

A shout behind them. Remi and Daniel whirled around to see the soldier running into view, having a shouted exchange with the priest as he approached.

Nothing to fear. Good. She didn't think she could take any more.

Remi leaned hard against the wall. It was all over. The maniac was dead.

What had he been after? What did he think the secret commandments of God to Moses really said? And how did he convince himself that four thousand years of Bible history were all a vast conspiracy?

Remi decided the details didn't matter. He was just a sick man, a twisted man, who had obsessively studied religion and decided it wasn't good enough.

She rubbed her eyes. They kept coming across people like this. Marginal figures willing to devote their lives to uncovering some secret, willing to kill for it.

You're not that different.

No, I wouldn't kill to get the cryptex secret.

You'd steal from a church, though. What else would you do?

Remi shuddered.

She felt a hand on her shoulder. Daniel.

"You didn't kill him," he said, telling her exactly what she needed to hear.

"I … would have."

"To save that priest. To save me. To save yourself. It was the right thing to do. That doesn't make it much easier, but it's the right thing to do."

And it's something I probably will have to do, sooner or later.

Remi shuddered again.

The soldier helped the priest to his feet. He gestured at Remi and Daniel, pointed at the priest's wound, and then pointed at the way out.

"Yeah, let's get him medical attention," Daniel said.

While the soldier didn't understand the words, he caught the tone, and they began to move for the exit.

"Shouldn't we search the man?" Remi said.

"No. It's an affair for the local police, or army, or whoever does that around here. We've done enough. The main thing is that it's over."

Remi felt a profound sense of relief. She didn't want to search a dead body, and Daniel was right. They had done enough.

They passed down the corridor on the way back to the spiral staircase. As they did, Remi got a second, closer look at the catacombs. Her interest in history never faltered, even in a situation like this. Now that she had time to look around her instead of rush headlong into a gunfight, something that was just now giving her a case of the shakes, she noticed that in several spots on the walls were written short lines of text in red or black paint with the same unfamiliar local alphabet she had seen on signs on the street. The letters looked almost Gothic in style but were totally different than Latin script.

"What are these?" she asked.

"Prayer," the priest said.

"Verses from the Bible?"

"Bible, yes."

Remi wished she could ask more, but the man's limited English, and her nonexistent Tigrinya, prevented it.

Then she saw something that nearly bowled her over.

A portion of the dirt wall was a slightly different color. She could tell that it had been dug out at one time and packed back in, disturbing the natural earth and changing its consistency and texture.

The excavated space was about two meters long and one meter high.

A little bigger than the Ark of the Covenant.

Could it be?

As the priest passed the spot, he brushed his fingertips along the wall and muttered a prayer. Remi's eyes went wide.

They buried it, Remi realized, trying not to let her emotion show in her face. *They buried it in this holy spot to keep it close but keep it protected.*

It was right there, probably just a few minutes' of digging away. She could make up some excuse to stay behind for a bit say that she had to investigate the crime scene. Then she could dig in there and …

No. She'd leave it where it was. If that bit of wall really did hide the true Ark of the Covenant, then it should remain there. It wasn't for her to touch or see. It was already in good hands. Even if they hadn't tracked that madman down, he would have never gotten the true Ark.

Besides, her job hadn't been to get the Ark, but to get the killer.

Mission accomplished.

Now all they had to do was find a way to get out of this warzone in one piece.

CHAPTER TWENTY NINE

They emerged from the catacombs to find a troop of soldiers preparing to storm the Chapel of the Tablet. The priest explained everything in Tigrinya. The troops saluted them and a couple of officers, after quickly bandaging his arm, went back downstairs with the priest.

Remi and Daniel, exhausted, staggered out into the sunlight.

At the gate to the church complex they saw Captain Kebede still sitting in the Jeep. He had revived a little, and someone had wrapped up his leg with some proper bandages rather than the earlier hasty field dressing.

Remi gasped in surprise when they saw who stood nearby.

Lucas Mekonnen.

"Where the hell have you been?" Daniel shouted. "You ditched us in the middle of a warzone!"

"I had things to do," Lucas replied in a cool tone. "Besides, the deal was to get you here, not babysit you."

Captain Kebede cut in. "So you stopped him? You protected the Ark?"

"We did. We shot him and the Ark is safe," Remi replied.

Although she answered the captain, she studied their driver. He showed no surprise at the mention of a gunfight or the Ark of the Covenant.

I'd like to learn more about you. I suppose that's not going to happen, though.

"Thank God!" Captain Kebede said.

"How are you?" Remi asked.

"The medic says the bullet passed through muscle and no arteries. I did not bleed too much. I think I will not be walking for some time, though."

"You'll recover soon, buddy," Daniel said with a smile. "You're plenty tough."

Lucas Mekonnen stepped forward, holding out a pair of SIM cards to Daniel.

"I saw you obsessively checking your phone like some Zoomer, so I went to the telephone exchange and got you some credit."

Remi blinked. "There was an armed uprising and you decided to go to the telephone exchange? Was it even open?"

Lucas gave a casual shrug. "It was for me."

Remi frowned. "I'm beginning to tire of your International Man of Mystery act."

The International Man of Mystery laughed. "I have access to an airplane and have orders from your boss to fly you out of here when you're done. The local authorities won't ask any questions. They're just glad you accomplished your mission."

"A plane?" Remi said with surprise. "What about your truck?"

Lucas treated her to a smug smile. "It wasn't my truck."

Remi shook her head. This man was truly annoying.

"So shall we go?" Lucas asked.

Captain Kebede extended his hand. Remi and Daniel both shook it.

"It is best that you leave before there is any more trouble, my friends. Thank you for all that you did. Even though I do not understand everything that has happened here, I know you are on the side of right. You are welcome any time in the Republic of Tigray."

"Good luck to you, and get well soon," Remi said.

"If it makes you feel any better, we don't understand everything that happened either," Daniel said. "All right, let's go."

Lucas led them out on to the street where a car was parked. He hopped into the driver's seat. Remi decided not to ask where he got the car, or the truck, or the plane. She wouldn't get a straight answer and it didn't really matter. They were getting out of here.

"So where shall I fly you?" Lucas asked.

"I suppose Djibouti City would be best," Remi said. "From there we can get a flight to Europe and then the United States."

And perhaps a stopover in Paris for a couple of days. I think we've earned it.

Daniel, sitting in the passenger's seat, was already putting the Ethiopian Sim card into his phone. Lucas was right. He showed the eagerness of some of her undergraduate students to check their phones after a long lecture.

She might as well too. As Lucas drove them to the airport through a city that was slowly returning to normal activity, she opened the back of her phone, removed the Egyptian SIM card and put in the Ethiopian one. Then she turned her phone back on.

Besides a couple of text messages in one of the Ethiopian languages welcoming her to her new phone service, there were not text messages from anyone. That surprised her until she realized she had only been gone from the U.S. for a few days. It seemed like a year.

Next, she checked her email and felt a tug of disappointment to see nothing from Cyril. She grimaced. It looked like he wanted to make a clean break.

She brightened immediately when she saw an email from Professor John MacDonald, her Canadian colleague.

The subject line read, "Breakthrough!"

She opened it.

"Remi, I didn't think I'd break it this fast and for a while I was stumped until I realized the language wasn't Greek or Latin, but Coptic. What a surprise! So I ended up with a decoded message I still couldn't read. I know you want to keep this secret, so I didn't contact anyone for help. Instead, I borrowed a Coptic dictionary from the university library and puzzled it out myself.

"It's a simple message: St. Bishoy Monastery, Main Chapel painting.

"The St. Bishoy Monastery is one of the early Coptic monasteries in Wadi Natrun northwest of Cairo. It was founded in the fourth century and is one of the oldest continually functioning Christian monasteries in the world. Looks like we have an Egyptian twist to this tale.

"I'd be happy to join you on a trip to Egypt if you like. I must admit I'm as intrigued by this as you are. It would be worth a long flight."

A long flight? Remi thought with a smile. *Not so long from here. Sorry, John, but I think I'm going to be taking this trip alone.*

She looked at Daniel sitting in the front, entranced by his phone.

No, not alone. With my partner.

She nudged him. When he looked at her, she didn't say a word, only held up her phone so he could see but Lucas could not.

Daniel read it, then looked at her, a smile forming at the edges of his mouth.

"Is this about what I think it's about?"

"Yes."

"And I take it you want to go there, like right now?"

Remi cocked her head and widened her eyes a little.

"Puppy dog looks are not appropriate between FBI agents," Daniel said.

"Is that a yes?"

Daniel shook his head and laughed. "You're unbelievable."

"Is that a yes?"

Daniel turned to Lucas, who was giving them curious glances.

"What's the range of your plane?" Daniel asked.

"It will get us to Djibouti City. Don't worry."

"How about Cairo?"

"Cairo is a lot further away. I'd have to refuel in Khartoum."

"OK, let's do it," Daniel said.

Remi squealed with delight and gave Daniel a hug.

"Ooof! Don't strangle me!"

Remi squeezed him tighter, then remembered herself and let him go.

"You want me to fly you to Cairo via Khartoum?" Lucas Mekonnen asked. "Do you realize there's been a coup in the Sudan?"

"Is it an anti-Western coup?" Remi asked.

"Not at the moment," Lucas grumbled.

"Then let's go," Remi said brightly.

"Look, I've been instructed to get you out of the country, not take you on some junket to Egypt."

"We need to go there," Remi said, imitating the cool, detached tone of voice he always used, "and you don't need to know why."

Daniel and Remi both laughed and gave each other a high five.

CHAPTER THIRTY

Remi looked out across the dusty parking lot toward a tall, featureless brown wall of mudbrick baked in the Egyptian sun. The wall must have been at least ten meters tall and nearly a kilometer long and was completely featureless except for a gate at the center.

The Monastery of St. Bishoy.

It had taken them almost two days to get here. Lucas had flown them out of Axum in a six-seater Cessna, flying high above the savannah of South Sudan, where, when they saw no trace of any human habitation, they dropped their weapons out the window. They couldn't rely on any understanding from the Egyptian authorities. Even Lucas threw out his guns.

They continued north, out across the vast Sahara before picking up the meandering course of the Blue Nile, one of the Nile River's two tributaries. Soaring high over this glittering ribbon, they spotted numerous villages and tidy farmer's fields, dwarfed by the vast desert stretching to the horizon on either side.

At last, they came to where the Blue Nile and the White Nile met at the city of Khartoum, the capital of the Sudan. Here they landed and Lucas refueled as quickly as possible. They were back in the air within twenty minutes.

From there they headed north, always keeping the Nile in sight. Lucas flew low so they could spot the great monuments of Egypt. First, they passed over the giant quartet of statues at Abu Simbel, four seated pharaohs looking south. Then they saw, dotted between the modern villages and cities, a series of temples before making it to Luxor, where they could see the vast temple complex of Karnak with its forest of columns covered in hieroglyphs, and the narrow Valley of the Kings on the opposite bank. Remi took a moment to remember poor Dr. Salah, and to wonder what Professor Hale had come to him in secret to talk about.

So much they didn't know. Most of all, she and Daniel didn't know why the FBI had allowed them on this mission at all.

From Luxor they continued north, past more temples and then the great pyramid fields of Dashur with its famous Bent Pyramid; then Saqqara with the Step Pyramid, the first ever built; then Abusir, before at last passing over the famous pyramids and Sphinx at Giza.

Lucas circled around the pyramids a couple of times before taking them to the airport.

They said goodbye on the tarmac. Lucas wasn't passing through customs. He was refueling and taking off to … somewhere.

"Best of luck to the two of you," he said, and sounded like he meant it. "You're two of the most interesting people I've ever come across."

Remi took that as high praise.

From Cairo it was easy to hire a taxi driver to drive them two hours into the desert to the fabled Wadi Natrun, the site of some of the earliest monasteries of the Coptic Church. They passed through a vast stretch of featureless desert into salt flats. The early monks had chosen this place because it was far from civilization and desolate. They had chosen well.

Remi figured they wouldn't recognize it now, though. The driver explained how the government had tapped into ground water far beneath the surface, and irrigation was reclaiming parts of the desert. Here and there they saw farms and date palm groves where there had once been only sand.

At last, they had made it here, to the gate of the Monastery of St. Bishoy. A small group of tourists stood outside. They joined them. A young priest with a neatly trimmed black beard and wearing white robes and a cowl addressed them.

"Ladies and gentlemen, welcome to the monastery. We will begin our tour in a couple of minutes. Entry is free of charge but if you wish to make a donation, feel free to put something in the box over there."

Remi saw a metal box set into the wall with a slit on it. She remembered her grandmother always giving to the collection box at Mass. Remi went over and put some Egyptian pounds through the slit.

As she returned to the group, she nearly fainted to see who had just joined it.

Father De Sanctis of the Association of Devout Students, along with two other priests. They looked as surprised as Remi and Daniel.

Then Father De Sanctis laughed. "Who says God doesn't have a sense of humor?"

Remi glanced at the crowd of tourists, then jerked her head toward the parking lot. She and Daniel stepped away from the crowd. Father De Sanctis followed, leaving his two companions at the gate.

"How did you know we were coming here? How could you have followed us?" Remi demanded.

Father De Sanctis raised his hands in a helpless gesture. "I didn't. I came here, following the same line of evidence as you did."

The code. How could he have gotten the code? John wouldn't have given it to him. Could they have hacked his computer? Or perhaps used some different evidence from their archives? They have some of the best archives in the world.

Daniel snorted. "You expect us to believe that you showed up right at the same time out of sheer coincidence?"

Father De Sanctis smiled. "My son, if you were a godly man, you would know there is no such thing as coincidence. Ah, I see the priest calling for us. We don't want to miss the tour."

They went back to the gate, Remi fuming. The Coptic priest raised his hands.

"Welcome to the Monastery of St. Bishoy. My name is Kosma Erian, and I have lived here for fifteen years. The monastery is part of the Coptic Orthodox Church, one of the most ancient churches in the world, founded by St. Mark the Apostle in the first century. St. Bishoy, who we honor here, moved to Wadi Natrun to become a monk in the fourth century. He later moved to Upper Egypt and died there. When this monastery was founded shortly afterwards, it was named in his honor. Come in. You are welcome."

The monk moved through the gate. The crowd followed. Remi let Father De Sanctis and his companions to go first so she could keep an eye on them.

Inside was a sanctuary from the desert. Carefully tended gardens cooled the air somewhat, and tall adobe buildings offered shade. There was a large main church with three domes, and a tall ancient tower. Brother Erian showed them the original well, and the world's oldest grain mill dating to fifth century. He even turned it a little to show that it still worked after 1,500 years.

Normally she'd find all this fascinating, but she was in no mood for sightseeing. She wanted to get to the main chapel and see the paintings.

Remi felt seriously tempted to ditch the tour and sneak off to find the chapel. She couldn't risk getting kicked out, though, not with Father De Sanctis here. If he got the clues and she didn't …

She kept a sharp eye on the three members of the Association of Devout Students. They seemed uninterested in the tour as well.

"Now let us see our church," Brother Erian said, leading them to the largest building in the compound. Remi studied it as they entered. The interior was richly decorated with elaborate woodwork. Icons hung on every wall. The building and art looked relatively modern, however.

"When was this church built?" Remi asked.

"The late nineteenth century. It replaced the original chapel in the tower that you will see shortly."

So far too new to be the one mentioned in the code.

Father De Sanctis grinned at her. "Thank you. I was wondering that myself."

Daniel leaned in and whispered in her ear. "For a priest, he sure is a smarmy bastard."

"Shh. We're in a church," she whispered back.

"Maybe you should pepper spray him again."

That gave Remi a case of the unholy giggles.

Brother Erian, if he noticed, decided not to say anything. "It is here where we hold Mass. Song is a large part of the Coptic church, and we always sing several songs in the Coptic language, which is descended from the language spoken in the time of the pharaohs."

The monk puffed out his chest and began to sing. The language was strange, unlike anything Remi had ever heard. The music seemed strange too, on an unfamiliar tonal scale, although the notes sounded a bit like the Greek Orthodox liturgy.

Remi stood still, looking around at the icons as the ancient music filled her ears. It gave her a strange tingling feeling, and even though she didn't understand a word it gave her a sense of peace.

Apparently, it did for Father de Sanctis too. He stood in the middle of the nave, his eyes closed, a serene expression on his face.

Not so with his two companions. One watched her, and the other kept an eye on Daniel. Remi noticed they were both fit and looked like they could handle themselves.

The song lulled her back into her thoughts. Once again, she got the impression of the song's great age. What had Brother Erian said? That

Coptic was descended from the language of ancient Egypt? Yes, she could hear the echo of centuries, of millennia in those strange words.

Remi had always been fascinated with time, and with things that had endured, like great works of art or architecture. But while she had devoted her life to studying such things, she had forgotten other things that endured as well.

Like religion.

And just like beautiful works of art or well-constructed buildings, religion endured because it had value.

She promised herself not to forget that again.

The song finished. Several of the tourists praised the monk, who bowed humbly.

"Now let us see the old tower, and the original chapel."

Father De Sanctis opened his eyes, suddenly alert. His companions looked a lot more interested now too. Brother Erian led them out of the new church, across a broad courtyard, and to the tower, a massive structure that rose sheer to the sky, with only a few windows high up.

"This is the tower the early monks would use when attacked by nomads. Since we would not shed blood, our only choice was to lock ourselves inside and wait for them to leave. We have sleeping quarters, a well, a large storage room for food, and of course a chapel."

They entered a small building beside the main tower and walked up a couple of flights of stairs to the roof before crossing a drawbridge into the tower.

"As you can see, the drawbridge is far above head level. Once closed, there is no way for any attackers to access it from the ground."

Their footsteps made a hollow clunking on the ancient beams as they passed over the drawbridge and into the tower's cool, dark interior. A single bare bulb illuminated a narrow staircase leading upwards. It took all of Remi's self-control not to shove her way to the front of the line.

They came to a short hallway with its floor covered with old hand-woven carpets. The monk led them down this to a long room with an arched roof. Faded paintings covered all four walls.

"These frescoes are the oldest art preserved in the monastery," Brother Elian said. "They date to the ninth century."

Before the cryptex was made, Remi said, her heart threatening to tear from her chest. *This is what the code is referring to.*

One wall was made up of portraits of saints in orderly rows, with a larger figure of Jesus standing at one end. On another wall was a more faded image of Saint George slaying the dragon. On another was a painting of Heaven. Another showed a scene in Hell. Interspersed with the paintings was writing in the Coptic language.

Remi started taking photos with her phone. Daniel did too. She was not surprised when the three members of the Association of Devout Students did the same.

All five of them did a very thorough job. Remi was amused how they all made way for each other, Remi pausing as one of the priests finished taking a closeup of Saint George, Father De Sanctis getting out of the way as Remi took a wide shot of the scene with Jesus and the saints. It was almost as if they were on an Easter egg hunt, more fun than competitive.

A year ago, she would have simmered with rage having them here, but after passing through a civil war and getting bombed by jet fighters, she had to put things into a different perspective.

That didn't affect her focus. She noted that there was nothing particularly unusual about any of these paintings. Done in a simple Early Medieval style, they did not have a great amount of detail, nor did any of their content have an obvious relation to whatever the cryptex might lead to. Perhaps the clue lay hidden in the writing, or perhaps the paintings created some sort of rebus. She had seen that in medieval art before.

So, as usual with the long trail of clues the cryptex had led her onto, she would not get her answer immediately, but only after days or weeks of study.

She had to make sure she found the answer before Father De Sanctis and the others in his association.

At last, they were done, and Brother Erian, standing at the doorway with much more patience than the other people in the tour, said, "Let us visit the rest of the tower."

Father De Sanctis came up to her. "A fascinating tour, don't you think?"

"After all the globetrotting I've been doing in the past few days, it's nice to enjoy a bit of tourism," she replied in as innocent a voice as she could.

"What was your favorite part?" the priest asked.

"When the monk sang. That was beautiful."

"Wasn't it? I enjoyed that too. I didn't see you taking any pictures of him, though."

Remi cocked her head and smiled. "You didn't either."

Father De Sanctis extended a hand. Remi took it.

"May the best man win," he said.

"Or the best woman," Remi replied.

CHAPTER THIRTY ONE

Standing outside the office of Deputy Director Burton, Daniel adjusted his tie and took a deep breath. He had been summoned to a meeting at the Deputy Director's office. Good. He had some serious questions for that guy. Not so good, because he had been specifically told "not to inform Trainee Agent Laurent."

That meant either an ass chewing or a discussion of something above her pay grade.

Passing through the door, he came to the outer office where Burton's personal assistant, Flora Whitaker, held court. A hunched woman in her sixties whose faced drooped from the weariness of seeing many deputy directors come and go, and the massive workload she managed to get through, she was one of the most capable people in the building. Although she didn't look like much, you underestimated her at your peril.

"They're waiting for you," she told him without looking up from whatever she was writing on her computer.

"Any idea what this is about?"

"I wasn't told anything."

Daniel cocked his head. Flora Whitaker knew everything. She was one of the best-informed people in the entire FBI. She sounded sincere, though.

Curious, Daniel walked across the outer office and knocked on the door.

"Come in," Deputy Director Burton called out.

He passed through the door and was confronted by a long meeting table. At the end sat Burton. To his right sat Assistant Director Ochiai of the Antiquities Division. To his left sat someone Daniel didn't recognize.

He had a military bearing, sitting erect and with a crew cut much like Burton, although he looked in his early forties rather than his late sixties like Burton. He wore civilian clothing and studied Daniel with steely blue eyes.

"Sit down, Agent Walker," Burton said, gesturing to a seat at the other end of the long table. This was one of Burton's little psychological tricks. The interviewee would be isolated at one end of the table while the bigwigs clustered at the other.

"Welcome back, and thank you for coming in," Assistant Director Ochiai said.

Another psychological trick. He didn't have a choice about coming in, so thanking him for doing so was a subtle way of pointing out that he had lower seniority.

"I'm glad to be back," Daniel said, then turned to the stranger. "I don't think I've had the pleasure."

The man nodded. "I'm here as an observer."

There was a pause as Daniel waited for the stranger to introduce himself. He did not.

Okaaay.

Deputy Director Burton spoke. "I'm sure you have many questions regarding your most recent assignment."

That's putting it lightly.

Daniel didn't reply, only kept up the attentive expression one was expected to have in these meetings.

"You did very well in an unusual set of conditions. While we would have preferred to get the suspect alive, we are not surprised that ended up being impossible."

"Even if we had captured him, I don't think we would have been allowed to extradite him. The Tigrayan authorities wanted him for local charges, and we had no jurisdiction."

He put the slightest emphasis on his last few words. Deputy Director Burton seemed to get the point.

"Yes, about that. We are aware that we asked you—asked you, not ordered you—to go well beyond your authority, but we did it because it was necessary."

"It seems a bit of an overreach to send two agents unfamiliar with the territory after a murderer. If he was that important, why not send the CIA or Special Ops or something?"

"That would have been seen as an escalation," Deputy Director Burton said.

"An escalation of what?"

“As you have no doubt become aware through your various cases, there are certain forces at work unseen by the average person, or even by the average law enforcement agency.”

“And there’s been an escalation of tensions recently,” Daniel said. “Yeah. I’ve been going back into the files for similar cases and not finding much.”

“Exactly,” Assistant Director Ochiai. “Hence the creation of the Antiquities Division.”

“All right,” Daniel said quietly, unsure how to proceed. “But why me? And why Trainee Agent Laurent?”

“In your work at BAU you proved yourself to be tenacious and resourceful, as well as, how shall we put it? Assertive.”

So I wasn’t really demoted for beating the crap out of suspects. I was turned into a guinea pig.

“And Trainee Agent Laurent?”

“She had made it her life’s work to investigate lost items of this nature.”

The cryptex. You’re talking about the cryptex. Jesus Christ. That’s why you hired her for the first case, but is that why you kept her on?

“So could you tell me a bit more about these forces that are at work, and why we can’t escalate by sending qualified people to a warzone rather than two agents who didn’t speak the language and had no contacts with local authorities?”

He knew he shouldn’t be so blunt, or so heated, but these people had seriously risked their lives.

“I’m afraid that’s impossible,” the stranger said. “Just take pride in the fact that you are helping your country.”

“I could help my country a whole lot more if I knew what this was all about.”

Deputy Director Burton gave him a reassuring smile. “In time, Agent Walker, in time. It’s just that the situation is a bit … delicate at the moment. But you have done well. Both of you. As recognition of your achievements and the unusual nature of these assignments, we are raising both of you to the next pay grade, effective immediately.”

A few extra grand a year is not going to make me accept being left in the dark.

“Thank you, sir,” Daniel managed to say. “I hope that Remi—I mean Trainee Agent Laurent—will get a chance to finish her accelerated training before our next case.”

Burton looked grim. "I hope so too, Agent Walker."

Oh, crap. Looks like we're in for more craziness, and soon.

The deputy director stood, walked around the table, and shook Daniel's hand.

"Thank you for your excellent service, Agent Walker. Take the rest of the week off. You've earned it."

Daniel tried to think of something to say. He looked at Assistant Director Ochiai and saw a poker face. He looked at the mystery man and saw a coldness that would have frightened Vladimir Putin.

He nodded and left. There was no point in hanging around. No one was going to tell him a damn thing.

As he left the FBI building, he put that out of his mind. He had long since learned to not stress about assignments he didn't have yet. Some agents got all wound up like that. He did not.

When he was on a case, it was a different story.

What really wound him up at the moment was the situation with Veronica. He still didn't know what to do about her.

But tonight, he'd put that aside, because he was having Remi over for dinner. He was cooking up the finest cuts of filet mignon he could find at a gourmet butcher, and he wanted to see what a real-life Frenchwoman thought of them.

He had invited his old partner Carmella Nomellini over too. He wanted the two of them to meet and he didn't want it to be just him and Remi. That would look too much like a date, even though … well.

One assignment at a time, buddy. One assignment at a time.

* * *

Remi shouldn't have felt nervous about coming to dinner at Daniel's house. They had eaten countless meals together over the course of their investigations, and she was interested to meet this old partner of his he had talked about so much. Plus, it would make a welcome change from the long hours she had put into staring at those old Coptic paintings, trying to tease out some hidden meaning that still eluded her.

For the moment. She would get the answer in the end, and she would go wherever that answer would take her.

But not tonight. Tonight, she would relax with her partner, and friend. Just a meal like all the others. It was ridiculous to feel nervous about such a thing.

Still, she had butterflies in her stomach as she clutched an excellent bottle of Pinot Noir and rang the doorbell of his apartment.

The apartment complex was not the nicest, looking more suited to young couples in their twenties just starting out, but Remi supposed that this was just a transition home since he had lost his house in the divorce. Hopefully he would move to something nicer soon, but given how driven he got at work, he probably didn't have the time to go house hunting.

Neither do I, she thought wryly.

Daniel opened the door. For once he wasn't wearing his black suit. Instead, he wore slacks and an old sweater. He looked more relaxed, and the casual clothes suited him. He beamed a smile at her.

Feeling warm, she smiled back.

"Glad you could make it, come on in."

She entered a modest living room with a few photos of landscapes on the walls. She was surprised to see one of Assistant Director Ochiai's works, a large black and white photo of three Japanese-American cowboys roping a steer with some rugged mountains as a backdrop.

Sitting on the sofa was a woman in her early forties, thin and Italian-looking with frizzy hair. She raised a beer bottle.

"You must be the professor. I'm Carmella, Daniel's old partner before they stole him from BAU."

They shook hands. Carmella indicated the wine.

"Nice one. I brought a bottle too. Daniel only stocked beer because he's a barbarian."

"I'm not a barbarian," Daniel objected. "I'm cooking you up a gourmet meal."

"Oh, shut up, Danny Boy! When you Googled that recipe, I had to tell you how to spell mignon, and then talk you out of serving it with French fries."

Remi and Carmella both laughed.

"Humph. Well, it's going to be the best filet mignon you've ever had, and it would have gone great with fries."

Remi turned back to Carmella and they both smiled.

"I was wondering about your last name," Remi said. "Are you related to Plinio Nomellini, the painter?"

Carmella's eyes widened. "Wow. No one at the bureau ever guessed that one before, but of course you were a professor before you went insane and joined the FBI. Yeah, he was my great-grandad."

The BAU agent elbowed her former partner. "You never figured that one out, did you, Danny boy?"

"Art isn't really my thing."

"He knows far more than he lets on," Remi said.

A shadow flickered over Daniel's features. Carmella stiffened.

What did I just say wrong?

The old partners recovered quickly.

"Shall I open up this bottle?" Daniel asked. "Have a primer before getting to the main course?"

"That would be lovely, yes," Remi said.

Carmella sat down and patted the sofa beside her. "It's nice to meet someone who knows about my great-grandfather. He's kind of been forgotten outside Italy. Let me tell you some family stories I got about him. I even got a couple of his sketches on the walls at him, hung high up to avoid the hellions."

"The hellions?" Remi asked as she sat down.

"Her twins," Daniel called from the kitchen to the accompaniment of a cork popping. "A pair of little tornados."

Carmella leaned in a little closer and whispered, "They love him to death. He's great with kids. He'll make a wonderful father one day."

Remi found herself blushing.

The ringing of the doorbell cut off what Carmella was going to say next.

Daniel walked out of the kitchen.

"Did you invite someone else?" Remi asked.

"No," he replied, looking confused.

He opened the door to reveal a woman about his age with blonde hair tied back in a severe bun. She wore an expensive business suit and carried a finely tooled leather briefcase.

"Oh, shit," Carmella muttered under her breath.

"Veronica," Daniel said, taking a step back. "What are you doing here?"

"I needed to see you. Are you all right? Where were you? Out of the country?"

She looked beyond her ex-husband and saw the two women sitting on the sofa.

"Oh. You have company." She did not sound happy. "Hello, Carmella. And who are you?"

Remi rose and went to take her hand. "I'm Remi Laurent. I'm Daniel's new partner."

Veronica looked surprised. Daniel looked away.

"Oh," Veronica said. "He didn't mention that his new partner was a woman."

He didn't?

Remi put on a smile as she shook her hand. "Well, considering the success rate he had with Carmella, I suppose the FBI decided a man and woman team would be the best."

Veronica said nothing. The pressure on Remi's hand increased ever so slightly.

They locked eyes, and for a moment there was that unspoken and universal communication between women that Remi had felt with that female soldier on the border between Djibouti and Tigray.

But this wasn't a supportive look she was getting; this wasn't a look that said, "I am on your side and will protect you."

No, quite the opposite.

Remi let go of her hand, her smile broadening.

I think a lot of Daniel's problems have to do with you. Not all, certainly not all, but far too many.

I don't think you deserve him.

Veronica's eyes narrowed a little, as if she could read her thoughts.

Daniel tried to cut through the tension by adding to it.

"I'm just cooking up some filet mignon. Would you like to stay for dinner?"

Please say no. Please say no. Please say no.

"Oh no, I wouldn't want to break up your little party."

Remi almost gasped in relief.

Daniel made a helpless gesture at the living room. "Can I offer you some wine?"

Not my wine.

"I should get going," Veronica said, then fixed Daniel with a look. "But we need to talk."

"Sure," Daniel said, looking flustered. "I have the next couple of days off."

"Good." Veronica gave him a long kiss on the lips. "Tomorrow. I'll call you."

She turned to Remi, her eyes cold, a boardroom smile on her lips.

"Very nice to finally meet you."

"Likewise," Remi chirped.

Because now I know what I'm up against. And if you think that expensive suit and that fat bank account are going to intimidate me, you have no idea what I've been through.

Veronica left. Daniel closed the door with a sigh. Remi moved close to him, brushing her hand against his and making it look like an accident.

"How about some of that wine?" she said.

"All right," Daniel replied, rallying.

"And I promise I won't make fun of you if you have a beer."

He grinned. "It's a deal."

NOW AVAILABLE!

THE DECEPTION CODE
(A Remi Laurent FBI Suspense Thriller—Book 5)

A billionaire is murdered and an ancient Egyptian relic is missing, one rumored to be cursed—and to be a clue to the greatest lost tomb ever known. The FBI needs brilliant history professor Remi Laurent more than ever as the case sends them on a wild hunt across the globe. Can she stop him in time?

THE DECEPTION CODE (A Remi Laurent FBI Suspense Thriller) is book #5 in a new series by mystery and suspense author Ava Strong, which begins with THE DEATH CODE (Book #1).

FBI Special Agent Daniel Walker, 40, known for his ability to hunt killers, his street-smarts, and his disobedience, is singled out from the Behavioral Analysis Unit and assigned to the FBI's new Antiquities unit. The unit, formed to hunt down priceless relics in the global world of antiquities, has no idea how to enter the mind of a murderer.

Remi Laurent, 34, brilliant history professor at Georgetown, is the world's leading expert in obscure historic artifacts. Shocked when the FBI asks for her help to find a killer, she finds herself reluctantly partnered with this rude American FBI agent. Special Agent Walker and Remi Laurent are an unlikely duo, with his ability to enter killers' minds and her unparalleled scholarship, the only thing they have in common, their determination to decode the clues and stop a killer.

The lost Egyptian relic points to many ancient Egyptian clues, all thought to have been dead ends, and leaves Remi just hours to decode a puzzle that has baffled archeologists for centuries. What exactly is the killer after? Where does he think the clues will lead him?

And can Remi outsmart him in time?

An unputdownable crime thriller featuring an unlikely partnership between a jaded FBI agent and a brilliant historian, the REMI LAURENT series is a riveting mystery, grounded in history, and packed with suspense and revelations that will leave you continuously in shock, and flipping pages late into the night.

Book #6—THE SEDUCTION CODE—is also available.

Ava Strong

Debut author Ava Strong is author of the REMI LAURENT mystery series, comprising six books (and counting); of the ILSE BECK mystery series, comprising seven books (and counting); of the STELLA FALL psychological suspense thriller series, comprising six books (and counting); and of the DAKOTA STEELE FBI suspense thriller series, comprising three books (and counting).

An avid reader and lifelong fan of the mystery and thriller genres, Ava loves to hear from you, so please feel free to visit www.avastrongauthor.com to learn more and stay in touch.

BOOKS BY AVA STRONG

REMI LAURENT FBI SUSPENSE THRILLER
THE DEATH CODE (Book #1)
THE MURDER CODE (Book #2)
THE MALICE CODE (Book #3)
THE VENGEANCE CODE (Book #4)
THE DECEPTION CODE (Book #5)
THE SEDUCTION CODE (Book #6)

ILSE BECK FBI SUSPENSE THRILLER
NOT LIKE US (Book #1)
NOT LIKE HE SEEMED (Book #2)
NOT LIKE YESTERDAY (Book #3)
NOT LIKE THIS (Book #4)
NOT LIKE SHE THOUGHT (Book #5)
NOT LIKE BEFORE (Book #6)
NOT LIKE NORMAL (Book #7)

STELLA FALL PSYCHOLOGICAL SUSPENSE THRILLER
HIS OTHER WIFE (Book #1)
HIS OTHER LIE (Book #2)
HIS OTHER SECRET (Book #3)
HIS OTHER MISTRESS (Book #4)
HIS OTHER LIFE (Book #5)
HIS OTHER TRUTH (Book #6)

DAKOTA STEELE FBI SUSPENSE THRILLER
WITHOUT MERCY (Book #1)
WITHOUT REMORSE (Book #2)
WITHOUT A PAST (Book #3)

www.ingramcontent.com/pod-product-compliance
Lightning Source LLC
Chambersburg PA
CBHW030618310726
48979CB00003B/772